Ghost Marina on the Mississippi

DEXTER JAMES

Ghost Marina on the Mississippi

OTHER BOOKS BY DEXTER JAMES:

Genesis Déjà vu – The Beginning

Genesis Déjà vu – The New Eden

Heist During the Rio Games

The Ultimate Conspiracy

Of Ghosts and Aliens

To

Ray Thomas

A stalwart on our boat trip which was

the inspiration for this novel

Contents

THE QUEST FOR THE TRUTH

Chapter 1 – The Quest – Modern Day

For the last couple of years, the life of Jason Clifford had been decidedly rough, to say the least. Mary, his dear wife of twenty-four years had succumbed to breast cancer, his youngest daughter, Shirley, had almost died from a drug overdose and his only son, Seb, had been killed in an automobile accident involving a drunk driver.

Although the life insurance from his wife's death and the compensation received for his son's accident in no way relieved his sorrow it provided him with enough financial stability to be able to take early retirement from his job as a teacher. It was also felt, by the powers that be at his faculty, that because of all the potential phycological repercussions he may experience due to these unfortunate series of events, he would also receive a disability pension until it was time for his retirement pension to kick in.

All these events had left Jason with a sense of withdrawal, a lack of motivation and more poignantly, a will to live. Prior to all these problems, Jason had been in great health, each week-day morning he would drag his slim, six-foot frame out of bed and visit the gym where he would put his body through rigorous cardio sessions and strenuous exercise routines. His light-brown tousled hair, damp with sweat, would cling to the forehead of his handsome face, tanned by hours of outside activities in the summer and skiing in the winter. Now, he looked pale and gaunt, he was listless and had lost weight. Basically, his life was devoid of purpose and despite the efforts of family and friends rallying around to lift his spirit, there remained a growing concern that he was turning suicidal. That is, until an unassuming conversation took place during a family Thanksgiving dinner at his parent's home.

Both Jason's daughters had accompanied him to the event, together with their respective partners. Jeannette, the eldest, who was with her long-time fiancée Allan, and Shirley, escorted by her partner Allison. The whole family had accepted Shirley's sexual preference ever since she first came out, and now that she was with Allison, she had reverted to the old Shirley, the one they had all known and loved.

As usual, the evening went well and they all enjoyed a great dinner and Jeannette drove her father home, albeit a little worse for drink. Once Jeannette departed, Shirley insisted she stay the night to make sure he would be O.K. Jason equally insisted that he was fine, and no chaperone was required. When Shirley was finally gone, Jason poured himself a nightcap, something he rarely did, then he sat in his comfy chair and began thinking about the conversation he had after dinner with his father. It had all started with the usual question about his grandfather's mysterious disappearance just before the end of World War II, and he began to recall the conversation as he sipped his whiskey.

"Well, all my mother was told was that your grandfather was flown by private plane from Canada, where he had just docked," William Clifford began, "he landed in Knoxville where a car was waiting to take him to meet with some top brass in a hotel. Next thing she knew, him and another sailor were put on a cabin cruiser to sail up river somewhere. That's the last my mother ever heard of your grandfather and of course, I was born that year in 1944."

"Didn't grannie ever try to discover more details of his disappearance?" Jason asked.

"Oh sure, but all they ever told my mother was that he was categorized as 'missing in action' while carrying out war-related maneuvers. But what war games he could have been playing in a cabin-cruiser on a river, beats the hell out of me." William replied philosophically.

"Surely grannie could have pursued this to obtain more information." Jason pleaded.

"You have to remember son, things were different in them days, the war was still going on, the government told you nothing and they made you feel as though they were doing you a favor by giving you a small death benefit each month." William replied. "It's not like today, after all this time, a lot more information is available and with the internet not only can you dig deeper it's also more difficult to cover things up. But in those days…." William just shook his head as if to say there was nothing more that could have been done.

But it got Jason to thinking, he could carry out some research as to the disappearance of his grandfather. The statutes of limitation on most of the war's events had expired and a lot of the information is now available on-line if you knew where to look, and he did. This was to be Jason's new quest and it gave him a real purpose that he hadn't felt since his college days.

Chapter 2 – From Halifax NS to Knoxville TN – May 1944

Seaman Raymond Clifford of the U.S. Navy had been assigned to a converted cruise ship which had been crisscrossing the Atlantic transporting U.S. and Canadian troops to and from England. At 6:00 AM the ship had just docked in Halifax, Nova Scotia, now devoid of passengers, except for a few injured military personnel returning to North America for recuperation. Ray had just finished securing some lines and was looking forward to grabbing breakfast when a bosun came up to him and told him to report immediately to the bridge. This was of some concern to Ray as no one got called to the bridge unless it was a serious matter. Ray's first thought was that there was a problem with his wife who was eight months pregnant. Ray hurried nimbly up the steps to the bridge and when he arrived he was greeted by a surly Petty Officer who asked him who he was and what his business was there.

"Seaman Clifford, I've been told to report to the bridge sir," Ray replied with some trepidation. The Petty Officer was about to say something crass but was interrupted by the Captain of the vessel.

"Ah yes, Clifford, follow me," the Captain said warmly and began walking to a small office area at the rear of the bridge. Ray dutifully followed, under the disdainful eye of the Petty Officer, "come in lad, shut the door." Ray did as he was told and when the Captain sat down at a small desk that was in the room, Ray remained at attention. The Captain gave Ray a quick visual once-over noting the seaman's weather-beaten face that highlighted his ice-blue eyes.

"At ease lad, at ease, take your hat off." The Captain said and Ray removed his hat to reveal a thatch of dark hair as the Captain began to fill a Meerschaum pipe with tobacco from an oilskin pouch, "young man, it appears you have some very special skills that are required by a certain individual on a very top-secret project that has the propensity to change the course of the war." At first, Ray thought the captain was making fun of him for some reason and began to get even more perturbed about his situation. The Captain struck a match, waited for the sulfur to burn off, then gently waved the flame over the tobacco as he took a couple of sucks on his pipe and waved the match to extinguish the flame before placing it into an ash-tray that was well beyond full. Meanwhile, although relieved it wasn't a complication with his wife's pregnancy, Ray was left wondering what possible skills he could have that would be required on a top-secret project.

"Now, I don't have any details, need to know basis you understand," the Captain continued, "but you are to immediately pack your kit and you will be met by MPs at the gangplank." The Captain then stood up, shook Ray's hand, wished him good luck then dismissed him. A surprised Ray just stood there, not sure whether he had unknowingly breached security and was being taken away, or what? This was all too sudden.

"Am I in trouble sir?" A nervous Ray asked the Captain.

"Absolutely not lad." The Captain replied, still puffing on his pipe, "really, I know nothing more than I have told you, I don't even know where the MPs are taking you and it is not my business to ask." Then with a kind smile the wizened old Captain added, "don't worry lad, I'm sure whatever it is, it will be better than avoiding bombs and torpedoes in the Atlantic. Now off you go, don't keep the MPs waiting, from my experience, they tend to get antsy."

Ray quickly returned to his cabin and began packing his gear into his Navy issued duffle-bag. Fortunately, there was nobody else in the area, so he wasn't exposed to any difficult questions regarding where he was going. Fifteen minutes later he was walking down the gangplank where a military police jeep was parked with two burly MPs sitting inside. The MP on the driver's side climbed out of the Jeep.

"Clifford?" the MP said. Ray nodded, "Id. please," the MP added. Ray produced his identity card; the MP nodded his head and returned the card to Ray before telling him to get into the back of the jeep. As soon as Ray was sitting down the jeep roared off, he wanted to ask them where they were going but between the noise of the jeep and the sullen looks of the two men he decided to say nothing. But it was only approximately thirty minutes before they were pulling up at the gates of RCAF Station Dartmouth. The driver pulled out some documents, which the Canadian guard read briefly before pulling up the red and white security barrier. The jeep sped through the gate and headed directly to the airfield where there was a U.S. Military Cessna Bobcat waiting.

The jeep stopped beside the open door of the plane where an Army officer was standing. Nothing was said but Ray assumed that this was where he got out of the jeep. Gathering his things, he climbed out and thanked the two MPs for the ride and was about to say it had been nice talking to you but thought better of it. No sooner was Ray out of the jeep it sped away once more and he thought to himself that if he was ever asked he would never be able to recognize those two men again.

"Clifford?" The smiling officer asked, looking over the tall, slim young man that had just arrived.

"Sir." Ray replied as he fumbled in his pockets for his identification card.

"No need," the man said, "Flight Officer Daniels, at your service. I will be your pilot to-day, come aboard." The pilot then assisted Ray onto the plane and directed him to his seat.

"Have you had breakfast?" The man asked.

"No, I haven't, it's all been a bit of a rush." Ray replied, realising now he was very hungry.

"Worry not, there's a flask of coffee there, some bacon sandwiches and a couple of muffins I just procured for you from the kitchen," the pilot explained before continuing, "now, buckle up, we have about a four-hour flight before we touch down. There is a toilet aft if you are desperate, but we will be able to get out and stretch our legs when we refuel. Any questions?"

"Yes, where to?" Ray nervously asked, not only because he didn't have a clue as to what was going on but mainly because he had never been on a plane before.

"All in good time," Daniels replied, "but we will have to land to refuel before we arrive at your destination and hopefully we can arrange for some lunch to be brought to us. So, eat your breakfast, relax and enjoy the scenery, the weather is expected to be clear all the way."

Which is what Ray did, he ate his breakfast, relaxed and enjoyed the view from the plane. Ray had not really traveled much in the U.S. prior to joining the navy but during this flight he had an excellent view of the north-east coast and the New York city skyline was a breath-taking sight as they flew to their fuel stop at Willow Grove, Pennsylvania. They did indeed get out of the plane while it was being refuelled and he made a quick rest-stop. On their return to the plane, there were more sandwiches, some fruit, a couple of Cokes each and another flask of coffee. Ray boarded the plane while the pilot did a few checks and verified the fuel situation. Satisfied that all was well, the smiling pilot boarded the plane, received clearance and they were airborne once more.

Once they were in the air, Ray tucked into some of the food that had been delivered to them and after a quick cup of coffee he settled back and before he knew it he was asleep. It was the touch of the wheels on the tarmac that awoke him, despite the gentle landing made by his pilot. As the plane was taxiing Ray saw a sign on one of the buildings that read, 'McGhee Tyson Airport' but it still didn't help him as to his whereabouts. Finally, the plane rolled to a stop and once the whirr of the engines ceased and all was quiet, Daniels came through to the passenger area.

"Welcome to Knoxville," Daniels said.

"Knoxville?" Ray said in total surprise, "what the hell am I doing here?" Daniels merely smiled.

"I have no idea, my job was to get you here, but I'll tell you something, someone with clout is behind this. All the red-tape was cut to get you here, whatever it is you will be doing, bon chance." Daniels said and held out his hand to shake. Ray dutifully obliged but was now more confused than ever.

Ray disembarked the plane with his kit-bag expecting to be met by more MPs but this time it was a regular taxi. Standing beside the car was a scruffy looking driver with a cigarette dangling from his mouth. The man held open the rear passenger door and almost imperceptibly beckoned Ray in. Ray did as was indicated and settled down, holding onto his kit-bag as though it was a security blanket. The driver then got into the car and immediately, dispensed with his cigarette and morphed into a totally new persona.

"O.K., there are some civilian clothes on the back-seat you need to change into them, and I mean everything, even your underpants and socks," the driver said with some authority as he turned to look at him. Ray looked first at the driver then looked to his left and saw some neatly folded, expensive-looking clothes beside him. "Take-off your dog-tags, place any identification papers into this bag," the driver handed him a paper bag, which Ray slowly took.

"From now on, you are simply Ray Clifford, a rich playboy type, and here is some new id." The driver handed him an identification card, a driver's license with an address in St. Louis and a few other documents that Ray wasn't given a chance to read. "You are booked into a hotel in Knoxville where I'm going to drop you off. Later, someone is going to call on you to tell you your next steps. Do not, under any circumstances, leave your room or call for room service until after the visit, here's a few dollars for tips and such, be generous, you're a rich playboy." The driver handed Ray a bunch of money, which at first glance amounted to quite a tidy sum, then the driver turned back around. For a moment Ray was too stunned to move and remained immobile, but then the driver quickly glanced back.

"You're not changed yet?" The driver whispered through clenched teeth. "Come on, we haven't got all day."

"You want me to change here?" Ray asked incredulously.

"Unless you want to get naked on the runway, yes here." The driver replied. "You'll be leaving your kit-bag in the car, there will be plenty of clothes in your hotel room. I'll be putting your bag in the trunk so if there are any personal mementos you want to keep with you, take them out now. Photographs or anything like that you can retain but absolutely nothing that will indicate you are in the navy."

It took Ray about five minutes to get out of his naval clothes and into the new ones that had been selected for him. Some of his moves to dress were bordering on contortionism in the small space on the rear seat of the taxi. A further five minutes were spent retrieving some artifacts from his bag, including his shaving gear and personal hygiene stuff. Photographs of his wife, Gloria, he kept in his wallet which he saw no reason to give up. Once Ray had finished rummaging around, the driver got out of the car, went to the opposite side of the taxi that Ray was seated in, opened the door and hauled out the kit-bag and placed it in the trunk.

They passed through security at the airport gates and the driver began to provide Ray with further instructions.

"When we arrive at the hotel, go straight to room 1511, here's the key." The driver said and passed a hotel key to Ray. "Don't talk to anyone, don't stop to read newspapers or admire the architecture just go straight to your room. You got that?"

"Got it," Ray said subserviently.

"In an hour or so there will be a knock on your room door, it will be the man, and he will bring you up to speed. Meanwhile, no phone calls and don't leave the room, as I have already mentioned, you can get room service after the man has left." The driver explained as he was pulling up outside the Andrew Johnson Hotel in downtown Knoxville.

"Good luck kid." The driver said and made a flick of his head to indicate to Ray he should leave the vehicle. No sooner had Ray shut the car door the driver sped away leaving him standing in the middle of a town he was unfamiliar with, outside an expensive hotel, in brand new clothes with a wad of money. Ray looked up at the building, which was the tallest in Knoxville, and he thought to himself, 'is this a big prank, what the hell is going on here?'

Ray discretely, albeit self-consciously, entered the lobby of the hotel and fortunately saw the bank of elevators directly ahead of him so he didn't have to look conspicuous searching for them. He tried to walk confidently towards the elevators and pressed the 'up' button. It was only a few seconds before the doors slid open to reveal an empty elevator, much to his relief. Ray pressed the button for the fifteenth floor and stepped back as the doors closed with an almost imperceptible swishing sound. A few seconds later the doors opened, and he stepped out of the elevator on the fifteenth floor. There was a sign on the wall indicating the direction of the room numbers and he turned left to go to room 1511. Ray's room was approximately halfway down the hallway, he used the key he had been given to unlock the door and he entered a beautifully decorated room that he thought must be costing a fortune. After a brief inspection, looking at his new wardrobe of clothes and checking out the comfort level of the bed, he laid back to wait.

Fortunately, he didn't have to wait long before there was a knock on the door. Ray opened the door to reveal a man in a trilby hat and a light brown mackintosh. He was a large man, maybe a little overweight but nevertheless an imposing figure with a stubble of hair on his top lip that couldn't really be classified as a mustache. The man strode purposely into the room as Ray closed the door behind him.

"Clifford?" The man asked brusquely.

"Yes sir." Ray replied as he stood to attention.

"At ease, relax and close the blinds please," the man ordered and waited for Ray to do as he was told.

"From here on in until further notice you are a civilian. For all intent and purposes, you have never been in the navy. Is that understood?" The man reiterated what had been told to him by the taxi driver. "For the next two months you and another selected sailor will have the cushiest job in the entire U.S. Navy and if everything goes to plan you will not be sent to a war theatre for the remainder of the war. That should please your wife, I understand she is expecting is that correct?"

"Yes si-." Ray was about to fall into his naval nomenclature when he stopped himself. "Yes, that's correct, the baby is due in June," Ray replied nervously, albeit relieved.

"Well, I expect your first little expedition will be completed by then and we can arrange some leave for you to be with your wife and new baby." The man replied with some empathy.

"That would be terrific sir, sorry I mean...," Ray's voice trailed off, not sure what to call the man so he changed the subject somewhat, "but what expedition will that be exactly?" Ray asked.

"Take a seat, let me explain." The man told him and then indeed went on to explain, at a very high level, about the project, without divulging any real information. He finished up by telling Ray what he was expected to do. "So, we will provide you with a cabin cruiser to transport some goods that must be delivered to a location in St. Louis. Once you are in St. Louis you will then be provided with a car while one of my men will retrieve the goods from the boat and secrete it in your vehicle. You will then be given instructions as to where to deliver the goods at their final destination. You will also be given a radio that is set to a secure frequency and should only be used when you arrive at dock 13 in St. Louis or in the event of an emergency. Do you understand?"

"Yes," Ray replied, still a little confused.

"You will be given ample cash for food, fuel, docking fees and sundries," the man explained before continuing, "and it is important that you act like a couple of tourists. A couple of friends enjoying a boat trip but under no circumstances, I mean none, do you allow anyone on the boat while that package is on board. The same rule applies when you transfer to the car, nobody should get near that car or the package. That means no hitch-hikers or women of the night. Understood?"

"Understood," Ray replied curtly.

"Good, that's it then," the man said and with that, he stood up. "I'm just going to meet with your shipmate, his name is Tony Lawless and once I have spoken to him I will send him to your room, so you can both get acquainted. The same taxi driver who dropped you off this evening will be waiting for you both, outside at 08:00 hours. I suggest you call room service for your meals this evening and in the morning. The fewer people who see you the better. You may call your wife but offer her no details, is that understood?"

"Yes, but why me?" Ray asked.

"You have experience on the rivers, you know how to negotiate around the tug-boats and the hazards in the river do you not?" The man asked.

"I do." Ray merely replied.

"And we wanted military personnel to carry out this task," the man explained, then added, "and you will be the one in charge." By now, the man was standing by the door when he said this and was about to leave but he came back into the room and placed a strong hand on Ray's shoulder. "What you are doing here son has the propensity to shorten the war and one day you and your family will know just how important this contribution to the war effort really is. Any questions?" The man said it in a way that negated any further discussion and after a couple of seconds he shook Ray's hand and said, "good luck!" Then he left the room leaving a bewildered Ray to await another knock on the door that would herald the arrival of his new shipmate.

Chapter 3 – Research – Modern Day

That first Monday after the Thanksgiving weekend, Jason began pumping the internet for information regarding his grandfather. The only facts he had available to him came from the quick phone call his grandfather made to his grandmother. His grandfather had told his grandmother that he had been placed on special assignment, he was going to be sailing upriver from the Knoxville area to St. Louis in a cabin cruiser. Jason's grandmother also recalled that he had been flown from Newfoundland to Knoxville in a private plane and at the time of the phone call he was in a posh hotel in Knoxville. One other thing he had told her was that he would be incommunicado for a few weeks, but after that call, she had never heard from him again.

Even though there was so little to go on, Jason got to work and by March of the following year, he had built an itinerary of a boat trip that was made by two civilians along various rivers in the spring of 1944. Sure, he had substantial gaps in his timeline and much of what he had compiled was based on assumptions. But between various military records and de-classified documents he felt he had enough information to categorically say that his grandfather, with a ship's mate, named David Lawless, sailed as far as twenty miles short of St. Louis. But at some point, along the Mississippi, all trace of the two sailors disappeared. So, what happened to the boat, his grandfather and his companion? Furthermore, what was the point of the trip? It wasn't a vacation otherwise he would have informed his grandmother.

Jason was stymied, but not deterred, he spent a further few more weeks trying to determine what could have possibly happened to his grandfather on that short expanse of water along one of the longest rivers in the world. Jason researched charts, homing in on marinas that existed along the river at that time, especially those that had gas and marine toilet pump-out services. He didn't come across any marinas that had records that went back that far but amazingly, what he did uncover was an invaluable eye-witness. A chance email had been answered by one of the office workers at a marina and informed Jason that an old-timer, Chuck, who had only been seven years old at the time of Jason's grandfather's trip, still hung around the river. Telephone numbers were exchanged, and a conference call was arranged. Jason was expecting to hear a thick southern drawl but was surprised to hear a very articulate voice on the other end of the line. During the call, Chuck told Jason that he clearly recalled two men pulling into his family's marina late one afternoon all those years ago. Chuck remembered them for two reasons, he just loved the gleaming new boat that they moored alongside. The beautifully polished wood paneling and the gleaming fittings all added up to the finest boat he had ever seen, and he desperately wanted to go on board to take a look-see down below. For some reason, the men were adamant against allowing anyone coming on board and Chuck's disappointment was so tangible he remembered it to this day. The other reason why the event stuck in his mind so vividly was that a storm was brewing, and the two men were debating whether they should risk cruising the twenty miles to St. Louis or take overnight shelter at the marina. The marina offered approximately 300 feet of dockage directly on the Mississippi and they could have easily waited out the night to let the storm blow over. But despite Chuck's father advising them to remain at the marina, the two men decided to push on. Chuck felt that the two men thought his father was just trying to extort docking fees from them on what was a slow night. But according to Chuck, the storm on the river that night was one of the worst storms he had ever experienced. It was the last time Jason's grandfather and his shipmate were ever seen or heard from again.

For the umpteenth time, Jason reviewed what he had learned about the trip and for the umpteenth time, he felt he had come to the end of his research and was no nearer to solving his grandfather's disappearance. So, with the trail coming to a dead-end, Jason decided that the only thing left to do was to take a boat trip along the same stretch of water where his grandfather was last heard from and to somehow try to recreate the events.

Chapter 4 – Talking to his Wife – May 1944

After the man's departure, Ray re-opened the blinds and waited in his room, pacing the luxurious carpet and occasionally looking out the window at downtown Knoxville from the great vantage point of his hotel room. To say he was anxious was an understatement and what contribution could possibly be made to the war effort by sailing a boat on rivers in the middle of America was totally beyond him. After about ten minutes of wearing out the hotel's carpet, Ray decided to phone his wife. She was still in Cleveland, living at her mother's house, at least until the baby was born. With Ray away for who knew how long until the war was over it was felt being pregnant and living on her own was not a great idea. Her mother, Agnes, positively clucked at the suggestion like an old mother-hen and it certainly wasn't an inconvenience for her. As for Gloria's father, Wilfred, he just went with the flow.

Ray dialed the operator, told her the number he wished to call and waited. A few minutes later he heard the ring tone, after a couple of rings it was picked up, but to Ray's disappointment, it was not Gloria but her mother.

"Mrs. Stanbury speaking," Agnes said demurely, almost like a question.

“Hi Mrs. Stanbury, this is Ray. Is Gloria there?” Ray said excitedly.

“Oh Ray, it’s you, you’re safe, how are you?” Agnes Stanbury said, genuinely pleased to hear her son-in-law’s voice. “Gloria will be so glad you’ve called. We were worried about you with all the stories of U-boats and the such.”

“Yes, well the U-boat threat has pretty much disappeared Mrs. Stanbury, could I speak to Gloria please?” Ray said, trying to maintain his patience with his obviously relieved mother-in-law.

“But we heard a couple of convoys had been attacked from the air. Of course, no news is good news, but we were still worried about you!” Mrs. Stanbury explained, but by now Gloria was by her side and almost wrenched the telephone from her mother’s hand.

“Hi,” was all Gloria said but it was enough for Ray to take an involuntary intake of breath.

“Hi, how ya doin?” Ray asked.

“I’m fine, how are you?” Gloria asked swaying and fiddling with the telephone cord, oblivious to her mother asking her to ask Ray about things.

After a few seconds, Mrs. Stanbury thought better of it and retreated into the kitchen to finish preparing dinner.

"I'm fine and how is the baby?" Ray asked excitedly, "not long now."

"Oh, he's kicking pretty good," Gloria said.

"He? Do you think it's a boy? How do you know that?" Ray said beaming from ear to ear.

"Well, mom thinks it's going to be a boy, you know how she is with all her old wives' tales," Gloria said.

"A boy? Wow!" Ray exclaimed, then the realization of his situation kicked in, he only had a few moments before his new shipmate was expected to come knocking. "Look, just wanted to let you know, I have been taken off the troop ships and placed on special assignment, stateside. I'm in this doozy of a hotel in Knoxville right now, they flew me here on a private plane from Halifax."

"Oh, what a relief." Gloria said and then added excitedly, "does that mean you can come home to visit?"

“Yes, with a bit of luck, I’ll be home for the birth, isn’t that great?” Ray said equally as excited.

“Oh Ray, really?” Gloria whispered into the mouthpiece of the phone.

“Yes, isn’t it great, but after this call, I may not be able to contact you for a few weeks, I’m sailing a cabin-cruiser up the river. So, don’t go fretting if you haven’t heard from me for a while, O.K.?” Ray told her, just then, there was a knock at Ray’s door.

“Look, I can’t talk right now, all I can say is, tomorrow, me and another guy will be heading upriver on a cabin-cruiser, we’re going to St. Louis. I think that’s him at the door right now. Love you lots babe and miss you, see you soon.” Ray said, thinking that maybe he had already said a little more than he should.

Chapter 5 – Beginning of the Quest – Modern Day

"You can't be serious!" Jeannette shouted at her father, "you've hardly ever been on a boat."

"Of course I have, all that scuba-diving I used to do, how the hell do you think I got to the dive sites?" Jason laughed as he was having this verbal spar with his concerned daughter.

"Yes, but you weren't responsible for the driving of the boat." Jeannette retorted.

"No, but I went sailing as a kid, it's like riding a bike, I'll get back into it," Jason replied with a confidence he didn't really feel. "Matter of fact, I'm looking at a boat this very afternoon, I'll have a good month to practice, docking, swatting up on rules and regulations, I'll be fine, don't worry."

"You're crazy, you should at least have someone traveling with you," Jeannette replied, still standing in front of her father, arms crossed over her chest, not happy with the concept at all.

"Who? There isn't anybody. Anyway, I'll be just fine. After all, you're the one who has been trying to get me off my arse to do something constructive." Jason replied.

“Yes, but not to risk your life on some cockamamie chase along the rivers,” Jeannette said, now pacing up and down the living room in Jason’s house. It was a Saturday morning, Jeannette had called her father, as usual, to check whether he needed anything but when he told her about his plan to re-create his grandfather’s trip, she didn’t hesitate, she immediately drove over from her apartment to his house.

“It will be an adventure, I’ll report in every day, phone call, text, email, whatever,” Jason said smiling, indeed, now he had made the decision to accept the quest, he was thoroughly looking forward to it.

“I guess if you’re going to kill yourself that’s as good a way as any.” Jeannette said with some disdain, realizing she was not going to be able to talk her father out of the trip, then as an afterthought, she added, “is there any shopping you need?”

“No, no, got everything thanks,” Jason replied. Then Jeannette walked over to her father, who was seated at his computer desk and gave him a quick peck on the cheek.

“Catch you later, text me if you need anything. Bye.” Jeannette said and left.

Jason knew his daughter only had his welfare at heart, she had always looked out for him, even more so since his wife had died. It was a certainty she would be telling Shirley and it was only a matter of time before she would be on the phone berating him for putting them through all this unnecessary worry. But for now, he couldn't think about that, he had to get to the marina and give a once over to a boat that might just suit his needs for the trip.

Jason arrived at the marina a little early and was directed to slip 401 where the boat he was going to be viewing was moored. The owner of the boat had not yet arrived, so it gave Jason a little time to study its outside condition in peace. Jason stood on the dock at about mid-ship and looked at the fenders that were covered in black covers matching the black lines of the MacGregor 26X, which itself was meticulously polished and gleaming in the spring sunshine. There were even fender racks attached to the stanchions and at the back was what looked like an almost brand-new Honda 50cc outboard engine. Jason tried to peer through the tinted windows of the boat to look inside the cabin-area, but he could see very little. Fortunately, it didn't matter as an elderly gentleman came limping along the jetty to the dock.

"Mr. Clifford?" the man asked.

"Yes, that's me," Jason replied.

"John Winslow, good to meet you, come aboard." The man replied as he struggled, puffing and blowing, to climb aboard the boat. Jason followed the man, fortunately, he didn't have anywhere near the same level of difficulty boarding the boat. By the time Jason was aboard, still searching for any defects or blemishes, John had unlocked the cabin-hatch door and was placing it between the steering console and the starboard seats.

"I've learned from experience to always store the door on the side opposite to where you have docked," John explained, "safer that way, when you're getting in and out of the boat, but when you are in motion, you put it below."

"Good to know," Jason said, as he followed John down the steps into the cabin area. Jason loved the cabin area, he could stand to his full height and it appeared quite spacious. Although the brochure for the model said it could sleep six people, he thought they would have to be very friendly. On the port side, there was a kitchen unit housing a sink, a single-burner cooker, a water heater, and a small cooler. Underneath the unit were cupboards containing cooking and dining paraphernalia, in fact apart from vittles the boat was ready to cruise.

John also showed Jason the spare life-jackets, tools and spare accessories that were neatly stored away in large, plastic, containers in the aft section, underneath the outside seats. All in all, the boat was in excellent condition and there was little that Jason would have to purchase to begin his quest.

“So, Mr. Whinslow, why are you selling the boat?” Jason was curious to know.

“I’m getting a little too long in the tooth for this game Mr. Clifford. My wife doesn’t want to come out much and the kids are not interested, not technical enough for this new generation. So, for the last couple of seasons, the boat goes in the water in the spring and just sits there until we take it out in the fall. All I seem to do is maintain it. This phase of my life is now over I think.” Mr. Whinslow said with just a hint of regret.

“And you say it has a trailer?” Jason asked.

“Yes sir, I can show you that on the way out of the marina, it’s stored in the compound over there.” Mr. Whinslow said, indicating the direction with a nod of his head. "Just been serviced, nothing wrong with it. The trailer storage has been paid for until the end of the season, as has the rental for the slip."

It came to the point in the transaction where they were about to negotiate the price and Jason was beginning the obligatory *'humming and harring'*.

"I'm still not sure whether this is the right decision for me," Jason mused. "I haven't sailed since I was in my teens and I'm not sure of the waterways," Jason paused, "I just don't know."

"If that's all you are worried about I would be glad to take you out a few times, show you the ropes as it were. It's a great boat, you won't get a better deal than this one." Old man Whinslow said, trying to clinch the deal. Jason took another look inside, came out and walked to the front of the boat. Jason inspected the anchor, line, and chain stored in a chamber at the front of the boat then returned to face Mr. Whinslow and offered him a price. Now it was Mr. Whinslow's turn to *'hum and har'*, eventually, they settled on a fair deal, a price that Jason was happy with and the one that Mr. Whinslow wanted from the get-go.

After inspecting the trailer, they shook hands on the deal and arranged a time to go out together sailing, at which point Jason would return with a certified check for the purchase of the boat. Jason couldn't have been more excited and immediately went home to plan for the trip. Jason was even more elated when he was informed by John on their first session on the water that he had all the charts for the Mississippi and on one occasion had even stopped at the very marina where Jason's grandfather had last been seen. John also had a 'Waterway Guide' which he brought up from the cabin and began to flick through the pages until he came to the one showing the very marina. John went on to explain the benefit of pairing the guide with the charts to arrange dockings and fuel stops.

Between training sessions on his new boat, Jason carried out some research on his intended route. He toyed with the idea of being a real 'looper' which he had learned was the term for someone sailing the great loop through the Great Lakes, the rivers, the Intra-coastal waterways of the U.S. and Canada. Jason's journey would begin right there in Cleveland, from Lake Erie, cutting through the lakes and down the Mississippi. But in the final analysis, he decided the more practical route was to tow his newly purchased boat down to the historic town of Kimmswick, Missouri where his new-found friend Chuck lived. Jason had exchanged numerous emails with Chuck and the new arrangements had been decided upon. Jason would launch his boat in Kimmswick and sail upriver to St. Louis, leaving his truck and trailer in Chuck's safe hands until his return. Of course, that also meant he had to sell his nice sedate, sedan and replace it with a truck powerful enough to pull his new rig, an action which was not appreciated by his two daughters.

Over the ensuing few weeks Jason gathered items he would need for the trip and began storing them on the boat. Sleeping-bag, high-powered flashlight, battery-operated lights so that he didn't run down the boat's batteries when he docked overnight. Then closer to his departure, he purchased bottles of water, provisions and packed clothes for all-seasons. From talking to people who had made the trip down the river, at the time of the year Jason was making the trip, he could expect a whole gambit of weather systems. As a precaution, he also stowed his scuba-diving equipment in the event of a foul-up with his prop. or some other unlikely occurrence.

So it was, much to the chagrin of his two daughters, Jason left his house early one morning, boat in tow, to begin the search for his lost grandfather, or at least to try and determine a reason for his disappearance. In all honesty, he felt his chances of finding any clue to the mystery were less than slim, but he felt there was no chance at all if he just did nothing. What was the worst that could happen?

Chapter 6 – The Trip – May 1944

After hanging up the phone, Ray walked to the door and opened it fully to see a slim, well-dressed, young man standing there.

"Hi. Ray?" The young man asked.

"Yes." Was all Ray said as he eyed the young man from head to toe. The fellow was Latin looking, olive colored skin with dark hair and dark eyes, he was much shorter than Ray, about five feet six inches, and couldn't have been more than 150 pounds soaking wet. But he had a friendly looking face that was forever smiling as if he enjoyed life to its fullest.

"Tony Lawless," the young man said and held his hand out to shake Ray's. "I understand I'm your ship's mate." Ray shook his hand and beckoned him in.

"Wow, great view, I'm looking across at another building," Tony said as he walked towards the window. "So, what do you know?"

"Know? All I know is I'm meeting you and, in the morning, we're being picked up by a taxi and taken to a boat where we will head to St. Louis. That's it." Ray said categorically.

"Sure, and the tooth-fairy is for real, right?" Tony said laughing as he made a playful punch to Ray's arm.

"No, really, that's all I know," Ray said emphatically.

"But you're the captain, the head honcho on this trip, right?" Tony asked, hunching his shoulders a little and holding his arms out to his side in that time-honored way when you're trying to figure something out. In addition, he gave a more questioning look at Ray.

"That's my understanding, yes, but that's as much as I know," Ray explained, but Tony was still looking at him as though he didn't believe a word of it. "Look, Tony, this morning I was on a ship that had just docked in Canada and was minding my own business when I was told to report to the bridge. The next thing I know I'm here in this hotel being told I am sailing a boat to St. Louis. I'm as much in the dark here as you are." Tony sat down on the expensive looking couch in the room and looked up at Ray.

"You're for real, you ain't kidding me?" Tony said looking deadly serious.

"For real, I'm not kidding you," Ray repeated Tony's words. Tony's reaction was to look down and shake his head a couple of times. But then he smiled, and a light flickered in his eyes.

"But we got money, right? We can order chow, right?" Tony asked.

"Yes." Ray simply said, wondering where this next tact was going.

"Well let's eat, I could eat a horse." Tony said, "why don't you get on the blower and order us up a banquet. Yea the works." Ray merely smiled and for the second time that evening, he picked up the phone, only this time he ordered some food.

Over a meal of prime rib, baked potato and vegetables the two men learned a little about themselves. Tony had only recently started at the Naval training school in Newport, but yesterday, before he could even pass-out of the academy he was driven here. Tony was single, didn't have a girlfriend back home in Chicago, and wanted to join the navy because he had spent his life on the boats owned by the family business. The family had a fleet of tug-boats that transported goods up and down the Illinois Waterway to the Mississippi and sometimes beyond.

Ray warmed to Tony very quickly, there wasn't anything not to like, he had an infectious, positive, attitude and he was funny too. But before they knew it, the time had come to hit the hay and they still had to pack their fine new clothes into the newly supplied carpet-bags. Tony agreed to come back in the morning at 7:00, with his bag all packed and ready when they would order breakfast. Once they had finished eating they would go together to meet their mysterious driver outside the hotel. With that, they bade each other good-night and Tony returned to his own room.

Next morning, as arranged, the two smartly dressed, young, fellows walked out of the hotel when immediately their driver pulled up his taxi beside them. The trunk immediately popped up and the driver was out of the taxi and grabbing their bags and placing them in the back. He then opened the back door of the taxi and ushered the two men into the back seat. Within seconds they were away and not a word was spoken until they arrived at their destination, some thirty minutes later. Their destination was a remote poorly, maintained, boathouse on a small river. The driver parked the taxi around the back of the boathouse so that it couldn't be seen from the road. Their driver then produced a key and unlocked the sturdy padlock on the door to the boathouse and waved the two men through.

Much to the surprise of the two men, the outside décor of the building belied the sophisticated set-up that was inside and the first thing that attracted their attention was the boat moored there. Amidst all the expensive looking tools and machinery littering the walls, there sitting peacefully in the water was a 1940 Chris-Craft Double Stateroom cabin cruiser.

"Is this our baby?" Tony said, eyes wide open with wonder as he immediately went to check out the engine.

"It is," replied their mysterious man.

"This is a diesel engine, that's unusual in this type of boat," Tony said, a little disappointed. "that's going to limit our speed a bit."

"The boat has had a few modifications, some of which is to the engine and the hull, I think you will find it can reach speeds of up to 30-35 miles an hour." The man replied, "hop aboard, I have to show you a few things."

One by one, all three of the men climbed aboard, Ray and Tony were running their hands over the sleek wood finish of all the surfaces, it certainly was a top of the line boat. The man pointed below, and he followed the two men down the steps to the living area.

"O.K. now listen up. I'm only going to say things once. Here are all the charts you will need to get you to St. Louis." The man pointed to a collection of documents sitting on top of the chart table in the corner to the cabin. "You can stop wherever you like on the trip but no partying and under no circumstances EVER allow anybody on board. Your objective is to arrive at your destination as quickly as possible without jeopardizing your safety or the safety of the boat, is that clear?" The man stopped to look at the two men individually as they nodded their heads in acquiescence.

"Radios, you have two, this one," the man said with his hand on a radio that was fixed to the bulkhead of the boat, "which is what you will be using for day-to-day uses, weather, marinas, tug-boats etc. Then there's this one." The man held out a small radio the likes of which neither of them had ever seen before. "When you are an hour out of Dock 13 in St. Louis, you will call me on this radio. Clearly, state the code that has been assigned, 'Cardinals are in town', that will be the only time you use this radio unless you have an emergency, in which case you will use the code 'Halifax is in Canada'. If you are unable to reach anyone on this radio, then use Channel 16 on the marine radio and use the same codes. That's it guys, oh, one more thing, there's a safe here with some cash in it, it has two keys, one for each of you." He dug into his pocket and pulled out two keys and handed the men one each, "the safe is fireproof and supposedly waterproof but I somehow doubt that. Any questions?" The two men looked at each other then shook their heads, then after further consideration, Ray had a sudden thought.

"The man who visited us in the hotel said we will be delivering some goods, where exactly are they?" Ray asked as he looked around for some tell-tale package.

"You don't need to know. Now I suggest you get going." The man replied perfunctorily, obviously trying to deflect the query before any further discussion could be had. "The key is in the ignition, start her up and I will open the boathouse doors." The three men went top-side and while Ray started up the engines Tony untied the mooring lines while the man opened the doors.

No sooner had the man opened the doors Tony had unhooked the last of the lines and walked expertly onto the boat as Ray slid the boat out of the boathouse at just above idle speed to join the river. The man pointed in the direction of the river that Ray was supposed to go to and shouted out one last instruction.

"Follow the river to the merge, you can't miss it and then you will have to rely on the charts," the man said as the two men waved their acknowledgment, then under his breath the man muttered a few more words, “good luck you poor bastards, you’re going to need it.”

Chapter 7 – Launching the Boat – Modern Day

Jason had toyed with the idea of carrying out the whole trip by boat but after careful consideration, the communications with Chuck and in deference to his daughters' concerns he decided the best idea would be to tow the boat to Kimmswick. If he wanted to explore the Tennessee River or the lower Mississippi he could still do that and maintain Kimmswick as a base.

It was a 580-mile road trip from Cleveland to Kimmswick and under normal conditions, it was a distance Jason could handle in a single day. But he was hauling a trailer, so he scheduled to split the journey into two days. Jason planned a stop the other side of Indianapolis, he estimated it would take him 6 or 7 hours to arrive there. As it turned out, his reckoning was dead on, despite experiencing a few teething problems with the trailer during the first few miles. As soon as he had hit the freeway he began to get a little more confidence with his new rig and was feeling quite proud of his decision to make the trip.

The following day, Jason left the hotel at first light and was hoping to arrive in Kimmswick by lunchtime, he had even emailed Chuck to inform him of his pending arrival. Chuck replied, and suggested Jason should drive straight down to the marina and then they would go out for lunch, doesn't matter if he arrived a little late. So it was, at 12:40 Jason was slowly driving his rig down a hill and into a marina where an old guy was waving and directing Jason to where he should park. Jason drove into the spot indicated by the man and came to a stop, he turned off the engine and got out of the truck.

"Chuck?" Jason asked.

"Hi Ray," the wizened old man said. Chuck might be 81 years old, thought Jason, but he looked fitter than most people half his age. He had a thick thatch of white hair; his skin had the consistency of old leather from years of being outside in all weathers. His blue eyes looked sharp and when he shook hands with Jason it was firm and the muscles in his arm were taut and he didn't appear to have an ounce of body fat anywhere.

"Boy, you're the spitting image of your grandfather," Chuck said.

"Wow, I'm impressed, you can still remember what he looked like?" Jason asked.

"Sure can!" Chuck replied. "Boy, you can't imagine my disappointment that day about not getting on that boat and never hearing about the two men again. But didn't give it a thought at the time, we get a lot of boats through here that we never see again. But when you called to say they had disappeared I remembered, that night a couple of ships went down, one of them was 'The St. Louis Streamer'. It was a party boat taking some of the St. Louis elite on a junket down the river, over 30 lives were lost."

"There were other boats lost that night?" Jason asked incredulously.

"Yes, sir. It was some storm, just upriver there used to be another marina, The Missouri State Marina, it hadn't been up and running very long, bit upscale as you would say today, but not only did a couple of boats from there disappear but so did the dockmaster. It was a bad 'un." Chuck explained, "anyway, let's talk about this over lunch, I'm parched." Jason thought that was a surprising choice of words until they walked into an establishment and the man behind the bar had already poured and served a large beer for Chuck before he had even sat down. Chuck waved to a couple of men sitting at the bar and they looked around at him a little surprised and disappointed that Chuck hadn't walked over to join them.

"What can I get you sir?" The barman asked Jason.

"I'll have the same," Jason replied. When the man returned with Jason's beer he took their food order and while they waited for their meal to arrive they talked largely about Jason's trip from Cleveland.

Over lunch, Jason didn't really learn much more than he already knew, although he was intrigued about the losses of other boats.

"One of the problems on this stretch of the river, and something you have to be aware of are those wing dams," Chuck said.

"Yea, I read about those and the guy who sold me the boat also warned me about them too," Jason replied.

"At this time of the year, they are at their worst because the river is at its highest and you can't see them. You must rely on your charts and make sure you remain within the channel markers. That way you can keep clear of them." Chuck said.

"If they are so dangerous what is the point of them?" Jason asked.

"They deflect the current towards the center of the river and helps prevent river-bank erosion." Chuck explained, "but many a boat has been damaged hitting one of them."

"So, you think that's what could have happened to my grandfather and those other boats?" Jason asked.

"It's possible, the river and the winds were so rough that night, it would have been easy to be blown off course. But I wouldn't like to speculate." Chuck said.

For the rest of the meal, they discussed family matters and Chuck shared stories of his experiences on the river. Jason insisted on paying for lunch and after he had paid, Chuck gave Jason a brief tour of historic Kimmswick, the second oldest town in Missouri he told him. Once the tour was over they returned to the marina to launch Jason's boat and to encounter his first real test.

Anyone who has ever had to tow a trailer knows that until you have had some experience reversing a rig it could take a few tries before you get it right. To avoid Jason's embarrassment, the 81-year-old Chuck took the wheel and expertly turned and reversed the trailer down the boat ramp to the water. Jason was grateful, he felt he could still be trying after darkness fell. With the boat in the water and secured against the dock, Jason parked his truck and trailer beside a large workshop, as instructed by Chuck.

"It'll be safe there until you get back." Chuck said as they both walked back to the dock, "even if I'm not here it will be well taken care of until you return." He then called over a teenager who was working on the dock. "Hey Charlie, this is Mr. Clifford, he's going downriver for a trip, keep an eye on his rig for him O.K.?" Chuck nodded his head in the direction of Jason's truck and trailer.

"Sure thing Mr. Clifford," the boy said. "Doing a little fishing are you?"

"He certainly is, but not for fish!" Chuck replied with a smile, "no, something a little more important than that. I'll explain later, now get back to work, you young scallywag!"

"Bye Mr. Clifford, nice meeting you," Charlie said as he returned to what he was doing on the docks.

"Likewise," Jason said, and then he turned back to face Chuck. "Well, thanks for all your help Chuck, I doubt very much that anything is going to come of all this, but I feel I have to try." Jason said.

"You never know, but you're right son, at least you are trying," Chuck replied and held out his hand. "Good luck, I really hope you find something out about your grandfather's disappearance and if you do, let me know. I sure fell in love with that boat of his."

"Will do," Jason said as he shook his hand once more, "who knows? I may be back quicker than you think." Jason climbed onto his boat and once more went to review the charts showing the waters between Chuck's marina and St. Louis. He took careful note of the wing dams noted on the chart and felt they would not be difficult to avoid, as Chuck advised if he kept to the channel markers indicating the center of the river. The next thing he knew, it was early evening, he made himself a sandwich and a coffee and once he had eaten he sent an email to his daughters, using the marina's WiFi, to let them know he had made it safely to his first destination. All this effort and outdoor activity had made Jason very tired so, despite the fact that there was still plenty of light in the evening sky he decided to have an early night.

That night, Jason slept on the boat for the first time, sleeping diagonally across the forward double bed with some of his strategically placed luggage. The strange thing about a spacious boat, the amount of available space shrinks rapidly when you begin to load clothes, spares, food, and water into it. Most of his stuff was in the rear of the boat, evenly distributed underneath the seats. One of the pieces of advice old Whinslow had given him was to keep the dining table and the seats around it clear. He had said there was nothing worse after a hard day's sail than having to make room on the table and clearing the seats to sit down inside, away from the elements going on above deck.

In the morning, Jason recalled those words of wisdom as he sat at the dining table enjoying a breakfast consisting of orange juice, cereal, and a coffee. The early morning sun was streaming through the windows and the rear-hatch, it was a beautiful spring day. Once he had finished eating, he cleaned the dishes and put everything back securely in its place. He made one last check to ensure all doors and drawers were secure before deciding he was ready to set off.

Jason went topside to survey his surroundings. It was a little chilly but not a cloud appeared in the sky and there was very little wind. It boded well for his first day on the water. Jason had decided to leave the boat's mast and rigging at home because he hadn't envisaged doing any sailing along the rivers. This resulted in no visual restrictions and far more clearance walking along the boat when he wanted to dock or line up in locks. From an efficiency point of view, it would also mean he wouldn't need to use the water ballast which was required for stability when in sailing mode. The empty ballast tank would allow him to be able to employ greater speed if required in an emergency.

Jason turned on the engine and began itemizing his mental checklist. Centerboard down, rudders down, lines untied, no traffic, slowly pull out into the river. Once Jason had navigated to the center of the river he increased speed a little, centerboard up, rudders up, increase to desired speed, which was about eight miles an hour. He didn't want to go faster than that just in case he missed something, exactly what that something was he didn't know.

Chapter 8 – Beginning of the Trip – May 1944

The first few hours of the trip were very steady, and Ray and Tony took turns at the helm, getting the feel of the boat. There was some food in the cooler and at mid-day, Tony made sandwiches for lunch and he opened a couple of bottles of cola. The Clinch river wound its way around some beautiful, peaceful countryside but in terms of time, it took much longer than they had anticipated. As a result, that first night they didn't quite make the convergence with the Tennessee River and because of a distinct lack of marinas along the Clinch, they were forced to dock against an abandoned jetty that they came across just before dusk.

Over a spartan dinner of cold meats and a salad, they speculated on what they could possibly be transporting that necessitated such a covert journey. It begged the question, why on earth were they being dispatched to take a package to St. Louis in such a circuitous route when it would have been so much quicker to transport by road or rail? And more significantly, where was the package? They had both unsuccessfully scoured the boat in search of anything remotely important. But of course, they both agreed, they were in the military, theirs was not to reason why, theirs was but to do and die. After dinner, they cleared up their few dirty dishes and plates, spent an hour or two swapping stories before having an early night.

The next morning, they were back en route, and it wasn't long before they did indeed join the Tennessee River, which was going to represent the majority of their time on this trip. Along the river, Tony decided to buy various kinds of pasta and vegetables at stops along the way and he spent a lot of time in the galley preparing meals while Ray navigated the boat around the bends and eddies of the river. It took them almost a month, but eventually, they reached the convergence with the Ohio River and that evening they managed to dock at Paducah in Kentucky. They went through their normal ritual of dinner, clearing up and swapping stories before getting to bed, happy in the knowledge that in the morning they would be on the Mississippi and only one more sleep from their destination.

They were up with the dawn and on the river at first light. With Cairo, Illinois on their starboard side they knew they were rapidly approaching the Mississippi, which also signaled the imminent completion of their river trip. Up until now, except for a few rain showers, the weather had been kind to them, but as they turned to go upstream on the mighty river it was obvious that a major storm was on its way. They had a choice to make, if they gunned the boat they could make St. Louis that evening, the modified gas tanks were full, so they had sufficient fuel to make the trip. Alternatively, they could continue at cruising speed and be forced to stop for one, possibly two nights. They agreed that the former option was the one to take.

They were making good time but as the day progressed, so did the ferocity of the storm and they were beginning to have doubts about arriving in St. Louis before dark. Just ahead on their port-side was a marina and they decided to pull in to take a break and once more consider their options. The river had gotten very choppy and the swirling winds made docking extremely hazardous, but they were assisted by a man and what they assumed to be his young son. As Ray tried to keep the boat steady, Tony threw a bow line to the young boy, he thought he would pass it to his father to tie up but instead, the young boy adroitly tied up the line to a cleat on the dock. Meanwhile, the man had grabbed the stern line and tied it to a cleat. Ray turned off the engine and both Tony and he climbed from the boat to the dock.

"Thanks, guys, it's getting pretty rough out there," Ray said, pretty much stating the obvious.

"Sure is, but I think it's going to get worse before it gets better." The man replied.

"We're supposed to get to St. Louis this evening, what is it another twenty miles or so?" Tony asked.

"It is, but you may be better off staying here the night." The man said. Ray and Tony exchanged glances but neither said anything.

"Mister, that's a fine-looking boat, can I have a look inside?" The young boy asked, he was staring at the boat in awe and was dying to climb aboard. Ray smiled and was about to say 'sure' until he remembered his instructions.

"'Fraid not son," Ray said, maybe a little too abruptly and he tried to make amends, "I think we're going to push on. But thanks for all your help." Ray felt bad about the disappointed look on the young boy's face if only he could explain, instead he turned and got back on the boat. Tony untied both lines and he too climbed back onto the boat leaving the poor boy almost in tears at their refusal to let him go onboard and his father shaking his head in disbelief.

Chapter 9 – Enjoying the Outing – Modern Day

That first morning, Jason was in his element, out on the mighty Mississippi singing a few bars of 'Ole Man River' and not caring who could hear his atrocious rendition. He was on the water, enjoying nature and waving at the few other boaters he passed along the river, this was the best time he had had in a while. Jason almost forgot his purpose for being there, but, in reality, the quest was just an excuse to do something different. Although he had enjoyed the chat with Chuck and the research he had been forced to carry out for this trip, he really wasn't expecting to discover any new information. There was one thing he thought he could do since his meeting over lunch with Chuck the previous day. The marina that had come up in the conversation, The State Marina of Missouri, that was new information to him and quite the coincidence that it had opened only a short time before his grandfather's trip and had closed at about the same time as his grandfather's demise. According to Chuck, the marina had been appropriated by the government, nobody had known why. Jason would be sure to keep a close eye on the shoreline for a possible opening into the old marina. Chuck had said it was about five miles north of his marina, so after about thirty minutes of traveling he unpacked his new binoculars from its case and began to scan the river bank.

Amazingly, many miles of this stretch of the Mississippi is devoid of any habitation, trees, bushes or wildlife. In fact, it looks quite desolate and there are stretches where you could travel over 200 miles between gas stops. This made what Jason then saw even more surprising, as he continued to look through his binoculars, a large wall topped with barbed wire had come into his view. The wall was about 500 yards along and it appeared to be unbroken. On the wall, at regular intervals, were signs but he couldn't quite make out the wording, he would have to wait until he was slightly closer to distinguish what they said. He checked around for boat traffic and seeing it was clear he made a bee-line for the wall. It seemed a strange coincidence that this wall would be situated at about the same location as he expected the old marina to be.

Jason brought the boat as close to the wall as he possibly could while maintaining his position within the channel markers in the river. It appeared to be an old wall made of solid concrete, not those pre-fabricated sheets that fitted into columns. Now he could clearly see the signs, 'Restricted Area – DANGER Keep Out' they stated, in bold red characters.

The signs were of the old metal type and some were badly rusted and illegible. The stanchions holding the barbed wire on top of the wall were badly rusted, as was the wire and much of it was hanging in rusty strands down the wall. It seemed obvious to Jason that the original reason for building the wall to protect what was on the other side was no longer relevant. Something else, now that he was closer to the wall he could also make out a slight opening on the left side of the edifice, it was barely ten feet wide where the wall had crumbled and left a gap. Jason studied the gap for a full minute before letting the binoculars hang down from its strap that was around his neck.

"In for a penny, in for a pound!" Jason said to himself and headed towards the opening.

As Jason neared the gap he could see lumps of concrete protruding from the water. The good news was, his boat only had a draught of one foot, so he was relying heavily on his depth sounder to make him aware if the water level got too low. The bad news was, at a slow speed the boat's steering became less controllable when both the centerboard and rudders were in the up position. He would be relying solely on the engine as a rudder, but that was a risk he was prepared to take because it didn't look like his boat would be able to clear any underwater obstructions if the supplementary steering was employed. Jason felt a couple of bumps and scratches were made to the boat as he traversed the gap, but he made it safely through, except he couldn't help but notice that the perimeter wall must have been at least two feet thick, made of solid concrete and re-bars. There was something else, in the center of the concrete was an insert of some type, but he couldn't quite make out what that was. But Jason soon forgot all about that once he turned his attention to what he discovered within the confines of the wall.

Chapter 10 – Accident on the River – May 1944

Ray and Tony had traveled only a few miles up the river when the two men realized that the decision to travel to St. Louis that night was indeed a bad one. The winds had really picked up to gale force and the rain was lashing against their faces, reducing their visibility substantially. The poor conditions were taking all of Ray's efforts to keep the boat on a line and Ray was just on the point of returning to the marina when he spotted an opening on his port side. Despite the teeming rain and trees, he could still see lights and masts, albeit barely, and figured it must be another marina, although it wasn't shown on the charts he had. Ray checked his surroundings for other boats, not seeing any, he turned the boat to head for the gap leading to what he hoped was indeed a marina and a safe haven from the worsening storm. Ray left the main channel and was approaching the entrance to the marina when suddenly, a paddle steamer came out of the gloom at a considerable rate of knots, far too fast for the conditions, and made a rapid turn for the safety of the marina. The captain of the vessel had obviously not seen the cabin-cruiser, despite it's lights, and Ray was forced to make appropriate maneuvers to avoid a collision. Relieved that he had just prevented a major catastrophe Ray's relief suddenly turned to concern as they were caught in the paddle steamer's wake and was being buffeted around like a cork in a maelstrom. Ray was handling the boat as well as he could until a large wave shot them upwards and they came crashing down on a wing dam with enough force to send Ray falling to the deck and throwing Tony over the side. Fortunately, they were both wearing life-jackets, Ray recovered very quickly, he tossed a line to Tony who was floating just a few feet from the boat. Tony scrambled back on board and Ray regained control of the vessel, which didn't appear to be any the worse for wear despite the force of the collision with the wing dam. At least now, because of the paddle steamer's actions, Ray was assured that the gap was indeed an entrance to a marina. Once more, Ray lined the boat up with the marina's entrance and gave the engine enough throttle to overcome the waves, wind, and current.

They were welcomed at the entrance to the marina by a crudely painted sign that said 'State Marina of Missouri' but Ray was more interested in watching the crew of the paddle steamer negotiating their docking into one of the vacant slips. There was an empty slip beside the boat and Ray aimed to pull into the neighboring dock, primarily to give the captain a piece of his mind for the man's reckless seamanship. But as Ray began to turn the boat into the empty slip the vessel felt sluggish, there didn't appear to be anything wrong with the engine but after a month or so on the boat, he had a pretty good feel for it and something was definitely wrong. Ray managed to dock the boat, albeit with some difficulty, Tony, despite being soaked right through, was immediately out of the boat and on the dock to secure the vessel. Ray went below, anticipating a cabin full of water but was surprised to find none. Ray checked the bilges, there was water in them but no more than would be expected given the inclement conditions.

"What's wrong Ray?" Tony shouted from the doorway.

"I don't know, it just doesn't feel right after that crash, but I can't find anything wrong," Ray responded, still trying to figure out the problem.

"Funny you should say that," Tony replied, "I thought it was my imagination, but it looks as though the boat is sitting a little lower in the water than it should be."

"Really?" Ray said and brushed past Tony to lean over the side to get a better look. "I think you're right Tony. Damn," Ray said, then stood and thought for a few seconds before continuing. "I think our journey ends here.

Perhaps mystery man can make the swap here instead of St. Louis. I'm going to have to contact him."

"But we should only be contacting him in the case of an emergency unless of course, we are in St. Louis, which we're not," Tony said.

"Well, that's just about true in both cases," Ray responded as they were both standing on the boat in the pouring rain. He saw the confused look on Tony's face, so he tried to explain, "I don't know what's wrong with the boat, but it has taken on water, it's too risky to take it any further. And we were supposed to call him when we were an hour from St. Louis, which we are. The only difference is, we're not going to be able to continue our trip to St. Louis, so maybe they could transfer the package here."

"I see what you are saying, makes sense. O.K." Tony agreed.

Ray went down below to retrieve the special radio that had been handed to them that first day on the boat, he pressed the call button, but there was no reply to his signal. He tried again, but still received no response.

"Maybe the weather has something to do with not being able to get through," Ray suggested.

"Maybe we should try the regular radio, that's what the man said," Tony suggested. Ray moved over to the radio in the bulkhead, he verified that the channel was set to 16 and said the code, "Halifax is in Canada." There was no immediate response and Ray was about to repeat the emergency code when there was a reply.

"Hold." Was the succinct reply. A moment later the familiar voice of the mystery man came through the airwaves.

"Switch to channel 70." Was all that the mystery man said. Ray followed instructions and repeated the code.

"What's the problem?" Mystery man asked.

"We're approximately 15 miles short of St. Louis in a marina named the State Marina of Missouri, on the west side of the river. Unfortunately, the conditions are bad out here and we were cut up by a paddle steamer, we don't think we can travel any further." Ray explained and waited for the mystery man's response.

"Stay put." The mystery man replied, and the radio went dead. Ray and Tony just looked at each other, no preamble, no explanation, just 'stay put'. They then realised that they were both soaked through and decided to get changed before their muscles ceased up. By the time they had changed into dry clothes, two things happened almost simultaneously. They began to hear music playing on the paddle steamer and a man in a sou'wester was standing on the dock crying out to them, "ahoy there, ahoy."

Ray came top-side and stood under the bimini to try and keep dry as he confronted the man who was calling to them from the dock. There were very little of his features that could be seen under all his foul-weather gear.

"Hi, what's up?" Ray asked politely.

"You can't stay here, this is a private marina, you have to move on." The man was quite officious and was giving them no dispensation for the terrible conditions. Ray noticed the man had a large bushy, grey, nicotine-stained mustache that went up and down as he spoke.

"We can't, we have mechanical issues." Ray calmly replied.

"I don't care, you have to leave, there's another marina just down river." The man was insistent.

"We came in here to shelter from the storm as did they," Ray said, pointing to the paddle steamer, then he added, "by the way, who are you?"

“I’m the dockmaster,” he said, pointing to himself, full of his own importance, then to accentuate the point he pulled down his hood to reveal his cap, resplendent with a badge that spelled ‘DOCKMASTER’. Then he continued, “and their presence has nothing to do with you. They are allowed to be here, you’re not.” The belligerent old man said, “you’ve got one hour to leave, or I’ll be calling the police.” Then, to avoid any further confrontation he briskly walked away. Ray and Tony smiled at each other, the fact was, they couldn’t go anywhere, and they were certain that the mystery man would soon arrive to take care of them.

What they didn’t know was just how he was going to take care of them.

Chapter 11 – Exploring the Restricted Area – Modern Day

As Jason passed through the gap in the wall, he noticed that to the left of him was just a continuation of the same concrete edifice that he had seen from the river. To his right was what Jason could only assume was once a marina, so he turned the boat to that direction. There were masts sticking out of the water indicating the presence of sunken boats, so he decided against navigating the entire marina to avoid the possibility of colliding with a submerged structure. To his immediate left was an empty slip, it was situated between two docks that were in a decrepit condition. The docks were built around wooden piles that allowed the platforms to rise and fall with the height of the water. The piles themselves looked rotten but Jason couldn't see any that appeared to be missing. Gingerly, Jason idled into the empty slip, constantly looking from one side to the other for any obstructions underneath the boat. He had pulled in with the dock on his port side and he discovered that what cleats were there on the dock did not look too secure, so he decided to hitch first a stern line to one of the piles, then a bowline on the pile at the other end of the dock. With the boat secure, he turned off the engine and began to look around.

The wall that he saw from the river appeared to encompass the entire marina and for the life of him, with the exception of the gap he had just come through, he could not see another entrance. There appeared to be no gate, door or entrance of any kind. Furthermore, there didn't appear to be anything nefarious that had occurred within the wall, it was just an old, neglected marina, so, his immediate thought was, why were there 'Restricted' signs plastered all over the outside? Jason decided to investigate.

As a safety precaution, Jason decided to keep his life preserver on as he sat on the gunwale of his boat and tested the dock, first with his left foot and then his right. Although parts of the dock looked rotten, most of it appeared to be stable. He put his full weight on the dock, while still hanging on to the gunwale of his boat as a precaution, thankfully, he didn't go crashing through. His mindset was to try and find an entrance to the marina from the land-side, so he began to walk, albeit with some trepidation, along the walkway between the docks towards the wall furthest away from the river. If there was going to be an entrance, that's where it would be. He had a good look around, everywhere was strewn with weeds and it didn't look as if any living creature had been here for many a year.

There were old, fancy wrought iron lamp posts on almost every slip, some still had their light bulbs intact and at the head of each of the slips was a tarnished, brass plaque indicating its number. Most of the docks were empty but what few boats were there had obviously not been used for some considerable time. They were all green with algae, rotten and forgotten and although, some of the boats were still afloat, many had succumbed to the elements and were either partially or fully underwater. Some had listed, others had turned turtle and there were also those whose lines, still intact, had prevented them from being totally submerged. There were even a few boats that had not sunk and had broken away from their lines and were beached in one corner of the marina where the winds and what little current had taken them. Most of the boats he could see were motor boats of various sizes ranging from small recreational fishing boats to grandiose cabin-cruisers, but all were in the same terrible condition. Littered among the motor-boats was the odd sail-boat, the canvas around their booms and headstays in tatters.

Walking cautiously along the walkway, Jason finally arrived on terra firma at what appeared to be a boat ramp. Leading from the boat ramp was pavement, badly deteriorated and pitted by weeds, but a road nonetheless.

Jason walked onto the pavement and followed it up a slight gradient only to be confronted by the wall. So, he had found what was once the entrance to the marina, but for some inexplicable reason, it had now been completely blocked off. As he returned to the ramp he noticed a building that was also on a floating dock with four piles, one on each corner. It looked as if the building was once a small marine store and just above the doorway, was a sign. Jason went to read what it said, chiseled on the sign, in large letters were the words 'State Marina of Missouri'. So, this was truly the marina Chuck had told him about.

Many of the windows in the wooden, slat, building had been broken and part of the roof had blown away. Jason walked to the door and tried the handle, it was locked but one of the panes of glass was no longer there, so it was no effort to reach through and unlock the door. He opened the door and continuing to test his every step before he put his full weight down, he gingerly walked in. The floor in the building had been sheltered from the elements to a certain extent so it appeared to be much stronger than the exposed docks. As he looked around the inside, there were shelves of marine supplies, confectionary, drinks and packets of food which were certainly well past their best buy date, even if they ever had one when these packets were manufactured. Jason saw charts, travel books for the area including routes along the Mississippi.

On one side of the store was a counter and placed at one end of it was an old-fashioned cash-register, Jason hadn't seen one of those since he was a kid. He walked around the counter, not being able to resist the urge to press a couple of the keys to see if the till would slide out with that familiar springing sound. Surprisingly, it still worked but what was even more amazing was that inside was a large amount of cash. Now that he was on the working side of the counter he could also see a desk and hanging above it was a sign that read 'Dockmaster'. On the desk were what obviously were the scraps of a sandwich that had once been wrapped in grease-proof paper that was now unwrapped and badly deteriorated. Beside the sandwich remnants, was a cup from a Thermos flask that was standing on a corner of the paper. There was also a dried-up apple core, it looked as though the dockmaster had been irreverently called away from his snack and had never returned. It reminded Jason of another maritime riddle, the Mary Celeste, an American merchant ship which was found bobbing around in the Atlantic Ocean. On board the abandoned vessel was found a table laid with food and in the hold, the cargo, still intact, but no sign of any passengers or crew.

Jason then saw a large book which appeared to be a log of some kind and beside it was a cash box. Jason opened the cash box to reveal a reasonable sum of money in paper dollars, he assumed these were docking fees that were kept separate from the proceeds of the store that were retained in the till. He closed the box and turned his attention to the log, which was of a very old type, leather-bound, thick cover which had certainly helped it to survive the ravages of time fairly well. Jason gently opened the book and began to read the contents on the first page. The writing appeared to indicate the comings and goings of transient boats and the fees they paid for the duration of their stay. Jason carefully turned the thick paper pages until he came to the last entries in the log. Using his finger, he scanned down the list of boats written on the page until he reached the final two entries. His heart skipped a beat as he read the details of the two boats written in the log:

05/20/44 16:45 Slip 360 St. Louis Streamer 1 night 5.00
Occupants: 32

05/20/44 16:46 Slip 361 Cabin-cruiser Uninvited – asked to leave
Occupants: 2

Jason was almost certain he had docked in slip 362.

Chapter 12 – Visit of the Mystery Man – May 1944

Since the meeting with the dockmaster, Ray had calmed down from the accident, although he still wanted to confront the captain of the vessel that forced him onto the wing dam. Consequently, both Ray and Tony covered their heads with a jacket, left their boat and followed the sound of the music that was coming from the paddle steamer. There was a gangplank leading from the dock to the bridge where someone was pottering about inside. They walked up the gangplank and tapped on the door. A look of surprise came on the elderly face of the man on the bridge, but he didn't hesitate to open the door to let the two men inside and provide shelter from the storm.

"Who are you, may I ask?" The man said with a hint of a French accent as Ray tried to evaluate him. He had a kindly looking face, but like everyone else who seemed to have worked on the river for any length of time, it was weather-beaten. The King Edward style beard gave him a look of authority which was accentuated by the navy-blue captain's hat that matched his smart uniform. He was a short man, stocky but he appeared well-built, and Ray was having difficulty putting an age to the man.

“We are the crew of the cabin-cruiser you forced onto a wing dam when you turned into this marina,” Ray replied with enough seriousness to sound indignant.

“What’s that you say?” The man said, “I saw no boat when I turned in here.”

“Obviously,” Tony added with a hint of sarcasm, which was met with an officious stare from the man.

“Young man, I was working on these rivers before you were born, in fact probably before your father was born and I have never had an accident,” the man replied indignantly but Tony wasn’t done.

“No, how could you,” Tony said, “you don’t see the other vessels that’s had to take collision avoidance moves to keep out of your way.”

“Alright, we’ve obviously got off to a bad start here,” Ray intervened. “but our boat is damaged. We were turning into the marina when you came out of nowhere and we were forced to turn sharply to avoid a collision. But then a wave hit us, lifted us right up and dropped us onto a wing dam.”

“Oh my, look I am so sorry, my company will pay for your repairs, don’t worry,” the man said, genuinely concerned.

"Oh, we're not worried, in fact, we are waiting for someone to come and take a look at the damage right now." Ray explained.

"In this weather?" The man asked.

"Our man is not going to be put off by the weather," Tony said, "he'll be here."

"Well, I doubt he will be arriving by boat. This storm is not supposed to die down until the early hours of the morning, even then, the water may not be safe enough to head out." The man explained then added, "oh how rude of me, let me introduce myself, my name is Jean Deschamps. I am the captain of this vessel, I have three crew plus eight entertainment and catering staff on board. We are carrying twenty passengers who are being entertained by a band for a fun night on the river."

"Hi, my name is Ray, and this is Tony. We are on the last leg of a trip to St. Louis but I'm afraid this could be our last stop." Ray said.

"My friend, I am so sorry about what has happened but really, I didn't see you." Jean said. The man was honest about not seeing another vessel when he turned into the marina, but it was probably more of a case of not expecting to see anyone else in these conditions.

"Is that a French accent you have," Ray asked.

"Oui monsieur." Jean replied in his native tongue before continuing in English, "I am originally from Quebec and have spent almost fifty years working the lakes and rivers. I have owned, lost, rented and worked on boats of all sizes and types, beginning with the small steamers working the St. Lawrence River near my home in Montreal. Then I gradually worked my way down to New Orleans and finally settled in St. Louis. A few years ago, I bought this baby and now I am quite content to run local excursions on the river."

"But surely you knew the storm would be too bad for a trip to-night?" Tony asked, doubting the captain's competency.

"Ah, my clientele does not mind if we are at dock, let's just say that they partake in various activities that they wouldn't be able to do on land or at least, a little cheaper. Did you know the government has introduced a tax on dancing?" Ray and Tony looked at each other and shook their heads in disbelief. "Of course, that's just one of the activities that goes on during our cruises. My customers pay me very well to rent my boat and for my discretion." Jean said conspiratively, with a little wink. "So, knowing we wouldn't be able to travel very far this evening, I made arrangements to stay at this marina, if we are forced to stay here until the early hours of the morning, then so be it. I don't think I will hear a complaint from my guests unless of course, we run out of drinks." Jean smiled, mischievously. Suddenly, Jean's eyes lit up "look, why don't you join the guests on board. There's music, drinks and plenty of food and I might add, there are also a couple of beautiful, unaccompanied women who would be glad to make the acquaintance of two handsome, young, men like yourselves." Jean added lecherously.

"No, really, I don't think...." Ray began to say, despite Tony eagerly looking through the window at the dancing that was taking place in the adjacent ballroom, he was just champing at the bit to have a little fun.

"Nonsense," Jean interrupted him, "we're going to be here all night because of this storm and in some small way it may compensate you a little for your inconvenience. Come!"

Without given them an opportunity to refuse Jean had opened a door to a room where a jazz quartet was blaring out some fast-paced music. Ray and Tony entered the room where they were immediately offered a drink of champagne and a choice of hor d'oeuvres from a silver platter. No sooner had they taken a sip of their drink, the first taste of alcohol since their trip began, they were approached by a couple of women. Most of the men were in a corner of the room playing what looked like roulette and if those chips were real, there was some heavy betting going down.

One of the women appeared to take a shine to Ray, she gracefully approached him and offered her hand that was covered in a black lace glove.

"Lady Ashdene, how do you do?" The lady said with a distinct English accent. All these people from so many different places, Ray thought, it was like a meeting of the League of Nations. Ray shook her hand and felt the softness of her fingers under the delicate lace, realizing he had not touched a woman since he had left home almost six months ago.

"Hi, I'm Ray, like a ray of sunshine." Ray almost stuttered out the words, intoxicated by her stunning, beauty, her perfume and the way she presented herself. Lady Ashdene must have been in her early thirties and she was wearing a beautiful black pleated dress that exuded elegance. Her dark auburn hair was cut short, just reaching down to her shoulders over the collar of the white tight jacket she was wearing that accentuated her slim figure. To top off the ensemble she was wearing what Ray could only describe as a gaudy necklace that appeared to be gold studded with small diamonds and rubies, with matching bracelet and earrings. Between the forefingers of her left-hand, she was delicately holding a diamond-encrusted cigarette-holder containing a freshly lit cigarette.

"That's a beautiful dress you a wearing Lady Ashdene," Ray said, struggling to think of anything interesting to say.

"Why, thank you." Lady Ashdene said, twirling to let the base of her dress brush lightly against Ray's legs. "I was in Paris you know, spring to be exact, just before the start of the war and I went to visit my favorite French designer, Robert Piguet," Lady Ashdene explained between short puffs of her cigarette, "the great man recommended a dress called 'Café Anglais' that was being designed by a young newcomer, Christian Dior, I think his name was. Well, of course, I just had to have it, me being English, I thought it was most appropriate, don't you agree?"

"I must admit, it looks beautiful on you," Ray replied. Just then, a loud cheer came up from the corner of the ballroom where the roulette game was being played. Both Ray and Lady Ashdene's attention were automatically drawn to the excitement and they watched as a man was being congratulated by all the other men positioned around the roulette wheel. All the men were smartly dressed in evening dress of various styles.

"It looks like Sinclair has made a killing." Lady Ashdene said, then after another quick puff on her cigarette she leaned into Ray and whispered in his ear, "once he's had a few more drinks he'll lose the lot." Her lips brushed Ray's ear, it was a brief, light touch but enough to send tingles through his body. She stepped back with the slightest of smiles on her face, she knew exactly what she was doing, Ray thought. She had still not let go of Ray's hand from their initial meeting and now she began tugging at his arm as she led him to a door that looked as though it led down to a lower deck. Ray's mind was in turmoil, as they walked past Tony who was dancing the jitterbug with another lady. Ray was a trustworthy, honest person and the thought of him being unfaithful to his wife was an abhorrence to him. Yet, this woman was leading him down a path to adultery and at such a stage in his marriage, he would have to live with this transgression for the rest of his life. Fortunately, his dilemma was solved when he saw a man walking past the back of the boat, heading towards his cabin-cruiser. It was the mystery man.

Chapter 13 – Looking for the Lost Boats – Modern Day

Jason picked up the log to return to his boat but before he did, he extracted all the money from both the cash-box and the till. He had qualms about taking the cash, but he figured it had been there for some 70 years and nobody had missed it up until now. He walked to his boat as fast as he could but still using enough caution to ensure his foot didn't go through any of the wooden panels on the docks. When he reached his boat, he looked down at the plaque indicating his slip number, it was indeed 362. He tried to look through the depths in the neighboring slip, number 361, but the water was too murky to distinguish anything. He didn't need to look at slip 360, the mast protruding from the water was proof enough there was a submerged vessel down below, but was it the St. Louis Streamer? Right then and there he decided to reconnoiter the area with his scuba-gear but as it was already lunchtime he was going to give the dive some thought over a sandwich and a coffee.

While he was preparing lunch, several questions began to cross his mind. If, indeed it was the St. Louis Streamer that was submerged in the next slip, why was it reported as sunk during the storm? If it sank here in the marina, surely the passengers would have made it to safety and if that was the case, what had happened to them? The same applied to the cabin-cruiser his grandfather was on. If he made it here to the marina, why would he have left a second safe-haven if the storm was as bad as Chuck had said it was? What if the cabin-cruiser is submerged in the very next slip? In which case, what happened to his grandfather and his shipmate?

Jason decided he would wait an hour to let his lunch settle then he would carry out an exploratory dive to verify two things. Whether the cabin-cruiser was there or not and check the name on the boat in slip 360. After lunch, Jason began preparing his diving equipment and secured his camera in its purpose-built underwater housing. Ninety minutes later Jason, in full scuba gear, was slipping into the cold, murky, waters of what had once been what appeared to be a thriving marina. The first thing he wanted to check was the existence of a cabin-cruiser in slip 361. Jason turned on his underwater light and while floating on the surface he checked his immediate surroundings for obstacles. Seeing none he made a couple of adjustments to his buoyancy control device and began to dive downwards into the gloom. After only a couple of seconds, the shape of a boat began to loom in front of him. It was indeed a cabin-cruiser that fitted the description Chuck had given him during his first telephone call with him. Jason continued diving downwards and he could clearly see the reason why the boat had sunk. On the starboard side of the boat, a large hole could be seen that had not only ripped through the hull of the boat but had also penetrated the deck. That must have been one bad collision to have made that happen, Jason thought, as he snapped off a couple of photos.

Moving slowly, Jason ventured out into the main body of water to move over to slip 360. Jason flicked his fins a few times to get close to the prow of the boat in the next slip. On the side of the boat was some lettering but it was obscured by algae and grime. He rubbed off the muck with his gloved hand and he could just make out the wording, 'St. Louis Streamer' and again, he took a couple of photos. He swam towards the stern of the vessel and just like the cabin-cruiser, there was a large hole in the port side of the vessel which would have easily resulted in the sinking of the ship. Jason then ascended a few feet to swim to the rear of the boat, there was a large door that was swinging idly with the movement of the water and he felt the entrance was large enough for him to enter without fear of getting his equipment snagged.

Inside were obviously the remnants of a party. Plates, tureens and eating utensils were scattered along tables. In one corner was an old drum set, a saxophone and a clarinet together with other instruments lying around a small stage. In another corner was a roulette wheel with chips floating on the ceiling, unable to escape from the room. Jason noticed a sign above a door leading to the bridge that said, 'Max. Persons 36'. If he remembered correctly, the dockmaster's entry reported a total of 32 people on board, so the boat had certainly not exceeded its safety numbers.

Realizing there was nothing more he could discover, Jason decided to surface and return to his boat but as he headed for the door he felt a tug on one of his fins. He immediately turned and looked down but there was nothing there. It must have just been a shift or a slight current that gave the illusion of a tug. Although, on second glance, he did notice a door he had missed when he was reading the sign. The door appeared to lead below deck somewhere, but he certainly wasn't going to risk taking that route. The chances of getting stuck became exponential when you were diving in cramped spaces like stairways, it's right up there with cave diving, which is something that had never appealed to him. Without giving it another thought, Jason returned to his boat, discarded his equipment on the transom and climbed aboard.

Jason went below and despite the dive in the cold water he was sweating profusely after wearing his tight wet-suit, so he opened the forward hatch to allow a little breeze to flow through the cabin. Once he had stripped off and changed back into regular clothes he began to evaluate the sizeable holes that were in the two boats. Was it a collision that had caused them? It would have been a side on side collision although he couldn't quite understand how a crash of that nature would have caused so much damage to both boats. Regardless, neither boat would have been able to continue motoring with so much water deluging the boat and yet there they were in the slips designated by the dockmaster. Did it occur as the two boats were moving into the slips? Possible, but then it would have been almost certain someone would have managed to survive. This whole situation with the wall, the boats, the reported disappearances, suggested that something else had happened here. He needed to return to Chuck's marina and show him the proof of what he had found but he was also concerned that once he left through that small gap in the marina's entrance, the wind and the current may shift some of the concrete and he wouldn't be able to get back in. He decided to stay the night, and in the morning, he would carry out a little more exploring before returning to Chuck's marina after lunch.

Chapter 14 – Visit of the Mystery Men – May 1944

"Oh, so sorry, we have to leave," Ray said, and he pulled his hand away in a desperate attempt to escape the wanton clutches of Lady Ashdene, much to her indignation. Ray tapped Tony on the shoulder and when he turned to see who it was, Ray pointed to the scepter-like person that could be seen through the rain-drenched window walking towards their boat. Ray tapped on the captain's door and waited for the captain to open it.

"Really sorry but we must leave, our man has turned up," Ray said as he grabbed his coat that was hanging from a hook beside the door they had just entered through.

"Why that was quick," was all the captain could say as Ray opened the door to leave.

"Thank you for your hospitality, maybe our paths will cross again someday," Ray said. Ray then put his coat across his head and made a beeline for his boat, closely followed by Tony.

They reached the boat at the same time as the mystery man who turned as he heard the footsteps of the two men running towards him. He was wearing a full-length, black, oil-skin coat and a black ranger's hat with the rain pouring from the brim onto the back of his coat, it made him look even more mysterious. He looked first at the two men then at the boat which they had obviously just come from, although he never offered any comment.

"Hi, as you can see, the boat is a little low in the water but what I don't understand is why there is no water coming in through the boat," Ray explained to the mystery man. The man ignored Ray's explanation but did go to the side of the boat, he went down on his knees and shone a high-powered flashlight at the bottom of the boat, towards the front. After a few seconds, he stood up and thought for a while.

"Did you talk to anyone on that boat?" The mystery man asked, nodding in the direction of the 'St. Louis Streamer'.

"Yes, we confronted the captain, it was his fault we hit the wing dam. Then he introduced us to a few of the passengers." Ray responded humbly.

"Get on the boat and stay there until I return. Don't leave the boat. I'm sending some people to you for the next phase." The mystery man said somewhat solemnly, which Ray thought surprising.

"What about the dockmaster, he wanted us to leave immediately," Ray added just before the mystery man turned to leave.

"I've spoken to him already," the mystery man replied and immediately walked away.

Before settling down to wait, Ray wanted to see if there was anything he could see from the side of the boat that could make the mystery man's decision-making finalize so quickly. He grabbed a flashlight and imitated the actions of the mystery man, looking towards the front of the boat. He pointed the beam of light down towards the bottom of the boat and at first, he saw nothing. Then, as he directed the beam in a certain way he could see, just below the waterline a pencil-thin stream of black liquid emanating from underneath the hull. Ray assumed it was oil and that was proof enough that there was serious structural damage to the boat and they could no longer continue with their trip. Ray turned off the flashlight, stood up and climbed into the shelter of the boat.

Ray dried himself off and prepared to make an entry into the ship's log-book, but he was interrupted by Tony, who had a question.

“The captain had a point. How did mystery man manage to arrive here so quickly?” Tony looked quizzical. “It’s almost as though he knew exactly where we were before we told him.”

“Remember almost every day we saw a small plane overhead, what twice a day at least?” Ray asked Tony. “They looked as though they were following us or at least keeping an eye on us.”

“Mmm,” mused Tony, “you really think that’s what they were doing?”

“That would explain how he knew we were so close,” Ray said and then began to write something in the log. When he had finished he placed the log in the safe, alongside their valuables. He didn’t believe he was going to have to write another entry and if they had to leave quickly he would only have one place to retrieve all their personal belongings.

Ray was about to sit back and relax while they waited for their next visitors but fortunately, they didn’t have to wait long. It was the belligerent protestations of the dockmaster they heard first as he climbed on board the boat and uninvited, climbed down into the cabin area.

“What’s going on?” Ray asked as the dockmaster came down the steps. Feeling quite indignant at the dockmaster’s presumptuousness to just come aboard uninvited like that. Surprisingly, the dockmaster was being closely followed by two men dressed in the same garb as the mystery man.

"You tell me. These two guys c..." But they were his dying words as Ray and Tony heard a dull, phut, sound, then the dockmaster fell headlong into the cabin with the tell-tale, crimson, blush of a bullet-hole in the back of his head.

Chapter 15 – Nightmare in the Marina – Modern Day

That night, after a light dinner of cold chicken and a garden salad straight from the packet, followed by yogurt for dessert, Jason sat outside with a coffee enjoying the peacefulness of the deserted marina. There was no artificial light in the area and he was able to see a multitude of stars that he could never get to witness in the city of Cleveland. Today had been an interesting day, at least he had found what he believed to be the boat his grandfather had used for his trip. But there were still no answers to other questions, what had happened to the boat to make it sink? What had happened to the two men, the dockmaster and the people on the paddle steamer? It was a conundrum, much like the mysteries of the universe he was now gazing at. Where did it end? When did it start? What was there before? Is there a sign on a wall that says, 'this is the end of the universe'? If so, what's on the other side of the wall? Which provided a segue from his reverie back to his present surroundings. Maybe in the morning, he would discover some more clues and the reason for the wall.

With that in mind, Jason began to think about what he could do in the morning other than to have another scout around to see what he could find. After all, at this time last night, he didn't feel he had a chance of finding out anything, but he had certainly turned that notion on its head. Then he suddenly remembered he had to touch base with the girls, he knew there would be no WiFi to transmit any emails, but could he get a signal for his phone? He located his smartphone down in the cabin and returned topside in an attempt to find a signal. Whether it was the wall or lack of cell-towers in the area was neither here nor there but his phone, to all intent and purposes, was useless as a communications device at that moment. The girls would just have to wait, he thought, but just then, a sudden tiredness washed over him. Having been out in the open all day, walking, diving, especially when you are not used to it, it can do that to you. So, Jason decided to turn in for the night but as he rose to climb down the stairs to the cabin the sound of a slight splash caught his attention. He was immediately drawn to the commotion but all he could see were ripples emanating from just above where the St. Louis Streamer lay. What actually had caused the ripples was hard to say in the dying light, so he merely shrugged his shoulders, continued downstairs to go to bed. Jason began to undress, most nights he would go to bed in pajamas or at least his underpants, but tonight, he thought, what the heck, there's no one around, so he climbed, buck-naked, into his sleeping bag. It wasn't long before he had fallen into a deep sleep.

It was the patter of rain on the roof of his boat that made Jason initially sit-up. Then, above the rain, he could hear the sound of music, a jazzy tune that he didn't recognize. He climbed out of his sleeping-bag to check first his MP3 player, then his phone but both were firmly switched off. Then he searched for any other electronic devices that were capable of playing music before it suddenly occurred to him that instead of being pitch black, as it was when he went to sleep, there was easily enough light to see what he was doing, even through the black-tinted windows of his boat. He looked outside to witness an amazing sight, all the lights in the marina were on, illuminating the docks which had been miraculously restored to their original condition. Beside his boat, in the next slip, the cabin-cruiser was afloat in all its magnificence, just as Chuck had described it. Beyond that, was the St. Louis Streamer in all its glory with party lights hanging all around its structure and up along the stays that were holding the radio mast in place. It could quite easily pass as a Christmas boat in a marina parade. The music he could hear was coming from the paddle steamer and he could see people moving around inside the boat. He was immediately drawn to the sound of the music and proceeded to slide open his hatch door.

Jason climbed out of his boat and oblivious of the rain pouring down he began walking towards the music coming from the paddle steamer. He caught a glimpse of a man staring over the side of the cabin-cruiser and was about to say something to him, but his attention was drawn to two men walking quickly towards him, their heads huddled under their coats to protect them from the rain.

"Hi!" Jason said, but the two men ignored him, it was almost as if they hadn't seen him. As they passed, Jason only managed to get a quick glance at the men, but it was enough to realise that the tall man hunched under his coat looked suspiciously like some of the old pictures he had of his grandfather. He turned to say something to them, but they quickly climbed into the shelter of the cabin-cruiser and were soon out of sight.

Continuing along the dock, Jason arrived at the paddle steamer, walked up the gangplank on the stern and opened the door. Immediately his body started responding to the beat of the music being played by an African-American quartet playing a type of swinging jazz he had never been subject to. Immediately, he was approached by a beautiful lady who proceeded to dance with him. For the first time since his wife had passed away, Jason was really enjoying himself until a man came in from the bridge of the boat wielding a gun and beckoning everyone through a door heading down to some steps. The music stopped, and everyone began to proceed down the steps indicated by the man. The last to leave was the lady Jason had been dancing with, she began to walk towards the step, trying to pull Jason with her. Reluctantly, he tried to pull away as her lips were trying to mouth something, but he couldn't interpret what it was she was trying to tell him. Jason tried to move closer to understand the wording as she moved her lips but the nearer he got, the more her lips began to shrink. Slowly, all the lady's teeth were revealed, then her gums began to recede and gradually, the skin on her face began to melt away until all Jason was facing were the bare cheek-bones of the once beautiful lady.

Jason recoiled in horror and made one last desperate effort to pull his arm away from the gloved hand of the lady. He succeeded, but in doing so, the force of his tug not only pulled the glove from her hand, it also brought with it the skin and the flesh of her arm revealing the white bones of her hand. The bracelet she was wearing went flying and settled underneath one of the catering tables against the wall. Jason's attention was briefly directed towards the jewelry but was more concerned about the body parts he had in his hand. Immediately, Jason let go of the glove he was holding in disgust and watched as it almost floated to the floor. Jason looked up from the loose skin and flesh wafting around on the floor only to see the almost skeletal remains of the lady receding through the doorway with all the other passengers, who had now also turned into skeletal replicas of their former selves. Still, the lady was reaching out to him almost pleading for him to follow her down the steps. But the man with the gun was herding everyone down the steps with the lady being the last to leave. Suddenly, the man turned to face Jason, by now, the man's face was a mask of decomposing flesh with flaps of skin falling around empty eye-sockets and his skeletal hand lifted to point the gun directly at Jason. Jason tried to reel back, but his legs were struggling to move and to make matters worse, it was then that he realised he was stark naked. Worse yet, the boat was sinking, he was desperate to get away from the gunman and off the boat. Jason was getting wetter and wetter, but the more he tried to move his legs the more resistance he was encountering, he was unable to escape.

Chapter 16 – Mystery Men's Task – May 1944

Ray and Tony just stood there dumbfounded as the old dockmaster fell at their feet. They then looked at their two new visitors and saw they were both holding guns with silencers attached. Unfortunately, they didn't have time to dwell on the matter as the mystery men each fired another shot, one at Ray the other at Tony. Both were killed instantly, and they fell on top of the dead dockmaster. The two mystery men went back into the rain, walking purposely towards the paddle steamer, leaving a third man applying explosive charges to the sides of first the cabin-cruiser, then the Streamer.

Like Ray and Tony had done earlier that evening, one of the mystery men went to the door of the bridge, unlike Ray and Tony, he barged through the door and ordered the captain into the area where the passengers were now being herded together by the other mystery man who had entered from the stern of the boat.

"Down below, now," shouted the mystery man who had entered with the captain, and he opened the door to show everyone the way. Amidst great protestations by some of the men they all went down the stairs, some of the women were crying and one of the caterers tried to make a break for it. The escapee made it through the captain's door and onto the bridge but as he opened the door to the gangplank, the third mystery man on the dock shot him expertly through the head. More screams were made by some of the women at the sound of the shot, some became hysterical as the dead man fell back through the captain's door and his torso hung in the doorway clearly revealing the hole in his forehead. Lady Ashdene was one of the more defiant ones who refused to go below but the mystery man first gave her an unceremonious shove towards the door which she countered. Then the man dragged her by the arm and as he did, her glove came away together with the bracelet she was wearing, and it went flying underneath one of the catering tables.

Once all the passengers and crew were down below they were forced into a storage room and the door was locked behind them. The room was already half-full with boxes and supplies and certainly didn't appear to have enough space for the influx of the entire ship's company, less the one dead caterer. Some men climbed on top of the boxes to make room for the others, but it was still extremely congested and some of the women were beginning to faint with the lack of air. Suddenly, there was a loud bang, then another which brought the onset of additional panic, but worse was still to come. Water began to seep in from underneath the door, gradually it rose to the ankles of the trapped men and women. It didn't take long before the water had passed their knees and the people nearest to the entrance began to pull, push and bang on the door with all their might, but to no avail.

On the dock, the one mystery man had waited for his compatriots to disembark the Streamer. The man had untied all the lines of the cabin-cruiser and all but one of the Streamer's. As the men reached the dock, they removed the gangplank and tossed it into the water, the third man untied the remaining line. The three men left the dock together and watched at a safe distance as the explosives were detonated.

The mystery men stood and watched impassively as the muffled screams of the boat's passengers gradually subsided as the once stately St. Louis Streamer sank beneath the waters of the marina. The other bang that the passengers had heard was the explosive charge that was set on the cabin-cruiser. The explosion should have sent the small craft to the bottom of the marina almost instantly but for some reason, it merely listed and refused to sink. One of the mystery men went to the dock and reached for the boat's bowline. He hauled the boat in close enough to place a foot weightily on the starboard gunwale. The pressure was enough for the cold black water of the marina to begin seeping over the side. As the water began to pour down into the cabin the mystery man stepped back, threw the bow line onto the boat and gave the bow a mighty kick to push the now sinking boat away from the dock. It only took a few seconds to sink to the bottom to join the St. Louis Streamer.

At the road leading into the marina was the mystery man that had once been Ray and Tony's taxi driver, he was guarding the entrance to ensure nobody else entered or left the marina. That included the three other mystery men who were making sure none of the passengers and crew escaped the watery grave of the St. Louis Streamer.

Chapter 17 – Stark Realisation – Modern Day

Jason suddenly sat up wide awake, his sleeping-bag was soaked through and it was sticking to him as he tried to extricate himself out of it. He then realized the source of the problem, it had been pouring with rain outside and he had forgotten to close the front hatch. Reaching up, he closed the hatch and secured it, it had stopped raining now, so it was a little like shutting the barn door after the horses had fled. The mattress was soaked, as was his bedding, so he wouldn't be able to continue with those sleeping arrangements. He still had some dry blankets stashed away and he could make up another bed by dropping the kitchen table across the two bench seats. But dawn was breaking and after the nightmare, he had just experienced he didn't think he would get back to sleep anyway.

Jason put on a swimming costume and a t-shirt then lit the burner to boil some water for a coffee. He tried to recall segments of the nocturnal sequence of events he had just experienced. Almost everything in the dream could be explained, the lights, the boats, he had seen all those things and his brain could quite easily play tricks with his imagination by embellishing the facts. It was the people he couldn't explain and the lady he had danced with, that was truly strange. While he was waiting for the water to boil he poured himself an orange juice and a bowl of cereal. Once his coffee was made he sat down at the table to eat his breakfast and tried to decipher what the dream was all about.

Jason was not prone to wild flights of fancy and his dreams to date had always bordered on boring, usually he didn't have any at all, certainly none that he could recall. But this one had been different, it was so vivid it was almost as if it had actually happened, but that was quite impossible. A thought crossed his mind, but he immediately dismissed it as folly, but it came to him again, the second time he knew it was his only course of action. He was going to have to dive into the bowels of the boats in an attempt to find answers.

First of all, diving alone is an absolute no-no, an action he had already carried out on this trip. But diving in unknown waters through wrecks and all the obstacles they could contain wasn't just a no-no, it was downright madness, especially when no one was aware of where he was and what he was doing. But he was determined to go through with it, the dream was a sign of some kind, he didn't know what, but he firmly believed a dive down to locate the doorway the lady had disappeared through in his dream would provide some answers.

Once Jason had finished breakfast, the first thing he felt he should do was bring out his sleeping bag and mattress to dry them out a little. With his bedding spread out on the top of his boat, Jason began to prepare his equipment for a second dive, remembering to add an extra knife to his kit. He ensured both his camera and underwater light were fully charged and at 10:00 AM, he was ready to enter the water. The clouds had cleared leaving a beautiful, blue, clear sky that would help a little with his visibility underwater. He entered the water with a little trepidation, he was beginning to have second thoughts as he submerged and began heading for the paddle steamer. He retraced his dive from the previous day until he entered the ballroom where his first action was to search underneath the table for the lady's bracelet that he had dreamt about. There was nothing to be seen except sunken garbage, silt, and weeds. In his heart, he wanted to be able to find some evidence to support his dream but in reality, this was what he had expected. He was about to abandon the dive as folly when a brief flash of light caught his attention. Rays of light had reflected on an object a few feet away. He finned slowly towards the source of the reflection, trying his best not to kick-up all the silt on the deck of the boat. There, almost totally buried under the debris was a beautiful bracelet. Jason picked up the object, gave it a quick inspection and placed it in the diver's bag attached to his weight belt. The bracelet was not exactly where he dreamt it was, but the current and even the sinking of the ship could have moved it from its original position. There was now no doubt in his mind that he had to go through with the remainder of his search.

Jason hovered at the entrance where he had dreamt the lady had gone, he calmed himself and pointed the flashlight down the stairs. There did not appear to be any obstructions and the opening was certainly big enough for him to proceed through, even with all his equipment. Cautiously, Jason slowly went down, pulling on the stairs to assist his downward progression to the bottom. Once at the bottom of the steps he shone his flashlight around, checked through all the rooms but there was nothing to see. Disappointed, he was about to ascend back up to the entrance when he noticed a closed door he had missed. The lever of the door was down, and a cotter pin, that was attached to a small chain, had been inserted to fix the handle in position. Using his diver's knife, he managed to pry out the rusty pin and attempted to pull up the lever, but it was rusted solid. He looked around for some sort of solid object he could use to bang the lever open but there was nothing in the immediate vicinity. Jason revisited the rooms and found a hammer and a crowbar, he returned to the closed door and began to knock open the lever. Working underwater, as he was doing was difficult, it was impossible to take big swings because of the resistance of the water. Additionally, he would be increasing the use of his precious air and he monitored his dials periodically to ensure he had enough supply to return to the surface. With the lever finally up, he used the crowbar to lever open the door. He slowly opened the door and what he saw was a sight that would be indelibly burnt in his memory for the rest of his life.

What faced Jason were numerous skeletons that had been packed into the room like sardines. His first thought, judging by what was left of the clothes that partially covered the bones, was that they must have been the passengers on the boat and they had been forced into this tiny room to die like drowning rats. What was even more disturbing was that the skeleton nearest to the door was wearing a necklace that matched the bracelet he had just retrieved upstairs. Was this the skeleton of the woman in his dream? It took all his composure to not throw up, there and then, which would have been fatal for him. He managed to take some deep breaths, wasting more precious air, but it was necessary to combat the nausea that had welled up inside him. Much calmer now, he remembered to take a couple of photos of the macabre scene and decided that he had spent sufficient time down there. He was about to leave when he debated about removing the necklace from the skeleton. For the second time in under 24 hours, he was contemplating stealing articles. This was a tomb and it was felt that taking artifacts from the dead is in fact stealing but he also thought that it may help in identifying the owner. Reverently, he gently removed the necklace from the bones of the person it had rested on for all those years. He opened his diver's bag and placed the necklace inside, next to the bracelet.

Jason returned slowly back up the steps but instead of leaving through the back door of the paddle steamer, he decided to exit through the door at the front. As he opened the door he was greeted by another skeleton, this one had a hole in the middle of the front of its skull. Again, Jason fought to keep his composure and left the boat through the bridge's entrance. Feeling calmer, he checked his instruments one more time and decided he had enough air to take a quick dive down to the cabin-cruiser.

Jason finned down to the cabin-cruiser but this time he entered the boat and looked down into the cabin. There, lying on the floor was a similar chilling sight to the one he had witnessed in the paddle steamer. The strange thing was, he could see three skulls, each one had a hole either in the forehead or in the back of it, could they be bullet holes? But who was the third person? There was also a strange hand-held radio beside the three skeletons that Jason retrieved, something he wouldn't have thought was available in those days. He paused to take some more photographs and thinking there was no more that could be gleaned from the scene he was about to return to the surface when he saw a cap lying at the bottom of the boat. It had badly deteriorated but on the front of it was a badge that spelled 'DOCKMASTER', that certainly could explain the third person. He picked up the cap and a few bits of cloth fell away from it but the front with the badge on it remained intact. Again, he was about to leave when something else caught his eye, it was a safe built into the body of the boat. Using his knife, he managed to cut away the wood, which was soft after being underwater for so long. Jason freed the safe, but it was too heavy to lift so he decided to surface with the cap and look for some rope he could secure around the safe to haul it up. There was no shortage of lines laying around the docks, so he chose one and tied an end securely to one of the piles and dove back down with the other end to tie around the safe. It didn't take long for him to secure the safe, which was just as well as he was beginning to find difficulty drawing breath from his demand-valve, his cylinder was running out of air.

Without panicking, Jason ascended slowly and once his head broke the surface he immediately spat out his demand-valve and took a deep breath of fresh air. He finned to the dock, unstrapped his equipment and rested it on the edge of the dock, ensuring the dockmaster's cap and his diver's bag were secure and not going to fall back over the side. There was a ladder at the end of the dock and after testing the rungs decided it would support his full weight. He climbed up the ladder, picked up the recovered articles and immediately went to his boat to fetch a bottle of water. His mouth was parched from breathing the air from the cylinder so now he needed some water to quench his thirst. He placed his diving bag and the retrieved cap on a seat on his boat before climbing aboard. Jason went down below and found two Ziploc bags, he placed the bracelet and necklace in one of the bags then the cap in the other. Then, he opened his cooler to extract a bottle of reasonably cool water and took a long swig. For a moment he wondered what the people on these boats would have thought if they would have heard about bottled air and water in their day.

After climbing out of his wet-suit, having a brief rest and downing a full bottle of water, Jason went to haul on the line to raise the safe. He gave the rope a couple of tugs and slowly, hand over hand, he managed to rein in a few feet of the line until it would come no more. The safe must have snagged on something on the cabin-cruiser. He gave it a few more futile pulls and decided that the only solution was to dive back down to the boat. Except this time, he would have to carry out a free dive because he had no way of replenishing his empty air-cylinders. He wrapped the line around the starboard winch of his boat before securing the end to a cleat. He really couldn't be bothered to go through the rigor of putting on his wet suit again, so he put on his fins, spat some saliva into his mask and wiped it around the glass with his fingers to prevent defogging. Then, he placed the mask in position and put the mouthpiece of his snorkel into his mouth. The boat was approximately 25 feet below the surface, so Jason knew that his working time at the safe would be just a matter of seconds. He moved to the side of the boat and took in a couple of deep breaths, then, without a second thought he lunged forward from a seated position into the cold water. He finned down quickly, but efficiently, a couple of times he was forced to pinch his nose and blow, clearing his ears to equate with the increasing water pressure as he descended. Fortunately, on his arrival at the boat, he could see that the safe had simply caught on the bottom rung of the stairs, leading up from the cabin. He managed to slide the safe away from the obstruction, he then stood on the boat, bent his knees slightly and by lifting the safe by the line it was attached to, he was able to haul the safe up through the entrance and onto the deck of the submerged boat. Quickly, amidst a cloud of disturbed silt and algae that had been settling there for over seventy years, he pushed off from the boat to return to the surface. Jason reached the surface just as his head was beginning to feel faint from a lack of oxygen and as his head broke through the water he took a huge gulp of air. Slowly, he finned to the dock and after taking off his fins and mask he climbed up the steps to continue hauling on the line. This time, instead of hand over hand on the line, he used the winch to haul in the line until the safe was at the surface. Once more he secured the line around a cleat on his own boat, he really didn't relish having to dive down for the safe a third time. Jason reached down to pull the safe from the water and placed it onto the dock. Jason then lifted the safe onto his boat just in front of the wheel-console, he dispensed with the line and began to inspect the box. There was a protective cover to the lock which was immovable without tools as it was welded shut with rust and grime. There should have been a key to open the safe, but it wasn't present, and he doubted if he would be able to find it even if he had more air for another dive. Neither did he have the ways and means to crack open the safe. He would have to wait until he returned to Chuck's marina where he was sure Chuck would know someone who could crack it open.

Still thirsty from his diving exertions, Jason retrieved another bottle of water from the cooler and headed back topside to enjoy what was a beautiful spring morning. He dried himself off and stood in the sun for a little while to rest and warm up. As he was reaching his head back to suck the last vestiges of water from the bottle he heard a small splash coming from the direction of the slip where the St. Louis Streamer had sunk. As he glanced over towards the source of the sound he could have sworn he saw a delicate hand receding beneath the surface of the water leaving behind in its wake a few gentle ripples. Jason contemplated what he saw for a moment and decided it must have been a fish breaking the top of the water. The sun reflecting on the scales of the fish could easily play tricks with his mind. A combination of light-headedness from his free dive and his brain still swimming with the sights he had just witnessed underwater, Jason dismissed the notion as fantasy and just a trick of the light. Even though he had not encountered a single fish during his entire dive.

With all his diving equipment secured he began to prepare lunch and think about a return to Chuck's marina and what he was going to tell the man about his discoveries. He had a quick meal consisting of a ham sandwich, a packet of chips followed by an apple, all washed down with a soda. He then changed into his jeans, sweatshirt and a jacket and put his still damp mattress back into the cabin. He opened the front hatch hoping that the through-draft would help to dry out the mattress, making a mental note to close it again before he went to sleep that evening. His sleeping-bag he reversed and secured it on the lifelines, he was hoping that the breeze during the return trip would complete the drying out process and he would still be able to use it that night.

Jason started the engine, untied the mooring lines and reversed out of the slip, he was retracing the track he had taken when he entered the marina, so he was confident he wouldn't encounter any underwater obstructions. What he hadn't expected was that more of the concrete would have fallen at the marina's entrance and there was a sizeable chunk blocking his exit. He pulled the boat parallel with the spit of land at the entrance and held onto the line until he secured it around a tree. There was no way he could lift the lump of concrete that had fallen but all he needed to do was somehow move it clear so that he could navigate his boat through the entrance. He looked around for something he could use as a lever, a long piece of wood or a metal bar. He had his emergency oar on the boat, but he didn't think it would be strong enough to counter the weight of the concrete. Then he spotted a couple of re-bars sticking out of the wall that might do the trick. He pulled on one of the metal poles and after a couple of good tugs, it began to ease out of the concrete encasement. When the end finally broke away from the concrete, Jason was face to face with one of the most gruesome sights he had ever seen. Stuck to the bottom of the re-bar was the head of what had once been a man that took on a striking resemblance to the man with the gun in his nightmare. This time Jason was unable to fight back the gall in the pit of his stomach, he dropped the rod and threw up into the water. After about a minute, he wiped his mouth and forced himself to turn and look at the ghastly sight he had just uncovered. Was there no end to the ghastly goings-on that had occurred here? The head was badly decomposed, all Jason could assume was that the head had only recently been exposed to the air after being buried in concrete for all these years. He still needed to use the rod as a lever to get out of the place, so he was going to have to extract the head, but he couldn't put it back in the encasement, he would need it as proof. He decided to compromise by retrieving a couple of large Ziploc bags from his boat with the view of placing the head into those. First, he had to slide the head off the re-bar, which he managed to do, constantly gagging and fighting back nausea. He then slipped a bag over the head, zipped up the bag and repeated the task with a second bag. He then secured the bundle against the wall, surrounding it with some of the broken concrete. Based on his findings to date, Jason was almost positive there were probably other bodies down there in the depths of the wall, but he had had enough of the macabre for one day and he was not going to look.

All Jason wanted to do was get out of that marina as quickly as possible, so he put all his efforts into the movement of the concrete obstruction. He pushed the end of the re-bar as far as he could underneath the lump of concrete and used another broken piece of the wall as a fulcrum. With one almighty push down on the pole, the concrete slipped into the water with a pathetic plop. Jason untied the mooring line from the tree, jumped back on the boat and slowly negotiated the entrance back out to the river. Although he couldn't resist having one more ghoulish, glance towards the head of the man he had uncovered. Yet another dead body, his grandfather, his mate, the dockmaster, thirty plus people on the paddle steamer and now this poor guy, not to mention the possibility of more buried down that shaft. What possible reason could there be for all these deaths and who was responsible for all these pernicious acts?

Chapter 18 – Building and Guarding the Wall – May 1944

Once the storm had abated a small coastguard vessel approached the entrance to the State Marina of Missouri and anchored across the opening. The mandate of the boat's crew was to prevent any vessel entering the marina and if by some chance the mystery men had missed any boaters who were staying within the marina, who were now trying to exit, they were to be brought to the mystery men's attention, fortunately, none did. During the afternoon, a small company of soldiers arrived and were bivouacked outside the marina operating an around the clock shift to prevent anyone entering the area within fifty yards of the marina.

Needless to say, the owners of the marina were outraged and demanded to know when they would be allowed to re-open. In addition, boat owners were livid that they could no longer gain access to the marina, many of them had made quite an investment on their boats. Even worse, there were a few boaters who lived on board but had spent the night on land to escape the wrath of the storm, they now had nowhere to go. As the disgruntled owners showed up to the secured gates of the marina the officer in charge gave them contact details to an office in St. Louis where a small staff was assigned to deal with ample compensation payments to appease everyone.

During the next few weeks, a small barracks was built to house the soldiers but more importantly, work commenced on erecting a large wall around the perimeter of the marina. The wall was being built to certain specifications with the last section, the entrance from the river, to be completed by a different company and would represent the final phase. The wall was designed to be two feet thick with a two-inch thick lead insert between the two one feet concrete pieces and the edifice would penetrate twelve feet into the ground. During the construction of the wall, the mystery man and his cohorts remained close by, supervising operations and ensuring no curious soldier tried to wander around the marina. Finally, the main part of the wall was complete and all that remained was to build the final section and to top the entire structure with barbed wire.

The day after the new company had dug the piles for the foundation of the section for the river entrance, the mystery man waited for the construction crew to return from the barge anchored just outside the marina's entrance to the building site a few hundred yards up river from the wall's perimeter. Once the builders had left, the mystery man and his associates went out on a small boat to inspect the work. It was approaching dusk as they moored the boat and climbed onto the tiny spit of land bordering the entrance. The mystery man walked over to the hole that had been dredged, dugout, then boarded, in anticipation of the concrete being poured into the casing.

"Damn, that doesn't look anywhere deep enough, does it to you?" The mystery man said and stepped back to let the other three men judge the depth of the hole. As the three men simultaneously gazed into the abyss the mystery man opened his jacket and pulled out a pistol with a silencer attached to the end of it. If there was anyone within hearing distance, which there wasn't, all they would have heard were three quick 'phuts' as each of the men were shot professionally in the back of the head. Two of the men fell forward into the hole, the remaining man fell first to his knees and then to his side. The mystery man wasted no time kicking the lifeless body into its muddy grave. With the largely vacant, construction pontoon in front of the entrance and the wall surrounding the marina, the mystery man was certain that his actions had gone unseen. Nevertheless, his eagle-eyes did a slow 360°scan, seeking for potential witnesses. Satisfied that he was in the clear he boarded his boat and calmly returned to the building site. Nobody had seen him leave with the three men and there was no one to see him return by himself. The mystery man moored the boat and walked briskly to his car.

Early the next morning a boat, specially designed to pump concrete arrived at the site to complete the final section of the wall. To show his pleasure with the successful completion of the project, the mystery man was adamant that he should ceremoniously, direct the pipe that would spout concrete into the foundations of the final piece of the wall. As soon as he felt there was enough concrete to cover-up the evidence of his crimes he raised his hands and cheered as the construction workers echoed his sentiments. The mystery man shook their hands and thanked them profusely before leaving on the same boat he had come in on during the previous evening. The workmen would be finished that afternoon and the final touches of barbed wire would be completed by the end of the week. For the final time, the mystery man moored his boat and returned to his car. Once inside his car, he picked up a radio and pressed contact. There was a click indicating acknowledgment from the man receiving the call.

“Containment procedures complete.” Was all that the mystery man said. A couple of seconds later there was another click, the conversation was over, and the two men never spoke to each other ever again.

UNCOVERING THE ANSWERS

Chapter 19 – Explanations and Investigations – Modern Day

Jason couldn't help thinking about all the bodies he had come across in the twenty-four hours he had been searching for answers to his grandfather's disappearance, so much so that he almost motored past Chuck's marina. It was about 3:00 PM when he finished securing his boat and he was approached by Charlie, Chuck's grandson.

"Hi Mr. Clifford, back so soon?" Charlie said. "You've solved the mystery, have you?" Charlie said sarcastically, smiling at Jason.

"You will be surprised by what I have found out Charlie. Where's your grandfather?" Jason asked.

"Usual spot, I don't suppose he's left yet, so you should be able to catch him," Charlie responded. The usual spot was the pub, aptly named 'The Lost Mariner', the place where Jason had lunch with Chuck the first day he had arrived. Jason brought out his mattress one more time to see if it would finish drying out, he gave his hair a quick brush, put a few items into a backpack and proceeded to the pub.

Jason entered the pub, there were only a few lunchtime stragglers around the tables and there was Chuck, sitting at the bar with a couple of his cronies. They all turned to see who was entering the bar and Chuck was the first to react.

"Heeey, Jason, my, I wasn't expecting you back so quickly," Chuck said, seemingly, genuinely pleased to see Jason, and he patted the stool next to him to indicate that's where he should sit. "What'll you have?" Chuck asked.

"Double whiskey!" Jason replied without hesitation. He was not normally a spirit drinker, although, he did have a bottle of Jack Daniels on board the boat, for medicinal purposes, but his nerves were still a little jittery from the last incident he had experienced before leaving the State Marina of Missouri. Chuck and his two friends looked at each other, smiled, nodded their heads as if some conspiracy was taking place but it wasn't, it was just that man thing.

Jason didn't say another word until the whiskey arrived, he said 'thanks', then downed the amber liquid in one swig. Then he ordered an 18-ounce beer. Jason now had the full attention of the three men and the barman.

"Tell me, what can you remember of the State Marina of Missouri?" Jason asked.

"Well, it opened up just before the war, as I mentioned to you before, the clientele was a little hoity-toity if you know what I mean. Then suddenly, for some reason, the army took it over as a top-secret installation." Chuck explained

"Do you know what it was used for?" Jason asked.

"Nope, no one I know ever worked inside there," Chuck said, shaking his head.

"In them days, I lived just a few miles away," the crony to Chuck's immediate right said, "I used to ride my bike there in the summers, but you couldn't get anywhere near the old marina. The army had a barracks built, they had armed guards all around the place. God knows what they were doing in there."

"When did the army abandon the place?" Jason asked as he took a hearty sip of his beer that the barman had now delivered. Chuck and his cronies looked at each other as though they needed to confer to answer that one.

“I should imagine it would be about 1950, around there I think,” Crony #1 suggested.

“Must have been, that would be about when they blocked off the road to the marina and they tore down the barracks and abandoned the place,” Crony #2 offered, he was the one sitting the furthest away.

“Didn’t anyone ever go down there to investigate?” Jason asked. “Curious kids, teenagers?”

“Nah, they still put those signs up, all sorts of rumors went around. Kids wouldn’t go near the place.” Crony #2 said.

“What types of rumors,” Jason asked.

“It was said that the government was manufacturing dangerous chemicals in there, gases for the war effort. The whole area was contaminated, your skin would fall off if you went in there without protective clothing.” Crony #1 said.

“Yep, that’s right, that’s what they used to say.” Crony #2 added.

Jason thought about that for a while, from what he had seen, there was no evidence of anybody manufacturing anything in the deserted marina.

"Did you see or know of anyone who actually worked in the facility?" Jason suddenly asked them. That appeared to require another conference between them until finally, they all shook their heads.

"What if I told you that the wall you can see from the river totally encircles the marina." Jason began to tell the men, even the barman was now listening in, "there is no entrance to the place, neither from the road nor from the river. Nobody has set foot in that place since they built the wall, they built the wall with all those boats still in there. The army was brought in solely to make sure nobody ever set foot in there." While the four men looked at each other askance, Jason took another swig of beer, which happened to be a local craft brew, it was very good.

"Nah, that can't be, the owners of all those boats would have said something." Crony #1 said.

"Sorry, I don't know your names, you are?" Jason said, reaching out his hand to Crony #1 who's name was Archie.

“Bill.” Crony #2 offered.

“Dexter,” the barman said. Jason later learned that Bill and Chuck had both grown up in the area and had known each other since kindergarten. Archie had come along a few years later and Dexter and his wife had moved into the pub relatively recently. The elderly trio were now widowers and spent their time mostly in the Blue Moon Café in the mornings and during the afternoons, the pub.

“When I went up the river the day before yesterday, you had told me about the marina’s existence, but I didn’t know exactly where the marina was,” Jason began to explain, “but then I saw a wall and there was a small gap where it had corroded. So, I went through it. I found the State Marina of Missouri and I can tell you, the marina was abandoned.” Jason reached into his backpack and pulled out his camera, he waited for the screen to show the first of his photos and he began to show them shots of the site. Before he got to his underwater photographs he paused.

The four men couldn’t believe what they were seeing, for years they had been told the marina had been converted into a military installation.

"It gets worse." Jason said, and now he had their full attention, so he continued, "I know where you can find the St. Louis Streamer, the dockmaster, and my late grandfather's boat."

"According to records, The Streamer sunk on the river," Archie explained, although the disappearance of the dockmaster always was a mystery. Old Zachariah Grimshaw was his name, he was an ornery old fart, liked a tipple. Because of the storm, it was a slow night and it was rumored that he'd had a little too much to drink, slipped on the wet docks and fell into the water. At least, that was the official verdict."

"Well, I carried out a couple of dives in the marina. The Streamer and my grandfather's boat are at the bottom of the marina in the slips that they were assigned, or at least docked in." Jason told them, "you know what else?" There was silence as the men looked at Jason, what else could possibly have happened?

"The bodies of all the passengers and crew of those boats, as well as the dockmaster, are still on those boats," Jason said, then he began to scroll through the remaining photographs on his camera. Finally, he reached into his backpack to pull out the clear, plastic, Ziploc bag he had used to store the remains of the dockmaster's cap. He gently placed it on the bar, like evidence in a judicious exhibit. "A major cover-up has occurred here, and I am determined to find out what it's all about."

Chapter 20 – Start of an Investigation – Modern Day

For a while, all four men were dumbfounded, their mouths agape and they just stared at Jason as though he was some kind of alien who had just dropped in from space.

"Dexter, you'd better get another round in, we could be here for a while," Archie said.

"Show me that photograph of the Streamer again," Archie asked. Jason scrolled through the photos stored on his camera until he came to the one showing the name of the boat at the bottom of the marina. Jason passed the camera to Archie, he studied it, first with his spectacles on, then at the top of his forehead and then again, back in their correct position.

"Looks like the Streamer alright." Archie confirmed, "and this is at the bottom of the marina you say?"

"Sure is." Jason replied, "but if you are not squeamish, look at the next few photographs, I'm warning you they are pretty ghoulish." In silence, the four men took turns at looking at the photographs. Dexter was the first to speak, he was tapping on the screen of the camera.

“This one isn’t underwater, what the hell is this?” Dexter asked.

“As I was leaving, I needed something to get some concrete out of my way, so I pulled out a re-bar that was in the broken wall. That head was on the end of it.” The four men looked at it again, shaking their heads in disbelief.

“I have more proof,” Jason said and reached into his backpack once more to pull out the log book he had taken from the dockmaster’s desk. He opened the book and flipped the pages until he came to the last two entries in the log. “There, see? St. Louis Streamer and a cabin-cruiser, my grandfather’s boat.” Jason passed the log over to Archie to read. Archie read the entries by repeating the same action with his spectacles. He shook his head, not in doubt but in amazement.

“That’s what it says alright,” Archie confirmed.

“O.K., my dad used to regularly visit that marina when it was opened to do on-site repairs to boats and docks. Old man Grimshaw used to make him register. Used to piss my old man off something awful,” Chuck said laughing about the memories of his father, “but what I’m saying, if that log is authentic, and I’m not doubting you for a minute son,” Chuck said, turning to Jason to reassure him, “but to prove the point, there should be entries in there for the 'River Worker'." Archie and Bill huddled over the log, flicking back over the pages.

"There," Bill said, proud that he was the first one to spot it and he read out the entry:

05/15/44 09:45 Slip 108 River Worker 1 day 0.00

Occupants: 1

They continued to flick through the pages and discovered other entries for Chuck's father, so now they were convinced that what Jason was telling them was true.

"Come on young fellow, what else do you have in that there bag of yours?" Archie asked.

"I have this," Jason said, and he pulled out the radio he had found on his grandfather's boat.

"Well, I never," Chuck said, cupping the six-and-a-half-inch long radio in his hands and lifting it up and down as if he was weighing it. "It can't weigh much more than a pound."

“I’ve never seen the like,” Bill said, and Archie did that thing with his spectacles again.

“That’s a job for Rusty,” Dexter said as he finished delivering the drinks.

“Rusty?” Jason asked.

“Sure, Rusty would know.” Chuck agreed as he turned the radio over in his hands once or twice. “I have no idea about this one.”

“Sorry, who is Rusty?” Jason asked again.

“Rusty used to have a radio shop, way before Radio Shack came along. He started out with ham radio when he was just a young boy and he never let it go.” Bill said, “is he still living on Route 21?”

“Last I heard,” Dexter said.

“Looks like we’re going to have a little road trip tomorrow,” Chuck said.

“Well before we do that, here’s a couple of other little items that needs investigating.” Jason once more reached into his backpack and pulled out another sealed bag, it contained the bracelet and necklace he had salvaged. This immediately caught Dexter’s attention.

“Are they rubies?” Dexter asked excitedly, pointing to the jewelry.

“They sure look like it, Dexter,” Bill concurred.

“They’ve got to be worth a few smackers,” Dexter said.

“Need to take that down to old Harry’s, he’ll soon tell you,” Chuck said.

“Harry’s long gone, his son took over about five years ago,” Bill stated.

“Harry is dead?” Chuck asked surprised.

“Nah, he didn’t die, he retired,” Bill admonished Chuck, “he was having trouble seeing through those little binoculars jewelers use.”

“You mean a jeweler’s loupe,” Dexter said.

“Whatever,” Bill said with a wave of his hand, dismissing Dexter’s pedantic correction.

“Well, Jason, why don’t you and I go and visit Harry’s son tomorrow to see if we can get any history on these jewels while Archie and Bill go visit Rusty with the radio? How’s that sound?” Chuck asked.

“What about me?” Dexter asked indignantly pointing to himself.

“Someone’s got to run the pub Dexter,” Chuck replied.

"Yes, but I can get my wife to do that." Dexter countered.

"Well, there is one more thing," Jason said, and the other four men looked to Jason's backpack to see what other goodies were going to be revealed. "There was a safe on board the cabin-cruiser, it is too heavy for my bag, I have it onboard my boat. It's solid and there was no key and I have no idea how to pry it open." The reaction Jason got was totally unexpected, the other four men all burst out laughing.

"What's so funny?" Jason asked.

"Dexter here used to be a locksmith, only one for miles around that's how he made enough money to buy this pub," Bill explained.

"Really?" Jason said, "great, I can drop it off before Chuck and I take off tomorrow and you can crack it open."

"Oh no," Dexter said wagging his finger to and fro. "You need to be present when I open the box, that's the way it is done. That way you can't accuse me of taking stuff out of the safe in your absence."

"O.K. why don't we all meet back here tomorrow?" Jason said as a compromise, "we can all exchange information on what we've learned, then we can all witness the opening of the safe. But it is important we don't tell anyone of what we have discovered, at least not until we know more. If there has been a cover-up of some kind the fewer people who are aware of what we have discovered the better. Hopefully, we will know more by tomorrow and between us, we can determine our next steps." They all nodded their heads in agreement, finished their drinks, Archie picked up the radio and they all left the pub.

Chapter 21 – Investigation Fully Underway – Modern Day

Jason decided to spend the night on his boat, despite the kind offers from each of the men to stay at their respective homes. Fortunately, by the time he had returned from the pub his bedding was dry, otherwise, he may have taken one of his new friends up on their gracious offer. The first thing he had to do after he climbed on board his boat was to send an email to the girls. To surprise them, he also attached a picture of their great-grandfather's boat, together with a couple of smug remarks about them thinking he was wasting his time. Although he didn't mention any of the gory details, he didn't want to worry them unduly. For the rest of the evening, he just sat on the boat playing music and thinking about the events to date and how he was going to unravel the conundrums he had created and what he was going to do about them. He still felt that he wanted to back off from talking to the authorities until he had as much information as he could so that he could paint a picture of what he thought had led to all these people's demise.

The next morning, around 10:00 AM, Chuck arrived in preparation to visit the jewelers. Jason looked around for a car but was told it was only a fifteen-minute walk up the hill to the store and the other two wouldn't be back until well after lunch, so they had plenty of time. Around twenty minutes later Chuck and Jason arrived at the entrance to the jewelers. Jason went to open the door only to discover it was a sophisticated electronic entry system controlled by a worker on the inside of the store. As soon as the person inside saw Chuck, a young lady pressed some security buttons, there was a loud click and the door began to slowly swing open electronically. As soon as Jason and Chuck had entered, the door quickly closed behind them.

“Chuck, how are you?” A smartly dressed man said as he suddenly appeared from the back of the store.

“Fine David, just fine. How’s Harry doing?” Chuck replied cordially, shaking the man’s hand.

“A lot of fishing, that’s how he is doing,” David said as the person who had opened the door for us, her part in the proceedings obviously over, disappeared into the same room David had appeared from.

“Hi, my name is David Horowitz, I own the establishment,” David said as he turned to Jason and shook his hand.

“Jason Clifford,” Jason said, eyeing up the man standing in front of him. David was tall, slim, clean-shaven, meticulously groomed with not a hair out of place and his perfect teeth, accentuated by a sincere smile, were immaculately white. His smart suit was obviously tailor-made, and his shoes were well-polished. Jason would normally pin this type of guy as a salesman and would say anything to make a sale but for some reason there was a demeanor about the man that he liked, and he felt he could trust him.

“I understand you have made quite an interesting find,” David said. Jason gave Chuck a quick sideways glare.

“He’s a busy man, I made an appointment,” Chuck said with a shrug of his shoulders.

“Yes, I have,” Jason said and withdrew the jeweled items from his backpack. David’s face was impassive when he saw the jewelry and began to don some white gloves before opening the plastic bags. Jason had only been able to provide a perfunctory clean to the items, but David dropped both the bracelet and the necklace into a bowl containing a clear liquid. He waited a few seconds then began using various brushes and cloths to clean out all the silt and algae that had accumulated on the intricate links of the jewelry. By now, the poor man's gloves were filthy but once he had the jewelry cleansed to his satisfaction he dried the items, discarded the dirty gloves and put on a new pair. Using a jeweler's loupe, he began to inspect the items, muttering incoherently as he did so. Finally, he laid the items down on a soft piece of cloth, took off his gloves and walked into the back room. He returned about ten minutes later carrying a binder, it was open at a page showing an old black and white photograph of the very bracelet and necklace that was lying on the jeweler's counter.

Throughout this entire performance, neither Jason nor Chuck had uttered a word but as soon as they saw the photograph of the items Jason had salvaged they both exclaimed simultaneously.

"That's it!" They both said.

"It appears to be," David replied calmly. "I found the hallmark," David indicated the mark with a probe and I managed to find details in this old collection of jewelry. What I can tell you is that it was designed and created by Raymons of New York. It was a very successful company between the two World Wars and was responsible for some fascinating pieces. This particular collection appears to be a one-off design that was created circa

1925, as you can see from the photograph, there would have been a pair of earrings completing the set. You don't happen to have those do you?"

"Unfortunately, I don't," Jason replied.

"Pity, anyway, I can tell you that this is a marvelous piece of art-décor design, large rubies surrounded by small diamonds encrusted in platinum. The workmanship on the linkage of both the bracelet and the necklace is quite exquisite." David paused for a few seconds. "Do you know the owner of this collection at all?"

"No, that's one of the mysteries we would like to get solved. It may help us with other questions we have." Jason replied.

"Well, although Raymons is no more, their records may have been inherited by the company that took them over when the original owner retired. If you like, I can contact them to see if they have any history of the items." David said.

"Could you? That would be fantastic." Jason said.

"No trouble," David replied.

"Oh wait, how much would that kind of a search cost?" Jason asked.

“No charge, I would love to know who once owned these, she obviously had good taste.” David said. He had put on yet another pair of gloves and was placing the now completely clean items into a velvet protective bag.

“How long do you think it will be before you hear anything?” Jason asked.

“Difficult to say, it could be a few days or a month,” David replied. “I will contact Chuck as soon as I hear anything.”

“Well thank you David,” Jason said. For a few seconds, there was an awkward silence as Jason waited for David to return the items to him.

“Where exactly are you keeping the jewelry while you are in town Mr. Clifford?” David asked.

“On my boat,” Jason replied.

“Would you like me to secure them here? Again, no charge, I just think they would be far safer here.” David said casually.

“I hadn’t given it any thought. Why do you ask?” Jason said slightly confused.

“It’s just that the bracelet alone is worth approximately $350,000 and the necklace, probably, the same again!” David said, still as calm as he had been throughout, “had you have included the ear-rings you could probably add at least another $100,000. But where you leave them is entirely up to you of course.”

Chapter 22 – Swapping Notes, Opening the Safe – Modern Day

Jason did indeed accept David's kind offer and left the jewelry in his safe hands while they looked forward to hearing any news from Raymons' successors. On the way back to Jason's boat Chuck suggested they retrieve the safe and they could go onto the pub and have lunch there and await the others. The safe wasn't so heavy that Jason couldn't carry it a little way, but the thought of walking up the incline for about half of a mile to the pub with it in his arms may be a bit of a stretch, so he suggested driving up there. But Chuck wouldn't hear of it, instead, he walked down to the dock and returned with a beat-up dolly to save Jason's exertions. When they arrived at the pub, Jason carried the safe into the bar and placed it carefully on the counter, while Chuck wheeled the dolly around to the back of the building to where the deliveries came in. As soon as Jason walked into the bar, Dexter began pouring drinks, one for Jason and one for Chuck, who had yet to enter. No sooner had Jason set the box down, Dexter produced the two beers and began scrutinizing the safe, paying close attention to the lock. From under the bar, Dexter then produced a neatly folded black cloth package tied up with a black ribbon. He untied the ribbon and opened-up the cloth to reveal an assortment of locksmith tools, including a penlight. He also produced a small hammer and with one deft swing he knocked the lock covering to one side. He then took the small flashlight and shone it into the keyhole while he squinted his eyes in order to get a good look at the mechanism inside. Then, Dexter, selected one of the picks and began probing the inside, while still aiming his penlight in the keyhole.

"Not surprisingly, it's a bit rusty in there," Dexter said although he didn't look perturbed. Once more, Dexter reached underneath the bar and came up with a small can of WD40 with the small red tube attached to its nozzle. He gave a liberal spray into the lock then left it to let the solution work its magic.

"Do you think you can crack it?" Chuck asked as he walked up to the bar.

"Absolutely, but don't you want to wait for the others to arrive before we open it?" Dexter asked, looking at Jason for an answer. "We can let that spray soak for a little while."

"Sure, we'll have some lunch while we wait," Jason replied. Jason ordered a burger and fries while Chuck settled for fish and chips. By the time their food arrived the other pair of the investigative team had arrived.

"Whoa lookee here!" Archie said as he spotted the safe at the end of the bar.

"Leave it be Archie, we're going to open it after lunch," Dexter warned as he began pouring beers for the newcomers.

"No, I wasn't going to touch it," Archie said as he did that routine with his glasses. "No sir, leave that to the experts," Archie said quietly as he walked to a vacant seat at the bar, without taking his eyes off the object of their discussion.

"What did you find out about the jewelry?" Bill asked as he climbed onto a bar-stool. Jason and Chuck explained what David had told them about the history of the pieces but when they told the others the value, their mouths physically dropped open.

"See, I told you they were worth a bit." Dexter said, "I've been around too many safe-openings to know value when I see it. Bet you'll get three-quarters of a mil for them."

"I doubt it, they're not mine," Jason replied dejectedly.

"Why not, 'finders keepers' rule applies here, they're yours," Dexter said confidently.

"Nah, I think I have to go through due diligence to find the original owner, or in this case the person's estate before I can even think about taking the money." Jason replied, "anyway, not so worried about the money I just want to get to the bottom of this, sorry, poor choice of words under the circumstances."

"So, did you get to meet up with Rusty?" Chuck asked in between a mouthful of fish, trying to change the subject.

"Sure did," Bill replied, "he says hi."

"Good, how's he doing?" Chuck asked.

"Looks great, doesn't he Bill? Still building radios." Archie chimed in.

"So, what did you learn about the radio?" Chuck asked, again, trying to change the subject, Jason stopped eating and Dexter was fully attentive.

"Strangest thing, Rusty said that this type of radio never went commercial, well not in this form, it was basically the forerunner for CB radio," Bill replied, taking the radio out of his jacket pocket to give back to Jason.

"Well, what do you know?" Dexter said, turning the object over and over.

"According to Rusty the system was called the Joan-Eleanor system, it didn't come into operation until 1944 and was not de-classified until 1976," Bill added.

"The Joan-Eleanor system?" Dexter added surprisingly, "was it named after Roosevelt's wife?"

"Close," Archie replied. "Rusty said it was named after the inventor's wife, Eleanor Goddard, the inventor was Alfred Gross."

"I've heard of him, he grew up in Cleveland," Jason interjected before Archie continued. "Well, it used frequencies much higher than the Germans or Japanese could pick-up at that time, so it was mainly used by agents in the field. They would talk to planes flying overhead to communicate."

"That's right," Bill said, "but here's the thing, Rusty figured if your grandfather had one of these onboard in May'44 he was probably one of the first people to ever be using the system, so he must have been doing something so clandestine that the authorities didn't want anyone to know about it."

"Wow, no wonder your grandfather didn't want me to set foot on board his boat!" Chuck exclaimed, "it all makes sense now."

"Well, I'm glad it makes sense to you because I'm as confused as all get out." Jason said, then continued, "what possible earth-shattering operation could my grandfather have been caught up in? He was just an ordinary seaman."

"Well that's what we have to find out," Dexter said calmly and patted Jason sympathetically on the arm. "Maybe this little baby may help us," Dexter added as he walked to the end of the bar, picked up the safe and brought it to where the four men were sitting.

"Before I start to open this safe, I just want to warn you," Dexter said, "although this is a military grade, waterproof, fireproof safe, after being in the water for as long as this one has, the contents may have suffered. We should expect the worst but hope for the best." The others nodded their heads in agreement, not that there was anything else they could do but to acquiesce to Dexter's comment. Jason noted that Dexter's wife, Helen, had now entered the bar and was pulling pints and seeing to the other customers. Helen was a typical no-nonsense lady you would expect to see behind a bar. She was also a tall, blonde, buxom, attractive lady but actually had a heart of gold.

Dexter selected a couple of tools from his collection of instruments and began probing inside the lock. At one point he had four of the instruments sticking out of the lock like some metal form of acupuncture. It didn't take long before there was an audible click and the lid of the safe jumped a fraction. Dexter removed the probes from the lock, turned the safe around to face Jason and held out his hand to invite him to open the lid. He looked first at Dexter, then to the others, placed a hand on both sides of the safe and slowly lifted the lid.

Chapter 23 – Safe Contents – Modern Day

Amazingly, it appeared to Jason that the contents of the safe were still bone dry. On top was a log-book of some kind, he took that out and placed it to the left of the safe as he began to rummage through the remainder of the contents. There were two envelopes, one marked '*Ray*', the other '*Tony*'. Jason emptied the contents of the envelope marked '*Ray*' onto the bar. A few old photographs fell out of the packet, most of the photos Jason had seen before from his father's collection, but there were one or two of his grandmother that were new to him.

"She was a beautiful woman," Chuck said, leaning in to view the contents.

There were also a couple of old letters from his grandmother that he would probably read later, at his leisure, but for now, he wanted to continue foraging through the contents of the safe, to see if they could uncover any new information. Jason placed all the items back into the envelope marked '*Ray*' and placed it on top of the log-book. Jason now turned his attention to the envelope marked 'Tony' and repeated the emptying of the packet. There were no letters in Tony's collection, just a few photographs of what could have been a sibling and a portrait of what they thought must be Tony with his parents.

That just left one final object in the safe, another, slightly larger envelope. This envelope had no writing on it, Jason tipped the contents onto the bar. What fell out was a bundle of U.S. notes of various dominations all wrapped in an elastic band, which broke as the wad hit the counter.

"Jesus, there's got to be at least $2000 there!" Archie shouted. At that commotion, just about everyone in the pub looked across in an attempt to see what was going on at the bar.

"Jeez Archie, keep it down, will you?" Chuck reprimanded his friend.

"Sorry guys," Archie said, now whispering, "but that would have been worth at least twenty-five grand in today's money."

"They're old notes though," Jason said.

"Doesn't matter, still legal tender," Dexter said. "U.S. notes, no matter how old are still legal."

"Really?" Jason said.

"Not only that, some of them may be collector pieces, they look in mint condition, you need to have them checked out," Dexter added.

"But this doesn't really tell us anything does it?" Jason said, a little disappointed. "I was hoping there would be more here but that's it, we're stymied once again."

"What about the log-book? Anything in there that might help?" Bill asked. Jason placed all the artifacts, except the log-book back into the safe and closed the lid. He placed the log-book on top of the safe's lid and gingerly lifted open the brittle hard-cover. On the inside cover was written a list of the two men on board the vessel:

Captain: Ray Clifford
Crew: Tony Lawless

Jason then quietly read the first item in the log to the other men:

5/1/44 - Mystery man gave us money, charts, and a boat, we are to meet him in St. Louis. Also supplied a radio to be used only in an emergency or when we arrive at St. L.

5/2/44 – Leaving Clinch River, now on Tennessee

"Where in hell's name is the Clinch River?" Jason looked up and asked.

"Tennessee," Chuck answered almost instantaneously.

"Where specifically?" Jason asked.

"Not far from Knoxville," Chuck replied casually. Jason took out his phone and using his maps app. he keyed in Clinch River and there indeed was Knoxville, not far from the river. That made perfect sense considering, by all accounts, that was where his grandfather was flown to. Jason continued to carefully flip through the pages of the log, it certainly represented a roundabout route to arrive at St. Louis. There were the references to planes overhead and his grandfather even noted his disappointment in not allowing a young lad onboard the boat, which brought a nostalgic smile to Chuck. Then, there was the final entry where the mystery man was mentioned again when they noticed the oil coming from the bottom of the boat and that was the last entry.

So, the five men in the bar were indeed stymied, where does their investigation go from there? It all seemed an innocent trip, according to the log, nothing untoward happened on the journey, but who was the mystery man? He was only mentioned at the beginning of the log and at the end, he's the man who holds the key to the puzzle. The only thing was to go to the authorities with the information they have and the proof of the bodies in the marina. They would either open a new inquiry or another veil of secrecy would descend on their facts to continue the cover-up. None of them said anything for a while until Chuck had a thought.

“Read that last item in the log again, please Jason,” Chuck said. Jason went to the last page in the log and quoted:

“05/20/44 – MM shone a light underneath the boat, frwd, thin line of oil leaking down, guess engine shot, looks like our journey is over.”

“MM?” Dexter asked.

“Mystery Man, I suppose, he didn’t want to write it out in full, so he just used initials,” Jason suggested.

“But that’s not what’s bothering me,” Chuck said to no one in particular. “What possible reason could there be for oil leaking out from the front of the boat?”

Chapter 24 – Next Steps – Modern Day

They all looked at Chuck, it was a good point but what use was this snippet of information in solving the mystery?

"What else could it be?" Archie asked.

"I don't know, but I bet you dollars to donuts it wasn't oil," Chuck replied confidently.

"O.K. we know the beginning and end of the trip, we don't know the why and we don't know anything about this Mystery Man. What else do we know?" Jason asked the group.

"We know they had a company of soldiers guarding the marina immediately after the night of the storm," Archie said.

"Is there any way we can find out what brought them to the marina? Someone somewhere should know." Jason asked.

"Wait a minute. What about old man Laarsen?" Bill said.

"What about him Bill?" Dexter asked.

"He was from Minnesota way, he was posted at that barracks just outside the marina and he married Jessica Winslow if I remember rightly. He was stationed there until they closed the barracks down." Bill explained.

"I remember him, but even if he's still alive he would have to be in his nineties by now, probably can't remember a damn thing," Chuck said.

"What? You mean like you? You old fart." Archie chipped in.

"Alright, I get it." Chuck responded belligerently, "but where does he live now? Poor Jessie died years ago."

"I didn't keep in touch with him but my son and theirs were good friends. I'll find out." Bill said and immediately began to call his son on his cell-phone. While Bill was talking, the others skipped through the log-book once more on the off-chance they may have missed something. There was something bugging Jason, but he couldn't put his finger on it. Once he returned to his boat he would scrutinize each entry of the log and try to determine what it was that was nagging at him. But by then, Bill had finished his phone call to his son.

"O.K., apparently, Laarsen is in a small, private, old people's home out Barnhart way, he's not very mobile these days but apparently, his mind is still as sharp as a pin. Likes to watch Jeopardy every night on T.V. My son said he's always glad to have visitors, we could pop around to see him any morning." Bill explained.

"Well, why don't we go there tomorrow?" Chuck asked.

"What? All of us?" Archie said.

"Why not?" Chuck asked, his hands extended out as if to say, 'what's the problem?'

"No can do tomorrow, beer delivery in the morning," Dexter said.

"Well that's more important, but we can still go. I'll drive, meet at the marina at 9:30?" Everyone except Dexter nodded their heads in agreement.

"Wow, Lorla will think we have left town, that will be two mornings in a row we haven't gone to the café." Chuck said.

"By the way Bill, did you get the address of the home Laarsen is in?" Jason asked.

"My son is going to let me know tonight." Bill replied.

After another couple of beers, the masters of sleuth decided to disperse, one or two of them needed a nap. Jason decided to go for a long walk, buy some groceries and think about what he had learned during the last couple of days. It was early evening by the time he returned to his boat, still, none the wiser about the reason for his grandfather's demise. Should he just go to the authorities with what he already knew? After all, he thought, the corpses of more than 35 people and the suspicious sinking of at least two boats were certainly justification for an investigation. Jason decided he would wait at least another day before contacting the police and then, he would have to think very carefully on how it was reported because up until now it had obviously been a very thorough cover-up.

Jason snacked on cheese and biscuits and drank a soda while he checked his emails. Both of his daughters had acknowledged his previous communications and he sent them a quick update saying that he had made real progress and would fill them in presently. After his light repast, he flipped through the log book one more time, remarking to himself on the meticulous, neat, notes his grandfather had made. As Jason read of various places and items of interest mentioned in the logs he would google them when suddenly, a chill went through his entire body. As he looked at the map of one of the rivers that his grandfather had negotiated a nearby town caught his attention. Jason was then reminded of something Chuck had said earlier that day which prompted him to carry out a further search on google. The result of that search sent a shiver down his spine. Jason calculated a quick timeline of all that he had discovered to date and as incredible as it seemed to him, if he was correct, what his searches had just revealed would most certainly explain the cover-up and would also account for the events that had taken place all those years ago.

Chapter 25 – The Who is Revealed – Modern Day

The next morning at just before the designated meeting time, Jason was talking to Charlie when Chuck arrived. Pleasantries were exchanged and before long, Bill drove up in his six-cylinder Cherry Red 52 Chevrolet Styleline Deluxe convertible, his pride and joy. Archie was in the passenger seat, Bill had picked him up on the way. Jason suggested they make the trip in Bill's car, but Jason was told it was only used for short trips, even though Barnhart was less than a 10-mile round trip. It was probably a shorter trip to Barnhart than from the marina to Bill's house!

Bill told Chuck the address he had received from his son, Chuck said he knew where it was, and it would only be a short ten-minute drive to the home, be there by 10:00, he said. On the short journey to their destination Jason decided not to share the information he had gleaned from the log the previous evening, at least not yet, he would wait until they had talked to Laarsen to see if there would be anything he said that would corroborate his theory.

Sure enough, they were at the door of the home just before 10:00 AM and it was indeed a home, albeit a large one. Jason rang the bell at the front door and waited until a very pleasant looking lady opened the door.

"Good morning, can I help you?" The lady asked, surprised to see four men standing on her threshold.

"Good morning, my name is Jason Clifford and I am trying to trace the whereabouts of my grandfather. My research has led me to believe that a Mr. Laarsen, who is staying here, may be able to help me with my inquiries." Jason explained, maybe a little too official sounding because the lady was still a little doubtful as she looked at the three other men.

"Hi, I'm Chuck, the owner of the marina down the road, lived there all my life, I've known Mr. Laarsen since I was a youngster when he was posted to guard the State Marina."

"We're friends of the Laarsens, our kids played together." Bill added.

"That's how we knew of Mr. Laarsen and the fact that he may be able to help Jason here." Archie explained. The lady was warming to them a little, but obviously still not convinced.

"Would you mind waiting here for a moment," the lady said and was about to close the door when she opened it again, "sorry, what were your names again?" Specifically asking Chuck and Bill.

"My name is Chuck Bailey, and this is Bill Lawrence, old man Laarsen will remember us." Chuck said with a smile. The lady was only gone for a few minutes when she returned and opened the door.

"Come on through." She said with a big smile. "My name is Mary, my husband, Greg, retired early, and we didn't want a bed and breakfast thing, but we did like the idea of hosting guests. So, we compromised, bought this house and converted it to accommodate a few seniors in their old age."

"How's it working out for you?" Jason asked as they walked through a well-lit hallway to a conservatory at the back of the house. The conservatory was roomy with plenty of natural light overlooking a small creek running through the bottom of a well-kept garden.

"Love it, we've been doing it for a couple of years now, no regrets," Mary replied, "anyway, here's Mr. Laarsen. Would you gentlemen prefer tea or coffee?" Mary asked. To a man they all replied coffee.

"Whoa, look at you! How are you?" Bill said to Mr. Laarsen with a laugh and a light punch on the man's arm.

"Hey Bill, I'm doing fine, what's the occasion? My funeral isn't to-day is it?" Mr. Laarsen said with a soft but coherent voice, then he saw Chuck. "Oh, hi Chuck, what's happening?"

"Hi, Mr. Laarsen, same old, same old," Chuck replied.

"This here is Archie, not sure whether you know him, he moved in a few years after you moved out of town." Bill pointed to Archie and he reached in to shake Mr. Laarsen's hand.

"And this is the star of the show, Jason, he's got some questions that you might be able to help him with," Bill explained, then it was Jason's turn to shake the man's hand. The hand of the man was thin and bony, the skin was like parchment and his grip was feeble, but his eyes were a bright blue and full of life.

"Oh really?" Replied Mr. Laarsen, "not sure I will be able to help you, but I'll certainly try."

They exchanged a few more pleasantries until Mary returned with coffees and a tray of cookies that were not going to last very long with the gannets Jason had accompanied to the home. Just after Mary left, Bill stated the purpose of their visit.

"Mr. Laarsen, do you remember when you first got posted to the State Marina back in '44?" Bill asked.

"Sure do. That was my first posting after training, my only posting in fact. I fully expected to be sent to the front but was my mother ever happy when I got sent there." Mr. Laarsen replied with a nostalgic smile.

"When did you arrive there Mr. Laarsen?" Jason asked.

"May 21st about 3:00 PM. I remember because we had lunch en route and when we arrived, we had to get our tents up before we could eat dinner." Mr. Laarsen replied.

"Do you remember if the gates to the marina were open then?" Jason asked. The others were all listening intently to Jason's questioning as they began to devour the tray of cookies.

"They were closed, but we weren't allowed anywhere near them, we were ordered to stay outside of a perimeter about fifty yards away from the entrance. The day after we arrived another army engineering group came in to build a wall all the way around the marina. We were never allowed to fraternize with them but the strangest thing, they built the wall across the entrance so none of us ever knew what was so secret inside that marina. Whatever it was, no one could get to it, well not by road anyway." Mr. Laarsen said, as mystified that day as he was when he was just a teenage rookie sent directly from basic training.

"So, you were one of the first of the soldiers to arrive, is that right?" Jason asked.

"That's right, the first." Mr. Laarsen confirmed.

"So, where did your orders come from?" Jason asked.

"You know the saying, 'not for me to reason why, mine is but to do and die'. We just did as we were told." Mr. Laarsen replied.

For the time being Jason was stumped, it looked like he had come to another brick wall in his investigation.

"But someone must have known what had to be done surely?" Archie asked. Mr. Laarsen thought for a minute.

"Funny you should say that. When we arrived, the lead truck was heading for the marina, that was the address the driver had been given. But out of nowhere, this big guy suddenly appeared, flanked by three other suspicious looking fellows. The main man asked to speak to whoever was in charge." Mr. Laarsen recalled, "that would have been old Sherlock, his real name was Major Holmes, so everyone called him Sherlock. Sherlock came forward and the strange man produced some papers then he began pointing and gesturing."

"Was he military do you think?" Asked Jason.

"Oh yes, for sure. But he was dressed in old, dark clothes, as were the other three men but it was difficult to see their faces, they were a real mystery." Mr. Laarsen said. The other four men all looked at each other, thinking the same question. Was it just his choice to use the word 'mystery' to describe the men or merely a coincidence?

"Sorry, if they were not in uniform, what makes you so sure they were military?" Jason asked.

"Harry, my buddy, was Sherlock's right-hand man, he was standing beside him when the stranger told him his rank and name. He told us later what went down. Apparently, the man's name was Captain Beardsley, he didn't say who he was assigned to, but he pulled out a letter and showed it to Sherlock. Now, Harry didn't get to read what was in that letter but from there on in, Sherlock was like a doting puppy, even though he outranked the stranger, so whatever was in that authorization was pretty heavy-duty. Then, until the wall was built those guys hung around the entrance to the marina to prevent anyone getting close, never saw them talk to anyone but themselves. But once that wall was finished, never saw them again. It was like they never existed." Mr. Laarsen said.

Everyone just sat back and thought about what they had just been told. Jason was now convinced everything that happened in the State marina on May 20th, 1944 had to be down to Captain Beardsley, that's where the trail was now leading.

"One more thing Mr. Laarsen," Jason asked, "when did they stop having a guard around the marina?"

"We pulled out May '50, just upped and left. Of course, I was married to Jessie by then, the Korean conflict hadn't started so I was allowed to leave the army and stay put." Mr. Laarsen replied.

"That's it? No police or any other security organization took over from your company?" Chuck asked incredulously.

"Not as far as I can recall, the signs stayed though." Mr. Laarsen said casually.

"So that marina has just been sitting there empty all these years." Chuck said, then added, "whatever for?"

"Well, nobody could get in from the road, that's for sure." Mr. Laarsen said.

"Sure as hell couldn't get in from the river either." Chuck confirmed, "so why was a perfectly good marina just left to rot?"

"I think I can answer that," Jason said, stunning all the men into silence, "but I need to carry out some research on our Captain Beardsley before I can be certain."

Chapter 26 – The Full Realisation is Assumed – Modern Day

The four men hung around the home for another hour or so explaining to Mr. Laarsen everything they had unearthed to date, including the sinking of the boats, the skeletons and jewelry.

"I bet those mysterious men had something to do with that, they were shifty looking, always slinking around." Mr. Laarsen's eyes were reduced to slits as he explained his recollections of them, "they always appeared to be up to no good like old-fashioned outlaws with their hats and their long coats."

By the time they had finished swapping their stories and catching up on the neighborhood, the visitors decided to take their leave, the cookie tray had long been depleted.

"Thanks again Mr. Laarsen," Jason said, shaking the man's hand once more, "you've been a great help."

"Let me know what you find out eh?" Mr. Laarsen said.

"Sure will Mr. Laarsen," Bill said, then the four men left, on their way out they thanked Mary for the snacks.

"So, what are you thinking?" Chuck asked Jason as they were pulling out of the home's small parking lot.

"Tell you what, I need to check up on this Beardsley fellow. Why don't I meet you in the pub after lunch, I will reveal what I know?" Jason said cryptically.

"Sounds good," Chuck said, and the others nodded their heads in agreement.

Nothing further was said on the short return trip back to the marina. Once they arrived, Bill and Archie climbed into the convertible and drove away, Jason went to his boat and Chuck hung around with his grandson, Charlie, as they both fiddled around with lines on the docks.

Jason climbed onto his boat and immediately got to work on the internet, starting with government sites looking for Captain Beardsley's military records, it didn't take him long to hit pay-dirt. Unfortunately, Beardsley had been assigned to the U.S. 7th Armored Division and had been one of the men murdered during the Malmedy massacre on December 17th, 1944. Further research revealed that the soldier had only recently been assigned to the division. Beardsley had previously been a member of the

Office of Strategic Services before being seconded to the British Specials Operations Executive. Jason dug a little deeper and discovered that both the organizations Beardsley had been assigned to operated behind enemy lines performing sabotage and covert operations. But Jason could find no reference to anything that could link Beardsley ever being in the vicinity of St. Louis. Jason backtracked and began making more structured notes on Beardsley's postings to see if that would shine any light on the solution.

It wasn't until Jason found an insignificant headline in the archives of a local Atlanta paper, Beardsley's home town. It was just a snippet that mentioned the soldier had returned stateside to recuperate from an injury incurred during active service and that he couldn't wait to return to England to continue the fight against the Germans. The article was dated April 2nd, 1944. Maybe security wasn't what it should have been, after all, what spies would have been reading a local rag? But there it was, the place that Beardsley was going to be temporarily assigned to while he was back in the U.S.

"Bingo," said Jason out loud.

Chapter 27 – Theory of a Cover-Up – Modern Day

The five men sat in the pub at a round table in the corner of the room, they all had their beverages of choice and Jason began to address the others.

"Here's what I think and as incredible as it may sound, it is the only theory I can think of that explains everything," Jason said.

"This sounds exciting," Archie said.

"Shut up, Arch, let him talk," Bill admonished him.

"I think my grandfather was carrying some plutonium on his boat," Jason said then sat back to let that information sink in with the others.

"What? Plutonium?" Dexter said. "No!"

"Think about it. Chuck, there were two things you had said to us that brought me to this conclusion," Jason said and looked at Chuck, "Clinch River, Knoxville, right?" Jason asked, and Chuck nodded his head in agreement, "and what is there that would have been critical to the war effort?" Jason asked. The four men just looked at each other mystified.

Jason leaned forward and banged the tip of his finger on the table to accentuate his point, "Oak Ridge that's what. Where they made plutonium for the Manhattan Project. Where they made plutonium for the bomb! And what was coming out from the front of the boat? Not oil, as you correctly told us, it was plutonium. It would have been black and could have easily been mistaken for oil." His audience all shook their heads in disbelief.

"No, I need a bit more substance than that, that's just pure coincidence," Dexter said as he leaned back, arms folded across his chest.

"O.K., so try this for size. I did some research on our Captain Beardsley, he had been in the Special Operations Executive in England during the war until he got injured and was sent back stateside for recuperation. Ironically, for all we know he could have returned on the very ship my grandfather was assigned to. Beardsley had been taught to be a ruthless killer and he just happened to have been posted to Oak Ridge in April 1944. Is that another coincidence?" Jason explained, and then paused for comments, when none was forthcoming, he continued. "The deaths of all those people could only have been committed by someone who was a cold-blooded killer. The cover-up could only have been perpetrated by someone experienced in subterfuge and undercover work. Remember what Laarsen had said after

Beardsley had produced the letter, what were his exact words? *'Sherlock was like a doting puppy, even though he outranked the stranger'*. Then there was the radio, didn't Rusty say it was state-of-the-art and top secret in those days, only someone with Beardsley's training would have been aware of technology like that. I suggest to you that he is the man that set this whole thing up and then he had the authority to carry out a cover-up when it all went tits up. Why was there a wall built all around the marina, a two feet thick concrete wall with a lead shield in the middle of it? I'm telling you, it all fits." Jason said, now it was his turn to lean back to let the other men digest these facts. After a few moments during which an uncomfortable silence prevailed over the group, Dexter was once more the first to speak.

"The problem is, if what you say is true, where do we go from here? Who can we trust?"

Chapter 28 – Cover-Up Revealed – Modern Day

"Jeremiah," Chuck said, the other four men just looked at him. "Captain Jeremiah Cartwright of the U.S. coastguard. That's who we can talk to, he'll know what to do."

"Can we trust him?" Bill asked the question everyone else wanted to ask.

"Let me put it to you this way, the man should have reached the rank of Admiral years ago, but the stubborn, undiplomatic son of a bitch could never play the game. The man is as honest as the day is long. Yes, we can trust him." Chuck replied confidently.

"How do you know him, Chuck?" Jason asked.

"Been coming through here for years, started off as a young seaman apprentice and I've watched him come right through the ranks to Captain. He's held various posts but is only really happy working the rivers. I'll get in touch with him and set up a meeting. He is a busy man, so I don't know when he will be able to fit us in."

"Well, I don't think there is any more we can do until that happens," Jason said. "Maybe I should return home to Cleveland until the meeting is scheduled."

"What? Don't you like it here?" Bill said.

"Is it the company?" Archie asked.

"No, no," Jason smiled as he replied, "you've all been great but if the meeting is not going to be for a while I thought I should go home for the weekend and see the girls."

"It won't be that long, if he's in the area he could be here Monday," Chuck said. "Anyway, we've had so much fun the last couple of days couldn't bear to see you go yet. This is the most excitement we've had in years." Bill added and the others all murmured their agreement.

"Perhaps we could go and visit the marina?" Archie asked.

"I think not," Jason said positively. "For one, I wouldn't want to risk going through that tight entrance again until all the concrete is safely cleared. That's a job for a marine construction company. Secondly, now that we think we know what my grandfather was carrying, the area would have to be tested for contamination before anyone could set foot in there. In fact, I should be tested, I went diving to the boat where the damn stuff was stored."

"You're right!" Chuck said, with Jason believing he was thinking of his welfare until that is, he continued, "that will get Jeremiah down here in a hurry."

"Let me go and call him right now," Chuck said, then he got up and left the bar.

Dexter took the opportunity to leave the table to replenish the now empty glasses of beers and he returned a couple of minutes later with five more brews. For the next ten minutes or so, they swapped ideas and scenarios that would explain all the deaths of the people on the boats. Jason's grandfather and his mate could easily be explained because of their closeness to the operation but why the deaths of the others?

"I can understand them wanting to shut up old man Grimshaw, but the people on the Streamer?" Bill said.

"Maybe they came in contact with my grandfather and his mate and they too needed to be silenced," Jason suggested.

“What, all of them?” Bill asked.

“It seems a bit over the top, doesn’t it? But then there was the head buried in the wall, I can’t explain that one either.” Jason said.

“Maybe there are others buried in the wall,” Bill said.

“They could have been the other mystery men that Laarsen spoke of and this Beardsley fellow could have bumped them off too!” Archie said as though a sudden revelation had hit him.

“You know, that’s not a bad theory,” Dexter said, and Jason agreed.

“Which would mean Beardsley was the only person left alive that knew what had really happened in the marina, until now,” Jason said, to no one in particular.

Before any further assumptions could be made, Chuck returned looking all pleased with himself.

“I got hold of Jeremiah and gave him the gist of the story. He’s a desk-jockey now in St. Louis, he said he could drive down for lunch on Tuesday and we will meet with him at 1:00. Meanwhile, he will contact the Environmental Protection Agency to have someone get in touch with me to get you checked out as soon as possible." Chuck nodded his head towards Jason, "Jeremiah will also arrange for an EPA toxicological team to be on standby so that they can move in as soon as they can get access to the marina." Chuck managed to blurt out in his excitement, before adding, "how about that then? Impressed or what?"

"That is impressive, Chuck," Jason said, "let's just hope our suspicions are correct, otherwise we are going to have egg on our faces."

Chapter 29 – Testing for Plutonium Poisoning – Modern Day

After a little more brainstorming and swapping of ideas they believed that between the five of them, they had cracked the case, assuming of course that Jason's theory regarding the plutonium was accurate. To celebrate, they each had one more beer and then they parted company, each going their separate ways. Just as Jason reached his boat and was about to climb aboard he heard young Charlie call out and he was running towards him.

"My grandfather told me to tell you he has received a call from an Armanda Patel who works at the EPA in Lenexa, Kansas. She is scheduled to arrive on Monday at 2:00 to carry out tests on you." Charlie said all official.

"Wow, they don't mess around, do they? Great, thanks, Charlie." Jason replied and then climbed onto his boat. The first thing he felt he should do was to send an email to his daughters, but he certainly didn't want to tell them about the possibility of plutonium poisoning they'd be worried sick. It was bad enough having to be concerned about it himself, let alone have his daughters worry as well. But he could put a positive spin on the topic and tell them that they were to have meetings during the next couple of days to discuss the raising of their great-grandfather's boat.

Once Jason had read through his emails and reported into his daughters he decided that as he would be having a visitor he needed to clean up the boat somewhat. He spent the rest of the evening tidying up and putting things back in their place. He decided that in the morning, after breakfast, he would give the outside of the boat a clean and polish.

So it was, that the following Monday, Armanda drove into the marina in her SUV, complete with the EPA logo emblazoned on the door, both Jason and his boat were ready for inspection. Jason walked slowly towards the vehicle as Armanda exited with the mandatory clipboard government officials always seem to have when out on site. In addition, she was carrying a small machine that Jason assumed was a Geiger counter.

"Armanda?" Jason said and held out his hand.

"Yes, Mr. Clifford?" She replied and accepted Jason's outstretched hand.

"Obviously you can't think I am too badly infected if you are prepared to shake my hand." Jason said jokingly as he eyed the young lady. She was obviously of Asian Indian descent, her tall, slim body was dressed in jeans and an EPA golf shirt that accentuated her beautiful figure. She had long jet-black hair that framed a beautiful face highlighted by stunning dark brown eyes.

"I didn't think for a moment you would be Mr. Clifford," Armanda smiled as she replied, revealing her perfect pearly whites, "Captain Cartwright briefed me on your situation and I did some research on Oak Ridge. I very much doubt whether there would have been much more than 85 grams of plutonium being transported and after being in the water this long it would have dissolved and dispersed by now anyway." Her accent was totally American with no hint of an Indian accent, so, Jason thought she had either been born in the States or arrived at a very young age.

"Well, that's a relief," Jason replied, genuinely relieved and forgetting for a moment that he was in the presence of a beautiful woman.

"But, let's check you out anyway, I want to have justification for driving here for five hours," Armanda said laughing. "First I would like to test your boat." She walked over to the boat, placed her clipboard on the seat next to the wheel and began to use her machine to test along the hull. As she bent down she revealed the tightness of her jeans over her athletic body, Jason began to have stirrings he hadn't experienced since his wife had died. He was thinking about how this trip had turned his life around, in more ways than one.

"Doesn't look as though you have encountered any exposure above the norm, Mr. Clifford," Armanda said as she looked at some readings on her machine. That's not what Jason was currently thinking.

"What do you mean, 'above the norm'?" Jason inquired.

"Well, you would be surprised how much radioactive waste you can be exposed to during your daily life. In fact, on this river, you may be exposed to more radioactive products than you were in the marina. So yes, there are some traces but way below safe levels."

"What is that machine?" Jason asked.

"It's a FIDLER Detector, designed to find levels of plutonium." Armanda replied, "now it's your turn, are we going onboard?"

"Sure," Jason replied. He climbed onto the boat first and then assisted Armanda. "Welcome aboard."

"Thank you," Armanda replied. Jason then led the way down to the cabin area.

"Can I get you anything? Coke, coffee, water?" Jason asked.

"No thanks, this won't take long, I would like to get back on the road to get home at a reasonable hour," Armanda responded.

"Sure," Jason said.

"O.K., I have a questionnaire to quickly go through and then a couple of physical tests and we're done," Armanda said as she gripped a pen in her hand and began to ask him her questions.

"Sounds good," Jason said.

"What makes you think that you have been exposed to plutonium?" Armanda asked. Jason gave a quick explanation of his suspicions, without the gory details, and the reason why he was doing it.

"Any nausea? Headaches feeling ill since you dove down to the boat?" Armanda asked.

"No," Jason replied, shaking his head sideways.

"No loss of hair by the looks of things," Armanda said, looking at Jason's thick thatch of hair.

"Any open sores or cuts when you went diving?" Armanda asked.

"No," Jason replied, checking over his body as he did so. "Would that have been a problem?"

"Potentially. However, inhalation is the worst thing that can happen when it comes to plutonium but since you were diving and breathing from an underwater apparatus that's not applicable in your case." Armanda explained. "Interestingly, plutonium is far more poisonous than the cyanide used in the German gas chambers, yet people work safely with it every day, as long as it doesn't get into your bloodstream or it is inhaled. The only risk you would have had is taking in plutonium orally, but as it is absorbed poorly through the stomach and bowels it is expelled from your body before it can do any harm. So, you would still be reasonably safe, unless of course, the volumes were unusually high."

"Good to know," Jason said absently.

After a few more questions, it was time for blood and urine tests. The blood test was quick and painless, and Armanda vacated the boat for the urine test, even though the toilet on the boat was private with a door. Jason did his thing then climbed off the boat and gave Armanda his deposit, with just a little embarrassment but she accepted it as though this was a regular occurrence.

"Well, thank you, Mr. Clifford, I am sure the tests will prove negative and if they don't we will be in touch," Armanda said as she held out her hand.

"Thank you, are you sure I can't tempt you in a beverage of some kind over at the pub?" Jason asked shaking her hand and holding it maybe a little longer than necessary.

"Lovely offer but I'm already paying my babysitter overtime, I'm afraid I need to get back," Armanda replied with that beautiful smile of hers but simultaneously crushing Jason as he learned that she was a mother and probably happily married in Kansas.

"But hey, good luck with your project, I'll be following the results closely," Armanda said as she waved goodbye, got into her vehicle, quickly stowed her results and was soon driving away.

Jason absently watched as her SUV disappeared into the distance and was suddenly brought out of his reverie by a leery Charlie.

“What were you getting up to on your boat with that young lady Mr. Clifford?” Charlie asked lasciviously.

“Ha, it’s not what you think Charlie, not what you think at all,” Jason replied.

Chapter 30 – Meeting the Captain – Modern Day

After Armanda's departure, Jason walked up the hill to join the others in the bar. For once, they didn't talk about Jason's quest but just shot the breeze talking about sports, politics and righting the world. Although, they did briefly discuss the pending visit of the Captain the following day and the others also persuaded Jason to have a quick trip in the morning to view the State Marina of Missouri for themselves. Although Jason was still reluctant to return to the marina he conceded to the others' wishes but remained adamant about not attempting another negotiation of that entrance until it was cleared and deemed safe to do so. Any viewing would have to be from the river, the others agreed.

Jason didn't stay in the pub that long, he decided to return to his truck and have a quick drive around the area. He found some shops and had a look around then decided to buy a Chinese take-out for dinner. After dinner, he went through his usual routine of checking his emails and phoning his daughters. They were both pleased about his findings and also that he sounded more enthusiastic about life. Shirley even resumed her attempts to get him involved in online dating and was pleasantly surprised to hear him consider it instead of dismissing it out-of-hand.

The next morning the others turned up to take the brief excursion to the State marina. Everyone was surprised to find Dexter had turned up too and ribbed him about the fact his wife would even let him out.

"Well, there were no deliveries scheduled for today, so Helen can handle it by herself for a couple of hours," Dexter explained.

"Well, everybody, climb aboard," Jason said and turned on the engine. It was a beautiful, clear day with very little chop on the water, so Jason was able to gun the engine a little and within forty minutes they were approaching the entrance to the State Marina of Missouri. Both Bill and Chuck had brought their own binoculars while Dexter and Archie shared Jason's. Jason cleared the channel markers and while regularly checking his depth sounder he slowly motored as close to the entrance as he was prepared to risk.

The concrete and lead structure were clearly visible as they neared the entrance and Jason pointed out where he had stored the head that he had unwittingly unearthed, although, not wishing to see it again. From the south-westernmost point they could just see inside a small section of the marina and could make out a few of the masts and piles that still remained and of course the wall that completely encircled the marina. They could also clearly see the broken pieces of concrete penetrating the surface of the water at the entrance making entry completely out of the question. Jason turned the boat around and headed upriver to inspect the wall from the outside, something he didn't do on his last trip. But there was nothing to glean, the wall was solid everywhere else, which made it even stranger to Jason that the wall was still impenetrable after all these years, yet at the precise moment he went by on his boat, just a few days ago, the piece of the structure at the entrance had collapsed. Perhaps it was the interminable current of the Mississippi that had finally weakened the foundations because the rest of the wall appeared solid, or maybe something else caused it, something not of this world.

The return trip was uneventful and by the time they arrived at the marina, it was time for their meeting. Captain Jeremiah Cartwright had obviously visited Chuck's watering-hole many times before and they greeted each other like long lost friends, which indeed they were. Chuck introduced everyone, ordered drinks, and appetizers and they sat down in their usual little round-table in the corner of the bar. Jeremiah was not in uniform, so he wasn't conspicuous in that regard in a bar full of tourists. But what did attract attention was his deep jovial laugh that seemed to erupt from the pit of his stomach at anything that was even remotely funny. His clear blue eyes would begin to well-up and tears would fall down his red-faced cheeks in a fit of laughter as his whole rotund body would shake with the sheer mirth of it all. Yes, you could say, Jeremiah was a man who loved life.

"So, do you miss not going out on the boats Jeremiah?" Chuck asked.

"Not really, Chuck," Jeremiah replied, "it's a young man's game now and I can still get out there occasionally if I choose to, but Elena is pleased I finally have a regular 9-5 job."

"How is Elena?" Chuck asked, referring to Jeremiah's long-time wife.

"She's great and now that I have a job with normal hours she flies away to visit the grandkids in California," Jeremiah said and burst out laughing with a thigh-slapping gesture. It was an infectious laugh and the others were all laughing helplessly with the man.

The drinks arrived, brought by a smiling Helen, who was now in on the plot and supported her husband's participation in the proceedings, much to the relief of Dexter. Then it was Jason's turn to be center stage and provide an account and theory to what had been discovered to date. Jason backed up his statements with the photographs, his findings and all the evidence to date. Jeremiah sat stolidly throughout the explanation and did not utter a word or ask a single question. When Jason had finished, even though Jeremiah had arranged for Jason to be tested by the EPA, it didn't look as though the man had bought one iota of the story. In fact, for a full minute, nobody said a word, it was almost as if the excellent presentation of the facts and theories Jason had just provided was so incredible, it was difficult for the others to believe as well. Just then, Helen brought another couple of plates containing appetizers that included nachos, bruschetta, and calamari.

"That is just too unbelievable!" Jeremiah whispered as he shook his head in disbelief. Jason had been pinning all his hopes on Jeremiah for a path forward and his shoulders slumped in disillusionment.

Chapter 31 – Plan of Action – Modern Day

"So, you don't believe me?" Jason said, his disappointment palpable.

"On the contrary. It all makes perfect sense, but what to do?" Jeremiah said and looked a trifle bemused. "First, I'm going to have some bruschetta, I'm starving, and I can't think on an empty stomach." Then gave out another belly laugh.

After a few moments of munching and commenting on the quality of the food, Jeremiah outlined a plan of action.

"The first thing we must do is verify that the marina is now government property, which I'm sure it is. Next, we will have to gain access to the marina and let the EPA do its thing, even if it is not government property we will still have to do that, it's a potential safety hazard. If the EPA gives us the go-ahead, which I'm sure they will after all these years, the wall over the road will have to be torn down as well as clearing the entrance from the river. The National Transportation Safety Board would be very interested in this one and I expect they will want to take jurisdiction over the investigation, although just about every government department will be involved and if your theory is correct, I expect the military will want to take charge. Either way, salvage cranes will have to be brought in and arrangements for those would still have to be coordinated between the Coast Guard and NTSB. I will let both the EPA and NTSB know because they will also have to arrange for coroners." Jeremiah explained but then his brow creased a little before continuing, "you realize now that the investigation is out of your hands. Once you have explained your findings to whoever takes charge, either the military or the NTSB team, you will be forced to hand over your evidence and you will be out of the loop."

"I understand that," Jason replied.

"You've done a hell of a thing here and I expect the cover-ups haven't finished because if what you have told me is substantiated, there is no way the government is going to admit to shooting people and sinking ships." Jeremiah explained, "I would suggest that for your own good none of this goes any further than this table. And Jason, make no mention of the jewelry, money or the photographs you have found, otherwise you'll lose those too."

"But I've told you!" Jason said.

“I don’t recall that son,” Jeremiah said nonchalantly. Jason got the drift but still didn’t like what Jeremiah was saying.

“But according to government records my grandfather was missing in action, yet he was murdered on a boat here in Missouri, a boat he was ordered to operate.” Jason countered.

“Exactly, following orders and was missing in action,” Jeremiah said quietly and deliberately. “The government will stand by what they said originally, they have not lied.”

“But what about all those people on the St. Louis Streamer who were murdered? How are they going to explain that one away?” Jason asked. The others were now looking first to Jason and then to Jeremiah as though they were in the middle of a tennis match.

“It sank, which was what was originally suspected. The only difference is, now, thanks to you, we have located the sunken boat and can confirm all souls onboard perished.” Jeremiah replied philosophically.

Jason was close to tears, all the research, all the time he had spent in successfully finding the real reason for his grandfather’s disappearance only to have the truth suppressed once more. Then Jason thought of one more thing.

"Then there's the body at the entrance how would they explain that?" Jason asked.

"What body?" Jeremiah asked.

"The head I told you I found buried in the concrete wall." Jason said.

"Sorry, I don't recall you telling me that and certainly nothing was found by the investigating team," Jeremiah stated. "Did you take any photographs of the alleged body?"

"Yes, you know I did." Jason hissed, then added, "look, who's side are you on anyway? I thought you came here to help us." There was a pause, things were getting tense and Jeremiah realized this.

"Look, son," Jeremiah continued in a quiet sympathetic voice, "I have come here to help you. I'm playing devil's advocate that's all. Trust me, I have been involved in a lot of unscrupulous crap over the years, stuff that has never made it to the public domain. I've got a feeling that this is another one. You've opened a big can of worms here son and Uncle Sam is just not going to let the whole truth get out."

"Jeremiah is right Jason," Chuck chipped in, "look, your objective was to find out what happened to your grandfather, you've succeeded in that and you've come away with some expensive jewelry to boot. You know the truth and you have found the Streamer, I'm sure you'll get credit for that. Who knows, thanks to you, we may even be able to re-open the State Marina. Allow Jeremiah to run with it now and you can let it go." There were nods of approval from around the table.

"I can assure you that once I have reported this, things will move fast, and I will be like you, just a bystander in the investigation. Although the authorities may want to question you Jason and they may also need Coast Guard's help for certain activities but other than that, you and I can just stand back and watch." Jeremiah added.

Chapter 32 – Investigation Time – Modern Day

Jeremiah was right, things did move fast. The very next day a team from the EPA scaled the wall at the State Marina of Missouri. Using ladders and scaffolding the EPA operatives climbed over the wall, their theory was that if tests for radio-activity proved positive it would be best if the wall remained intact. As it turned out, tests proved to be negative and during the ensuing days, a construction team was brought in to tear down the wall that was built across the road at the marina's entrance. At the same time, a floating crane was despatched from St. Louis to clear the entrance from the river. Meanwhile, a team of F.B.I. investigators descended on the marina, complete with mobile offices and live-in trailers. Jason and the rest of the group were amazed at the flurry of activity that had been initiated by Jason's findings. But the disappearance of a few grams of plutonium was a big deal and the alleged deaths that had occurred because of it certainly necessitated an investigation. Jason was contacted as soon as the F.B.I. was ensconced in the marina and they sent one of their logo-laden SUVs to fetch him for an interview.

Jason was directed to one of the mobile offices in the marina and there he was greeted by Agent Gary Redmond. The G-Man came in at about the same height as Jason, around six feet tall, but that's where the similarities ended. The Fed. was broad-shouldered and extremely well-built with hardly an ounce of body-fat, he gave the impression he worked out with weights, a lot. His eyes were dark and beady, darting from one thing to another as though he was constantly watching every move in his immediate surroundings. The agent subsequently introduced Jason to another agent, Audrey Jordan, who on the other hand was short, petite and very attractive. The kind of girl Jason could imagine being used in an undercover sting.

The three of them sat down to discuss Jason's findings to date. Jason did almost all the talking, displaying his photographs, the dockmaster's logbook, his grandfather's log book and of course, mentioning the body at the waterside entrance to the marina. Because of Jason's research to date and what he had learned from Laarsen he also provided a theory about what had happened. Jason believed Beardsley had overseen his grandfather's mission. Because of the accident, the plutonium was compromised so Beardsley used his undercover operator experience to cover-up the whole mess by sinking the two vessels, with all hands on board, together with the dockmaster. He then arranged to build the wall and when that was finished he killed off the only other men who knew about the plot.

The two agents listened to Jason's facts and theories without blinking an eye-lid. Jason thought they either thought he was a crank or there was real substance in what he was telling them.

"Do you mind if we keep these log books, as part of our investigations, and take copies of your photographs for our records?" Agent Redmond asked.

"Not at all," Jason replied. Jason pushed forward the logs then ejected the memory card from his camera and handed it to Gary who went into a back office to copy the photographs.

"Just inquisitive, what made you take a second dive to look at the boats?" Audrey asked while they were waiting for Gary to return. At first, Jason didn't know what to say, he could hardly tell the agent that he had a dream where a beautiful woman had beckoned him onto the boat.

"It was just a feeling, it felt like unfinished business that's all," Jason said, trying to sound convincing.

"It's just that diving on a wreck by yourself is a risky business," Audrey replied with a hint of dubiousness. Fortunately, at that moment, Gary returned with Jason's memory card and the interview was effectively over.

"Right Jason, thanks for your help, if we need you, we know how to contact you. I'll have someone take you back to your boat." Gary said pleasantly but perfunctorily, then added in a more serious tone, "one other thing, it would be best if you kept your theories and any other information about this incident to yourself until our investigations are complete." Jason's recent conversation with Jeremiah in the pub suddenly came flooding back to him with all too much reality.

"Absolutely, but there is just one thing," Jason said, "I believe there has been a major cover-up perpetrated here, my grandfather, his shipmate and over thirty other people have been murdered to hush up a shipment of some radioactive substance. I would like to see justice carried out for all of them. I'm prepared to take it up with the media if necessary."

"Mr. Clifford, we would like to thank you for bringing this information to our attention. However, I believe your interest in this investigation is now terminated." Gary said, "we will be conducting our search for the truth in the most professional manner possible." Then his voice took on a serious, ominous tone, "however, your assumptions of a cover-up may be a little premature and I would advise you to keep any outlandish ideas of a cover-up to yourself. All you have here are a few fuzzy underwater photographs of skeletons, which quite frankly, could have been taken anywhere. The badly decomposed head you claimed you saw at the marina's entrance, probably just the remains of a foraging animal." Gary waited a few seconds as Jason let that information sink in before continuing on a more somber note, "I can also tell you, Mr. Clifford, that the government bought this property in May 1944, so remember, anything you discovered once you entered here from the river; you did while trespassing on federal land, ignoring the numerous 'keep out' signs that are clearly displayed and in the process, damaging government property, i.e. the wall, to gain illegal access to a restricted area. You then proceeded to remove articles from the property. Those actions would not be too highly thought of in a court of law if you decided to go to the newspapers trying to sell a story." Gary then smiled but it wasn't a smile of amusement it was cynical and was meant as a warning.

Chapter 33 – Killing Time – Modern Day

Jason did indeed get the point, he couldn't say he hadn't been warned by the old sea-dog, Jeremiah, but it certainly appeared that nothing detrimental to the government would ever be disclosed. In the SUV during the trip back to his boat he decided he would remain in the area for a couple of more days before returning home. In fact, Chuck was right, he had fulfilled his objective, he had discovered what had happened to his grandfather, he felt he had gone about as far as he could with his investigations. That was until the next morning when Chuck greeted him as Jason was sitting on his boat, relaxing and drinking a coffee.

"Ahoy there Jason, what say you?" Chuck hailed.

"Hey Chuck," Jason responded, "do you want a coffee?"

"We don't have time lad." Chuck told him with a big smile on his face, "David the jeweler just called. He's got some news for us, come on, let's go."

"What now?" Jason asked, taking a quick gulp of his coffee.

"Yes now, time for coffee later, or something stronger if the news is good," Chuck told him. Jason took another quick gulp, tipped the remains of his cup over the side of the boat, placed the cup on the seat and proceeded to climb onto the dock.

They walked briskly up the hill to the jewelers where the same young lady repeated the same process to let them into the store. David, immaculately dressed, as usual, was there to greet them.

"Ah, Chuck, Jason, good to see you both again," David said as he held out his hand to shake theirs. "I think I have great news for you." He added as he opened a file containing a single copy of an email. "The firm that took over from Raymons has replied and informed me that the collection in question was sold to a Lady Ashdene in July 1940." David passed the copy to Jason for his perusal.

"So now all we have to do is find out where this Lady Ashdene lived," Chuck said.

"Where do we start with that one?" Jason asked rhetorically.

"Well, we know she was in St. Louis in 1944," Chuck replied.

"May I suggest the St. Louis Post-Dispatch or even census statistics." David offered.

"Yes, but where do I start?" Jason asked, "I can't just start looking through archives of old newspapers from 1940 onwards."

"You don't necessarily have to," Chuck said, "from what you have discovered, the elite of St. Louis was on the Streamer when it sunk. Bet your bottom dollar that would have been reported, then you can take it from there."

"Good point," Jason agreed. "So, I need to do some more research." Then turning to David, "would you mind taking care of the jewelry for a little longer?"

"My pleasure," David replied with a smile before adding, "bye the bye, if you ever wish to place these items on the market I would be more than happy to help you fetch the best prices possible." Yes, thought Jason and you would also be happy to fetch the best commission possible. Then he thought again, well, of course, he would, that's his business, why wouldn't he? After all, to date, he had been very accommodating, providing all his assistance at no charge, why shouldn't he have a little of the action?

The men exchanged their farewells, Jason thanking David for all his help then Chuck and Jason returned to the marina where they were greeted by an agitated Charlie. "I'm glad you're back, the F.B.I. have been here," Charlie said

"Well, you knew where we were why didn't you come and get us?" Chuck asked with some frustration at his grandson's apparent incompetence.

"They weren't interested in talking to you," Charlie said, quite upset, "there were four of them, I tried to stop them, but they brushed me aside, they just wanted to search Jason's boat and his truck."

Chapter 34 – The Lady of the Streamer – Modern Day

Jason climbed hurriedly onto his boat expecting to see that it had been ransacked, but much to his surprise everything was pretty much as he had left it. It was obvious, however, that a thorough search had taken place, things were not quite as he had left them, but tidy nonetheless. His computer was still there but when he turned it on he discovered that all the photographs he had taken had been erased. Jason checked his camera; his memory card was empty. That annoyed him, but fortunately, he could console himself in the knowledge that he had sent emails to himself, with attachments as well as backing up the photos on the cloud. But after further checking, there was no trace of his emails and the files on the cloud had disappeared. The only other thing that seemed to have been taken was the radio and the safe he had found on his grandfather's boat. What the authorities were not aware of was the jewelry, left with David for safe-keeping, the photographs and money Jason had found in the safe; they were in his wallet. He also had a backup of the photos he had taken retained on a memory stick on his key-chain.

Jason was extremely angry by this affront and considered confronting Agent Redmond, but after careful consideration, he realized that nothing of importance had appeared to have been taken. Furthermore, the F.B.I. would not have carried out the search without the appropriate authorization. Consequently, he decided not to give Redmond the satisfaction of a confrontation which Jason knew he would end up losing anyway. Chuck had now boarded the boat and he could see that Jason was still seething.

“Anything taken?” Chuck asked sympathetically.

“Looks like the logbooks, the radio I found and the safe,” Jason replied, not wanting to mention the photographs.

“They didn’t leave it in a mess though, I suppose that’s something,” Chuck remarked. “Although, they could have done the washing-up while they were at it!” Chuck said nodding towards the dirty breakfast dishes sitting in the sink. At which point they both burst out laughing.

“Come on son, I’ll buy you a beer,” Chuck said, and he began to leave the boat.

"Bit early for a brew isn't it?" Jason replied after a quick look at his wrist-watch.

"It's mid-day somewhere in the world and you look as though you could do with a drink," Chuck told him.

"You've got that right." Jason agreed, and he began to follow the old man off the boat, taking his laptop with him.

When they arrived at the pub Dexter was behind the bar and he immediately began to pour them a couple of beers. It was still a little early for Archie and Bill, so Jason and Chuck sat at the bar and explained the day's events to Dexter.

"So, Jeremiah was right, it looks like the Feds. want to keep this under wraps." Dexter said once he had heard the gist of what had happened. "They seem to be eliminating all your evidence."

"Seems that way," Jason replied although he didn't tell them about his memory stick. Jason's thoughts harkened back to his conversation with Agent Redmond, the photos could be of anything and they certainly didn't have the resolution required to distinguish the bullet holes in the skulls.

By the time they were on their second beers, Archie and Bill had arrived and they too were brought up to date.

"So, are we all going into St. Louis to look through the paper's archives?" Archie asked.

"Not sure we have to," Jason replied, opening up his laptop, "let's see if they have anything online." At that, the others sidled their chairs around to get a better view of the screen, Dexter just stood over Jason's shoulder. Jason connected to the pub's WiFi and typed in a few search parameters and Jason selected one of the more promising results, which turned out to be exactly what he was looking for. It was a site containing St. Louis Post Dispatch archives dating as far back as 1874. There was a small fee necessary to enter the site, which Jason paid for by credit card. The excitement amongst the men was almost palpable and the only thing that could be heard was the clacking of the laptop's keys as Jason speedily entered data. It didn't take long before he hit pay dirt.

"Got something," Jason said, and the others huddled closer to his computer to read what he had discovered:

'St. Louis Elite Feared Dead'

was the headline on the front page of the edition dated May 25th and they all began to read the article which stated:

> The recent storm that barrelled through the area may be responsible for taking the lives of many of St. Louis's top businessmen and women. A representative from St. Lawrence Boat Cruises have informed us that the St. Louis Streamer failed to return to port on the night of the 24th May. There has been no word from the captain of the vessel, Jean Deschamps, and it is feared that the paddle steamer possibly encountered difficulties during what appeared to have been one of the worst storms on the Mississippi in recent memory. Amongst those believed to have been on board were Robert Sinclair (Sinclair Steel Manufacturing) and Lady Ashdene.
>
> More to follow as information becomes available.

In support of the article were a couple of stock photographs of both the Streamer and Robert Sinclair. The photograph of Sinclair showed him standing in the middle of a group of people that was taken during a recent benefit concert. On the edge of the group, although her face was turned away as the photograph was being taken, was what looked like Lady Ashdene. Jason could only surmise that was who it was because she was wearing the jewelry he had recovered from the boat.

Chapter 35 – Researching – Modern Day

"They're the jewels alright," Archie said as he did his thing with his spectacles.

"I'd like to print a copy of that, but I don't have a printer," Jason said, but more to himself than the group.

"I have a printer; can you copy it somehow and put in onto a memory stick," Dexter suggested.

"Sure," Jason replied and opened a program that could take a screen-scrape of the photo and save it as a JPEG file. In a matter of seconds, Jason handed his memory stick to Dexter, "there you go, the file to print is called photo.jpg."

"Not too imaginative, are you?" Dexter laughed as he took the stick and went to a room behind the bar to print off the photo. He was back with the printout and passed it to Jason together with his memory stick.

"Right, let's see if there's any other useful information," Jason said and began to search through the archives. Each subsequent day there was more information regarding the search for the lost vessel and a few bios on some of the people suspected of being on board, but no further mention of Lady Ashdene. It wasn't until Jason read one of the editions that was almost one month after the reported sinking. A decision had been made to call off any further searches and the newspaper printed a list of the known people who had perished on board the Streamer. In the list was the following item:

.......Lady Ashdene of Ladue, who leaves behind a young son

"Where's Ladue?" Jason asked.

"That's the expensive area of St. Louis," Dexter commented, "that makes sense."

"So, that's the next step, find the address of Lady Ashdene and see if we can locate this son of hers," Jason said, signing off the web site and closing his laptop.

"And how do you propose to find that out?" Chuck asked, "he may be long gone by now, dead even."

"There you go again, you're not dead yet, why should her son be?" Archie berated him, but everyone just ignored the comment.

"Well, do what David suggested, check out census data at the library in St. Louis," Jason said. "So, who's up for a road trip on Monday?"

"I can't, deliveries expected all morning," Dexter said.

"I have a doctor's appointment in the morning," Bill added, at which point everyone turned to look at him.

"Nothing trivial I hope," Archie said, jokingly.

"Nah, just a checkup." Bill replied although he didn't sound too convincing.

"Looks like it will be just the three of us then," Jason said.

"Wait a minute, I would like to be in on this, what about the Tuesday could we all make it then? Surely another day is not going to hurt!" Bill suggested.

"I could make the following day too, Helen could handle the bar for a day by herself," Dexter mentioned.

"Fine, we'll make a day of it then." Jason agreed.

"And what will we be looking for?" Archie asked.

"Census data that would contain names and addresses for 1944." Jason replied, "looking for any reference to Lady Ashdene, if we find any, we will take it from there."

"Right you are son, sounds like a plan," Archie replied.

"Maybe tomorrow you and I could take a quick boat trip to see if they have made any progress opening up the entrance from the river," Chuck suggested.

"Good idea Chuck let's do that," Jason replied.

With the arrangements made for the next couple of days, Jason decided to have one more beer with the guys before heading back to his boat to make the now routine connections with his daughters. His mind was in a little turmoil, yes, he had discovered what had happened to his grandfather, but he was still disappointed that the real truth may never surface. He found that a total injustice, especially because his grandfather was serving his country at the time. What he didn't realize was that his life was about to change, forever.

Chapter 36 – Further Investigation – Modern Day

The next morning Chuck climbed aboard Jason's boat and he motored the boat out of the marina into the channel and throttled back to a steady 8 knots towards the State Marina. The topic of conversation was Bill's health as Chuck had never known him to go for a check-up in his entire life. But Chuck hadn't noticed much of a difference in him of late, so he was hoping the problem was not serious.

As they neared the State Marina they could clearly see the huge floating derrick that had been brought in to clear the obstructions in the entrance, but there didn't appear to be any activity happening on the vessel itself. As they got closer the explanation for the inactivity became apparent. A marquee had been erected over the portion of the wall where Jason had found the head and the sound of jack-hammers could clearly be heard emanating from inside the tent. It was obvious that the wall was now a crime scene and all work on the entrance had been curtailed until that investigation had been completed. But before they could make any further conjectures about what they could see a small Coast Guard vessel appeared from beside the floating crane. One of the Coast Guard personnel on the boat was hailing them with a bull-horn, telling them to move away and that they were in a restricted area. Jason was happy to oblige as he turned away to rejoin the river between the channel markers. He didn't want to be caught snooping in the area and he was certain the Coast Guard crew wasn't aware of his involvement nor would they have recognized his boat. As far as the Coast Guard crew was concerned the boat contained inquisitive onlookers and they did their job and told them to go away, nevertheless, it provided a talking point for their return trip.

"You called it son." Chuck said, "the F.B.I. is looking for bodies under that canvas. You can bet they will find three bodies there and no one will ever know anything about it." He added, sounding very frustrated.

"Remember, we are making assumptions, we don't know that for sure." Jason offered.

"Your assumptions have been correct up until now, I think you have nailed this. They wouldn't be throwing this many resources at it for you to be wrong." Chuck said with some weight. Then Chuck began to shake his head in disgust before adding, "to think, that lovely boat was sunk because of a cover-up."

"I wonder what they will do with the boats when they salvage them." Jason mused out loud.

"I expect once they have removed the bodies they will just dump them," Chuck said.

"Could the boats be restored?" Jason asked.

"Unlikely, obviously the engine and electricals would all have to be replaced. As for the wood, don't know, would have to look at it." Chuck replied distantly, as he reminisced about that boat he had seen all those years ago.

"Do you think they will rip out all the docks and piles as well?" Jason asked.

"Who knows?" Chuck replied, coming out of his reverie, "I should imagine they would want to destroy anything that could possibly link the government to the marina, maybe they will restore it to its original state."

"What was that?" Jason asked.

"Not exactly sure," Chuck replied, "the marina had been built at about the same time I was being born so this is all I have ever known about the area. My father never brought me here, but I should imagine the inlet was natural, probably would have been a nice place to build a retreat, right there on the river."

Nothing much else was said for the remainder of the trip back to Chuck's marina and as Jason pulled into his assigned slip, young Charlie was there to take a line and help moor the boat. Chuck went off with Charlie to discuss some marina related questions while Jason was left to kill some time before going to lunch at the pub, so he pottered about his boat, cleaning up and checking his emails. While he was carrying out these mindless activities he began to think about what he was going to do, when, he managed to locate any of Lady Ashdene's descendants. Jason felt that after the trip to St. Louis he would give his investigations another couple of days before taking his boat out of the water and returning home to Cleveland. Perhaps, the following year he would plan a longer boat trip down to the Gulf, he had to admit, the experience gained from this trip had been a great one and he had met many kind people in the process.

By the time Jason got to the pub, all the others were in attendance and Dexter immediately poured him a beer. Chuck had been explaining what they had discovered that morning to the others. In a slight lull in the conversation, Jason dropped his bombshell and informed the others of his intentions to leave in a couple of days. The others were all a little crestfallen, he had brought a little excitement to their mundane lives, but they too realized his visit was temporary and it couldn't last forever.

As it was a Saturday, Jason decided he was going to take a ride around the area, to do a little sight-seeing and maybe stay in a hotel for a couple of nights. They all supplied him with a few suggestions, Jason returned to his boat, packed a few things, locked up then took off for a couple of nights to luxuriate in a bath instead of a cramped shower and enjoy some really, tasty, cooked meals instead of the packaged fare he had been preparing for himself.

On Monday Jason returned to the marina and went straight to his boat to unpack his things. By then it was time to meet the others in the pub, he walked in and everyone was there. They all asked about his trip and he told them it was a nice little getaway, some time to forget about the quest and the F.B.I.

They chatted about it for a while until Jason realized he hadn't heard how Bill had got on at the doctor's office.

"How did the check up go Bill?" Jason asked.

"Oh, I have to see a specialist." Bill reluctantly replied.

"Why, what's wrong with you?" Archie asked, suddenly concerned.

"Oh, it's nothing," Bill said waving with his hand to emphasize the point. "Doctor just wants to make sure it is nothing, that's all. He hasn't got a clue if you ask me." Then trying to deflect the subject, "So, what time are we heading out for the River City tomorrow?"

"I figure it will take us at least an hour to get there and find a parking spot," Dexter replied. "Last time Helen and I went to St. Louis the traffic was horrendous on the I270, creating jams all over the place."

"Why don't we leave about 9:30 then." Archie suggested, "that way we will miss the better part of the rush-hour and we will still have a couple of hours before lunch to do some research."

"Sounds good," Chuck agreed, and the others were nodding their heads in agreement.

"I'll drive, I know the best route," Dexter said.

"You cheeky young whipper-snapper, I've been taking that trip since before you walked the face of this earth!" Chuck admonished Dexter.

"Yes, but your horse and cart are gone now." Dexter quipped.

"Aaah." Chuck responded and smiled.

The next morning Dexter was at the marina with his Lexus SUV to greet the others.

"Someone is going to have to ride shotgun on the hump in the middle of the back-seat," Dexter said, and Jason immediately volunteered, noting that there were no objections from the others. Jason got in, stowed his backpack over the back seat of the car and fastened his seat-belt before the others got in. Once everyone was settled with their seat-belts on, Dexter began the drive to St. Louis.

"I expect it will take us about 45 minutes before we get there," Dexter told the others as he turned on a Classic Rock radio station transmitting out of St. Louis, which was greeted with many murmurings from the older passengers in the vehicle. That notwithstanding, Dexter had hardly driven out of the marina before there was a request for a stop.

"Aren't you going to stop in at Lorla's for a coffee to go?" Archie asked quite concerned.

"I hadn't planned on it," Dexter replied.

"Well, do you think you could fit it into your schedule?" Bill asked.

"Jeeeez, it's like taking a bunch of kids out on a day trip!" Dexter replied frustrated, as he made a bee-line for the Blue Moon Café. It was about twenty minutes later by the time everyone had gotten their beverages of choice as well as a donut. But then they had to repeat the belt-buckling performance, except, this time the two elderly gentlemen in the back were now attempting contortionist movements with their hands full and required Jason's assistance to complete the seat-belt clicking.

Eventually, they were back on the road and there was very little traffic congestion, so the 45-minute estimate turned out to be reasonably accurate. The next hurdle was to find somewhere to park which was hampered by a new complication, Bill desperately needed a washroom.

"That coffee has gone straight through me I'm afraid!" Bill said sheepishly.

"I could go straight through the city and go back home," Dexter replied which gave everyone else a smile.

"Look, here we are right outside the library, they're sure to have a washroom in there. Why don't I drop you all off, I will go park and catch up with you?" Dexter said, solving the immediate problem. Grateful murmurs were heard as Dexter stopped. Chuck, who was in the front seat and Bill, who was on the driver's side at the back both evacuated the vehicle, closely followed by Jason. Bill then slid across the seat to join the others on the sidewalk. As Jason was about to shut the car door he made eye contact with Dexter who was just shaking his head.

"We'll be old one day Dexter, I doubt if we will be any better." Jason smiled.

"Well, I hope I die before I get old," Dexter replied and as soon as Jason shut the door Dexter drove off to find a parking spot. Jason shepherded the three men from the vehicle and led them to the front doors of the St. Louis library.

As Dexter went to park, the others entered the building, Jason asked the first person he saw who looked liked they worked in the building for directions to a washroom. The three old men followed the man's directions and went off while Jason remained by the front doors for their return and Dexter's appearance. He didn't have to wait long for either, both parties turned up at much the same time.

Jason approached an information desk and they were subsequently directed to a department where they were met by a kind, elderly, African-American lady. She appeared to have a permanent smile on her face and enjoyed the flirting comments she was receiving from the elderly gentlemen. Once Jason explained what they were looking for the lady, whose name was Kobe, led them each to a desk and told them all she would be back presently. While they waited for Kobe's return they took the opportunity to browse through some magazines that were on the desks. The magazines were in plastic, protective coverings to provide a little longevity from clumsy fingers, like the ones who were handling them right then.

Kobe returned with six telephone directories and an explanation.

"The census data is online, but it may be difficult to access and understand so I wondered if, because it is Ladue, you might be able to find what you are looking for in one of these old telephone directories," Kobe suggested as she plonked the books on the table in front of them. "They appear to have been issued about the time period you are looking for."

"Great idea," Jason said and took one of the directories and began gently flipping the pages. All the others followed suit, except for Archie.

"Unusual name Kobe does that have some kind of meaning?" Archie inquired.

"It is African for born on a Tuesday," Kobe patiently replied, knowing full well what Archie was doing.

"And today is Tuesday!" Archie said enthusiastically, "it's fate Kobe, that's what it is."

"Oh, give it up Arch, she's far too young for you," Bill said.

"When you've finished, just leave the books on the desks." Kobe instructed them and after a quick tap on Archie's shoulder she walked away laughing. The others were smiling as they perused the directories for an entry for Lady Ashdene, it didn't take long.

"Got it," Dexter suddenly said. "Caroline Ashdene, 7845 Barnes Road, Ladue 4581."

"Well, the telephone number has probably changed by now but let's take note of the address," Jason said. There were scraps of paper and pens lying on the desk just for such a purpose and Jason took a sheet and wrote down the address.

"O.K. let's hit the road," Jason said.

"Maybe I'd better hit the washroom before we leave, you know, just to be on the safe side." Bill said nonchalantly, although Archie and Chuck groaned and rolled their eyes, they also went to the washroom with him.

While they were all in the washroom, Dexter decided to fetch the SUV, he thought that might save some time. As they went through the usual difficult procedures for putting on their seat-belts, Dexter keyed in the address into the vehicle's GPS.

"Looks like we've got about a 10-minute drive, so, sit back and enjoy the sights," Dexter said. It wasn't long before they were out of the metropolitan area of St. Louis and into a more suburban area, and the further they drove the further apart the houses were as they entered the much more expensive area that was Ladue. They drove past an expensive looking golf club before joining onto Barnes road and they all began to search for number 7845.

"It's an odd number so it's going to be on this side of the street," Chuck said, who was sitting behind Dexter.

"Which side is 'this side of the street' Chuck? I haven't got eyes in the back of my head." Dexter said with a little frustration.

"Your left," Jason said. "How do you know that Chuck?"

"I was the postmaster for a while, odd numbers are on the east side." Chuck calmly explained.

"There's a sign on this driveway," Dexter said as he began to slow the vehicle. There were no numerals to indicate what house number it was, but the elaborate sign read, 'Denes of Ash'.

"This has got to be it," Jason said excitedly.

Dexter pulled into the asphalt driveway that was on a tight curve, bordered by large trees and neatly manicured shrubbery which concealed the house from the main road. Dexter negotiated the turn through the driveway that prevented little light to penetrate through the myriad of leaves on the elegant trees. But as they came through the trees and into the bright sunlight they could see that the driveway led up to a beautiful mansion surrounded by what Jason could only describe as an old-fashioned English garden. Or at least, having never been to England, what he expected an English garden to look like. The driveway forked, one juncture changed from asphalt to gravel bordered by white brick that led up a circular driveway to the front door of the house. The other road remained asphalt and continued slightly downhill around to the back of the house, they assumed this would be the tradesmen's entrance. Dexter slowly continued towards the front door, the noise of the tires on the gravel must have been evident to anyone inside the house. Dexter stopped parallel with the front double door of the house.

"Well, off you go Jason, good luck!" Dexter said, and the others murmured their best wishes but unfortunately, Archie and Chuck were too intent on admiring the house to realize one of them had to get out to let Jason out.

"Archie, maybe you can let me out?" Jason asked Archie as he was putting his spectacles back on for the second time.

"What?" Archie replied, wondering what Jason was asking until he suddenly realized. "Oh yes of course!" Archie undid his seat-belt, opened the door and got out. As Jason turned to walk towards the house, Archie also wished him 'good luck'. Jason was beginning to think that if and when the door opened, corpses or something equally as ghoulish was going to appear as they did in his dream. So, it was with some trepidation that he rang the bell.

He waited a few seconds and turned to smile at the quartet in the car who was looking at him more like expectant fathers. The door slowly opened and for the second time since he had been on this quest, he saw a sight that would be indelibly burnt in his memory for the rest of his life.

Chapter 37 – Catching Up – Modern Day

The person standing before him was the woman in his dream.

"Hello, can I help you?" The lady said with a smile, as she looked first at Jason then the SUV in the driveway. "Are you lost?"

"Er no, no!" Jason feebly replied, still shaken by her appearance. She was indeed the real-life version of the waif in his dream, although her hair was much longer, shinier and she was absolutely stunning. The lady was probably in her late thirties, early forties but very young and athletic looking, dressed in office clothes consisting of a dark jacket, skirt and cream-colored blouse. She was about the same height as Jason and as her beautiful dark eyes met his, the images of his dream came flowing back, melting his insides as he tried to reply to her. "No of course not, no, my name is Jason, Jason Clifford."

"Well, Mr. Jason Clifford, if you are not lost, what can I do for you?" The lady repeated her question, albeit still, with that friendly smile.

"Ah yes, well, I'm trying to trace a Lady Ashdene." Jason stammered.

“I’m afraid Lady Ashdene passed away some time ago, 1944 to be exact.” The lady stated. Jason’s response was to slap himself on the forehead.

“Yes, yes, I am aware of her demise, sorry, this is not going to plan,” Jason began, deciding the best thing to do right now was not to look at the lady. “I’m trying to trace Lady Ashdene’s descendants and as this was the last known address that I have I thought I would ask here.”

“Well yes, you’ve come to the right place.” The lady replied, “I am Lady Ashdene’s granddaughter, and for the third time Mr. Clifford, what can I do for you?” The lady was not upset as she appeared to be enjoying Jason’s bumbling attempts at communicating with her.

“You are?” Jason said.

“Yes, I am, I just told you that!” The lady replied.

“Then I think I may have something that belongs to you,” Jason said. Now the lady looked a little skeptical and once more glanced over to the four faces peering at her from the SUV. Jason meanwhile pulled from his pocket a copy of the photograph they had found online when they were searching through the paper’s archives.

“Is this your grandmother?” Jason asked as he pointed at the lady in the cutting.

“Yes, that’s her, I have the original. Where did you get this from and what could you possibly have that you claim can be mine?” The lady said, now intrigued.

“That necklace,” Jason replied, pointing at the photograph. “I have it. I recovered it from the St. Louis Streamer.” The lady’s smile disappeared and for a moment Jason thought he had struck a nerve and that he was about to be asked to leave the premises.

“Well, you’d better come in then.” The lady said as she stepped back and opened the door wider. “Would your friends like to come in and join you?”

“They would be delighted.” Jason smiled and waved to the others to come in.

Jason stood by the door and introduced each one of them as they entered.

“This is Chuck,” Jason said.

“Caroline Ashdene.” The lady replied as Chuck shyly shook her hand and gave a slight bow.

“Archie,” Jason said.

“Hi, Archie.” The lady said.

“Pleased to meet you ma’am,” Archie said as he too shook her hand and lingered a little longer on the hold than would have been customary.

“This is Bill,” Jason said.

“Hello, Bill.” The lady said. Bill just nodded his head and gave a light shake of her hand.

“And finally, Dexter,” Jason said.

“Come in Dexter, pleased to meet you.” The lady said.

“Likewise,” Dexter said.

“Why don’t you all go through to the sitting room and I will put on some coffee.” The lady said as she directed them to a door on their left. She followed them in to retrieve something from a credenza, but as she went to pull the drawer it wouldn’t open.

"Damn, the lock has got stuck again," Caroline said.

"Here, let me take a look." Dexter offered as he stepped forward already with one of his many lock-picking tools in his hand. Within seconds he had picked the lock, so he pulled open the drawer a fraction and stepped back. As he walked away, Caroline thanked him then reached into the drawer to extract something from it which she secreted in an inside pocket of her jacket before leaving to prepare the coffee.

The room was expertly decorated, resplendent with leather seats and expensive artifacts. There were numerous photographs distributed amongst the walls and on top of bureaus and sideboards. Jason noticed a few pictures of Lady Ashdene with a young boy which he assumed to be Caroline's father. The others were also marveling at the contents of the room and Dexter nodded at Jason with wide eyes as if to say, *'there's money here'*.

It wasn't long before Caroline returned with a trolley containing a carafe of coffee and a tray containing various types of cakes and cookies, much to the delight of the elder statesmen of the group.

"Sorry, I wasn't expecting company," Caroline offered apologetically, "so this is all I have available." She needn't have worried, clumsy hands had already begun to reach out for the goodies.

"So, you said you have recovered my grandmother's jewelry," Caroline said skeptically. "Do you have it with you?"

"Er no, I don't," Jason replied, which made Caroline even more skeptical, she was beginning to think this was all some sort of scam.

"So, after some 70 years, during which there have been numerous searches and theories put forward regarding the disappearance of the boat, you, a complete stranger turns up on my doorstep claiming to have found my grandmother's necklace, but you don't actually have it with you. Have I got that right?" Caroline asked with some authority.

"Yes, that's correct," Jason replied gingerly.

"So why should I believe you and what do you want from me?" Caroline asked.

"I don't want anything from you," Jason replied, looking surprised, and was about to continue before Caroline verbally attacked him again.

"I better warn you, I am an experienced lawyer. A Harvard graduate worked in corporate law in New York for fifteen years. Don't try and intimidate me, you will be sadly disappointed." Caroline told the group and by now if there was anyone who was intimidated it was Jason who was now looking at her like a scolded puppy.

"I think you had better explain everything from the beginning," Dexter said, slowly and quietly, trying to add a little reason to the conversation. The others couldn't say anything because their mouths were too full of goodies. Caroline merely stared at Jason, he took a deep breath and related the series of events that had brought them to this point, although he omitted the bit about his dream, that was just his secret. Jason told her of his theory and even told her about the F.B.I. investigation, which he knew he shouldn't have done. Once he had finished, she looked at him for a minute then pulled a cell-phone from her pocket, scrolled down her contact list and dialed a number. As soon as the recipient replied she walked out of the room and the men could hear her talking but not what she was actually saying. After a minute she returned.

"Well, this is truly an incredible theory, although you have no photographs or any evidence to support your findings," Caroline said as she paced backward and forward in the room. “You do not have the necklace. Furthermore, I have just spoken to a contact of mine and he has told me he can’t find any reference to an agent Redmond in the F.B.I. nor is he aware of any investigation being carried out along the Mississippi. One of you obviously has safe-cracking skills,” she said, pointing her head towards Dexter. “You’re obviously the smooth talker,” directing her attention back to Jason. By this time her pacing had brought her to the long sliding doors that faced a beautiful, well-manicured ornamental garden. At this point, she reached into the pocket of her jacket and pulled out a gun. Then, pointing to the front door with some vehemence with one hand while aiming the gun at Jason with the other she added, “I don’t know what kind of scam you are trying to pull here but I think you had all better leave. Now.”

Chapter 38 – Realisation – Modern Day

"Wait, wait, I do have photographs," Jason said as he was fumbling in his pocket to retrieve his USB stick, completely ignoring the weapon that was being pointed at him.

"You told us the F.B.I. took everything," Chuck said just as unbelieving as Caroline was, now everyone was staring at Jason.

"Well, I'm not daft, I knew if I lost my computer I could lose everything, so I backed them up on this stick as well as the Cloud." Jason said sheepishly but everyone was still looking at him as though he had just committed treason "Well, I didn't tell you, I didn't want anyone to know I still had copies. I even took photographs of the logbook and the radio before the Feds. took everything."

"So, you can still prove to the lady you found the boats?" Dexter asked.

"And we have the necklace and bracelet, right?" Jason said pleading with his arms outstretched as though he was not only trying to convince the lady but also the guys as well.

"I just need a computer." Then looking at Caroline, "do you have a computer?" All through this conversation, Caroline had still been standing with her arm outstretched pointing the gun at Jason but now she slowly lowered it to reply.

"Of course I have a computer but I'm not letting you stick that into my port. It may have a virus." Caroline replied, not realizing the euphemism she had just said that fortunately brought a little humor to the situation.

"I brought my laptop, it's in the car," Jason replied and left the room to retrieve his device.

While he was out of the room, Dexter tried to pour oil over the turbulent waters. "We all saw the safe, the log-book and the radio. Miss Ashdene, I know you don't know us from Adam but why would we be here if it wasn't all true? The jewelry is in a safe place in Kimmswick." The others just nodded their heads in agreement.

"But what about my friend not knowing about the investigation?" Caroline asked.

"Can't explain that." Dexter replied "but think about it. If Jason's assumptions are correct, this is one huge cover-up, they are not going to advertise an investigation into it, are they?"

Before Caroline could reply Jason had returned from the SUV with his laptop. Within a minute the photos of the wrecks were being displayed on his screen. He scrolled through the photographs and just before the photograph of the skeleton of Caroline's grandmother was about to be displayed, Jason paused and took his finger off the arrow key that was being used to scroll through the images.

"What I am about to show you may be disturbing, I can assure you, that these photographs are real, I would never, ever try to fake what I am about to show you." Jason looked directly at Caroline when he said this. "Are you sure you want to continue?"

A look of concern had appeared on Caroline's face as the offered evidence was beginning to convince her of proof. She merely nodded her head, so Jason proceeded.

A gasp of breath emanated from Caroline and her hand reached to her mouth as if to suppress any sound. She could clearly see the necklace around the skeleton of what would have been her grandmother. She sensed then that everything she was being told was true. Quickly, Jason scrolled through the remaining images and when the last one was displayed there was a silence in the room.

Chapter 39 – Moving On – Modern Day

Once the initial shock had passed, Caroline composed herself and looked around at each of the men who appeared to be awaiting some kind of direction from her.

"O.K., what do you want from me?" Caroline asked.

"Want?" Jason asked with a questioning look on his face. "We don't want anything, we just wanted to know who to return the jewelry to."

"Surely you have come here to obtain a finder's fee or a price for the return of the necklace and bracelet, haven't you?" Caroline asked stoically, still unconvinced. "Isn't that what salvagers do?"

"I'm not a salvager!" Jason said in surprise at the lady's reaction. "Look, I told you the reason for my search, it was to investigate the disappearance of my grandfather." Jason emphasised with some frustration, "I didn't even know about the St. Louis Streamer before coming down here and talking to Chuck. Finding the jewelry has been a bonus. All I want to do is return it to its rightful owner. Are you that person?" Everyone looked at Caroline waiting for her response. She turned and sat down on one of the chairs in front of the men.

"Sorry, this is all a bit of a shock," Caroline said almost inaudibly, at least to some of the elder men in the room. "Yes, I guess I would be the rightful heir. Lady Ashdene, the title was not official, because she was British and sounded awfully posh to her new circle of friends she was always referred to as Lady Ashdene, but she was really just Mrs. Caroline Ashdene. Her husband, Captain Reginald Ashdene sent her to America for safety at the beginning of the war. She arrived, six months pregnant, unfortunately, my grandfather was part of the British Expeditionary Force in France and was killed during the beginning of the war. So, he never got to see his son, my father. My father, another Reginald Ashdene, married into St. Louis money but my parents were killed in a traffic accident while I was quite young, I was raised by my nanny, although I was sent to boarding school in England for many of my younger years. Fortunately, there was enough money in the kitty for my education and welfare, so off I went to Harvard and then to New York, where I earnt enough money to keep this place going." Caroline paused and smiled before she continued. "I wasn't bluffing about being a lawyer. But after a few years working in the Big Apple, I decided to return to St. Louis and just cherry-pick the cases I wanted to take on." She paused once more and held open her hands "so, what's the next step?"

Everyone looked to Jason who in turn looked around at them, "well, I hadn't really thought about it." He replied bemusedly, then finally turning to Caroline, "I guess you should come to Kimmswick and retrieve what is rightfully yours."

"Don't you want any documentation to prove it is mine?" Caroline asked, the lawyer in her coming out.

"No, not really, it's not mine to make any demands. We located you, you only have to look around at the photographs in this room to know that what you have told us is the truth." Jason explained innocently, not wishing to explain that she was the woman in his dream which was all the proof he needed.

"Yes, but you stand to make a lot of money on this transaction if you insisted on a fee," Caroline stressed, "I do have some idea as to how much that jewelry is worth."

"As I said, I'm not after money, I just set out to find out the truth about my grandfather, that I have now done, despite what the authorities may end up saying," Jason stated. There was a sort of an impasse with neither Caroline nor Jason knowing how to continue.

"Look, why don't you come down to Kimmswick, we can go and visit the jewelers and you can choose to either leave them there for now or bring them home." Chuck offered, "then we can all have lunch." At this, everyone muttered their agreement.

"That's a great idea, although I won't be able to make it until Friday," Caroline replied enthusiastically, "but I insist on paying, my treat."

There were more mutterings of agreement and after directions to the marina were given to Caroline, the men left.

Chapter 40 – The Return Home – Modern Day

On the trip back to Kimmswick, the guys discussed the meeting with Caroline, her house and the finery inside, although strangely, the fact that she had trained a gun on them was not even mentioned.

"There's obviously money there my friends," Dexter said.

"Is there ever, whew!" Archie added.

"Yes, but those Brits. were not very imaginative with their names, were they?" Chuck laughed, "Reginald or Caroline, that's it!"

"Really?" Bill said, "What was your father's name, Chuck?"

"Charles, you know it was," Chuck replied.

"But your given name is Charles, right?" Bill said. The rest of them were beginning to smile as they could see where this was going.

"What did you call your first son?" Archie began to chime in on the joke. "Oh, wait a minute, I remember, Charles. And what did he call his first son, your grandson? You know, the one who now works at the marina."

"Alright, alright, I get it," Chuck said waving them off with an arm.

After a few minutes of silence, Dexter decided to breach the subject that Jason was coincidently, quietly contemplating.

"So, Jason, you've found the answer to your grandfather's disappearance and you've located the owner of the jewelry. What are you going to do after Friday's lunch?"

"I was just thinking the same thing Dexter," Jason replied solemnly. "I guess I'm done here, there's nothing left for me to do, I shall go home." Although the prospect of returning to Cleveland to continue the same existence he had been living since his wife had died did not appeal to him, especially after the excitement of the last little while. In a few short days, he had seen the most horrifying sights he had ever seen, he had been raided by the F.B.I. and had a gun pointed at him by a beautiful woman. More action than he had ever seen in his entire life up until that point. There was also a murmuring of discontent amongst the others, Jason had been like a breath of fresh air and the search had galvanized them into action they hadn't enjoyed for many a year.

"I'll book Friday's appointment with David at the jewelers, have lunch and prepare to leave on Saturday," Jason said with a great deal of resignation.

His decision was met with silence as there really wasn't much more that could be said, the quest was indeed, over.

"Oh, I will try and locate the family of my grandfather's shipmate, Tony, but I can do that from home," Jason added as an afterthought. "I can return the few artifacts of his to them. That will give me something to do for a while."

Another silence fell upon the men, each of them absorbed in their own thoughts.

"You could always come back and see us in a few months time and let us know how you got on with Tony's family," Dexter suggested.

"Yes, I could do that, the authorities may have something to report by then as well." Jason replied.

"Unfortunately, I won't be around." Bill casually said.

"Why, are you going on holiday Bill?" Archie asked enthusiastically.

"I wish." Bill replied stoically, "I have pancreatic cancer, the doctors have given me three months."

Chapter 41 – The Last Supper – Modern Day

After Bill's bombshell nothing further was discussed during the trip home and when they arrived at the marina they merely bade each other good afternoon and went their separate ways. Jason returned to his boat, he managed to catch David on the phone just before he left the store. With the meeting for Friday now arranged he sat down to check his emails and send his obligatory texts to his daughters. He made himself a quick sandwich and thought about going topside to just sit and watch the sunset, but nature decided to throw him a curveball. The heavens opened, and it began to pour down with rain. He quickly rose to close the cabin door and ensure the front hatch was secure then he sat down heavily at the galley table. Bill's news, the end of the quest and now the rain was the last straw, he reached down and dug deep into a bag before pulling out an unopened bottle of Jack Daniels. He moved to the small camping fridge to extract a can of Coke and made himself a stiff drink. The next thing he knew was that the morning light was seeping through the windows of his boat and his head was throbbing terribly. In front of him was an almost empty bottle of Jack Daniels. Several empty Coke cans also littered the table that he had obviously crashed out on. But right then, that was the least of his worries, he had an almost uncontrollable urge to throw up and the gentle bobbing of his boat on the river, a pleasant feeling when trying to sleep, was not helping his dilemma. Fortunately, he just made it to the head before the results of his previous evening's shenanigans were brought back up. He flushed the toilet and laid on the floor of the head vowing never again to have another drink.

Jason didn't know how long he had been lying there, he must have fallen asleep again, but a cry of 'ahoy there' was penetrating his fuzzy brain, someone outside was trying to get his attention.

"Ahoy there Mr. Clifford," the voice rang out once more. As Jason's senses were slowly coming into focus he realized it was Charlie, he is the only one at the marina who addresses him as Mr. Clifford.

"Hi, Charlie. What's up?" Jason managed to reply from his semi-prostrate state between the head and the galley.

"Grandad and the others are going to the pub for brunch, I've been told to come and get you," Charlie replied innocently, not knowing the expression that was on Jason's face as he heard the reason for the early call. The thought of a fry-up right then made Jason turn to the head for another couple of gut-retching sessions.

"Are you alright Mr. Clifford?" Charlie asked.

"Fine, fine." Jason managed to reply, he stole a glance at his watch, it was 10:35. He couldn't believe he had been out cold this long. "Give me ten, I'll be there." Although he knew it would be at least an hour before he arrived at the bar.

"I'll tell them," Charlie replied.

As Charlie left, Jason extricated himself from his position and the first thing he did was have a large swig of water from one of the cold bottles in the cooler. He knew from past experience, dehydration was the cause of his throbbing headache and no pills or potions were going to fix him any better than water. Once he had drunk the water he proceeded to clean up the head, then he stripped off and took a shower. His toilet had been modified to accommodate a shower that consisted of a drain with an electric pump that had been inserted in the floor to extract the water and a shower head that extended from the heater in the galley through a gap between the toilet door and the bulkhead. He was told by the previous owner to just remember to turn on the pump and remove the toilet roll before showering. Up until this point, Jason had always managed to remember these two tasks, but this morning was an exception. He was standing immersed in a couple of inches of water before he realized the pump wasn't turned on and the toilet roll, a full one of course, was one big soggy mess.

By the time Jason was dressed and had consumed another bottle of water, he was feeling much better and gingerly climbed off the boat and made it to the pub. He entered the pub just as Helen was serving the first of the plates of food to Chuck, Bill and Archie.

"Good timing Jason," Archie said as Dexter was delivering two more plates, one for himself and the other for Jason. The others said 'Hi' but their attention immediately turned to the feast laid before them and so they were not aware that Jason really wasn't at his best. Jason, on the other hand, was not sure that he could stomach the offering in front of him, lamenting once more that he would never drink again. He first took a gulp of the large orange juice that was set before him before he realized it was a Mimosa, heavy on the sparkling wine. As the full realization hit him the others all picked up their glasses and Chuck proposed a toast.

"To the quest," Chuck said and they all repeated the words then took a large gulp from their glasses. Surprisingly, contrary to what Jason expected, he began to feel a little better, '*hair of the dog*' as they say. Furthermore, as he began to tuck into the cholesterol loaded fare that was in front of him his queasiness also started to dissipate and once brunch was over he was almost back to his normal self.

"Well, Jason, I for one am going to miss you when you've gone," Dexter said. "Once more, I'll be by myself stuck with these old farts." Dexter realized what he had said and looked to the heavens before turning to Bill.

"Sorry Bill, it just slipped out." Dexter apologized.

"No, you're right, I feel sorry for you, being alone with these two." Bill said unphased, "at least you could have an intelligent conversation with me." To which, everyone laughed.

"But you will come and visit, won't you Jason?" Archie asked.

"Sure, of course," Jason said feeling a little uncomfortable, although his demeanor defied what he was truly feeling because up until that point he hadn't given a thought of returning unless he decided on a boat trip down the rivers. "But I want to thank you for all your help, without you I wouldn't have found out about my grandfather. So, I would like to pay for this fine feast."

"Oh no you don't, this is on the house," Dexter said and began to pour out more Mimosas. Before Jason could protest Bill chipped in with a profound comment.

"I can't help feeling that this is not the end, but just the beginning."

After yet another bombshell from Bill that everyone was still trying to decipher the group parted company and Jason returned to his boat to begin securing items and packing his clothes. Although the first thing he did was to empty the remaining contents of the Jack Daniels down the sink, he wanted to remove all temptation. Once he had gone as far as he could with his preparations for departure, he sent emails to his daughters for them to expect to see him sometime Sunday evening. He also thought about taking his boat out of the water and sleeping on the boat on the trailer but decided against that, he thought he may try to squeeze in one more trip upriver before he left.

What Jason didn't know was that Bill was right. Jason would not be back home that Sunday evening and he would be making more trips upriver.

Chapter 42 – The Meeting – Modern Day

Just before 10:00 AM Jason was walking towards the gates of the marina dressed in the best clothes he could muster from his limited wardrobe. He was clean-shaven, wearing a little of his best after-shave and well groomed for the pending meeting with Caroline. Approaching was Chuck, who for the first time since Jason had met him, was wearing a suit and tie; and looked quite passable as a city gent. As they met and exchanged pleasantries, not least of which were the comments on how well they had both cleaned-up, Bill came driving along in his 1952 Chevrolet. Before anyone could say anything about their willingness to leave an impression on their guest a Porsche SUV was slowly heading towards them. It stopped behind the Chevrolet and Caroline popped her head out of the driver's side window.

"Morning everyone!" Caroline shouted, "where's the best place for me to park?" Chuck replied, using his arms to usher her into a parking spot next to Jason's truck. Bill proceeded to do the same, but it was Caroline who was out of her vehicle first. Her demeanor as she walked towards them was one of excitement with one big beautiful smile on her face. If there had been any skepticism or doubt about their discussion of a couple of days ago it had all dissipated now.

"Hi," Caroline said as she held out her hand to Jason. "This is exciting isn't it?" Jason shook her hand, but not for the first time, he was lost for words. Caroline again looked stunning, if she was wearing make-up there couldn't have been much, and her beautiful dark hair hung over a loose red top worn outside of tight, ice-blue, jeans. She was wearing canvas sailing shoes as if she was expecting to go out on a boat. The lack of a reply notwithstanding, she shook hands with Chuck and repeated her ritual as Archie and Bill arrived, although Archie, true to form, went one step further and reached in for a hug.

"Would you like a lift up to the jewelers in my car?" Bill asked.

"Oh, I was under the impression it was close by!" Caroline replied a little confused.

"It is, it's only a quick ten-minute walk up the street," Jason replied, finally finding his voice.

"Well, thanks for the kind offer Bill, but after the drive here it may be nice just to stretch my legs a bit," Caroline said, although disappointed, Bill was quite impressed that she had remembered his name. "But I'd love to have a spin in your car later, it looks lovely." Whether she was pushing Bill's buttons, or she genuinely meant what she said it didn't matter to Bill, he was beaming like a schoolboy.

Chuck led Caroline along the road to the jewelers with Jason flanking the other side of her, while Bill and Archie watched them leave. Chuck was giving her a little history lesson of every building along the route and she was fascinated with the quaint village of Kimmswick remarking on how close she had lived to such a marvel, all her life, without ever realizing the place existed.

At the jewelers, they went through the usual security procedures, but this time, David was ready with the jewels. Jason hadn't fully explained to Caroline how he had traced the items to her, but David showed her the maker's catalog and how the investigation developed from there. After much discussion with David, Caroline decided she would stew a little longer about keeping the items or selling them. Although, she promised that if she did decide to sell she would leave it to his expertise to find an appropriate buyer. Her decision would be based on the fact she would never wear the jewelry nor were there any other heirs to present it to. However, she was aware that David had to make a living and felt bad that he had been taking care of the jewelry at no charge. As a result, they agreed on a storage fee that would be waived in the event of a sale and agreed a commission structure that included a handsome finder's fee for Jason, although he protested vehemently that it was totally unnecessary. By the time all the paperwork was completed, it was time for lunch, so they headed back to the pub.

Bill and Archie had already got a head start on the others as they were on their second pint as the trio entered the bar. To emphasize the fact, the two men raised their glasses as the trio sat down at a table, specially prepared for them. They had hardly sat down when Dexter appeared with drinks for the two male newcomers

"What can I get you, Caroline?" Dexter asked.

"White wine please." Caroline replied, "better not drink too much, driving you know." She indicated with her hands a driving gesture.

The group began a little small talk until Dexter returned with the wine and a drink for himself. Then Caroline began the proceedings.

“I have a confession to make.” Caroline said solemnly, “do you remember I said my contact had never heard of an Agent Redmond?” There were murmurings of agreement from around the table, they remembered it well, difficult to forget when you have a gun pointing at you. “Well, my contact called back later after doing a little more digging. It appears that Agent Redmond had been brought in from Washington DC, he belongs to a Special Projects group. Very hush hush apparently.”

“So, you believe our story now?” Jason asked.

“Absolutely,” Caroline said emphatically.

“Well, I’ve been doing a little digging too,” Dexter said, and all eyes turned surprisingly to him. “I’m not without contacts either, some of the jobs I had to do during my locksmith days were working with the police helping out on criminal investigations. So, I phoned one of the guys I once worked with to check out our Caroline Ashdene to see if she was who she said she was.”

“You didn’t tell us?” Chuck asked with some indignation, but a smile appeared on Caroline’s face.

“That’s good, what did you find out?” Caroline asked.

"You are who you say you are," Dexter said succinctly but a little sheepishly now that the other guys were upset with his subterfuge. "Well, you never know!"

"You're right. I'm glad you checked me out." Caroline said, "now we all know where we stand, and we have no more secrets."

"I'll drink to that," Bill said and that relieved the tension, but before they could elaborate any more, Helen arrived to inform them that the food was now ready to be served. She introduced herself to Caroline who, in turn, asked her host where the washrooms were. Helen escorted her to the facilities and they could be heard laughing in the background as Chuck chided Dexter for his actions. Before Dexter could reply the dulcet tone of his beloved wife beckoned him.

"Dexter, you can give me a hand with this food!" For once, Dexter was grateful his wife had innocently rescued him from the remarks from the old men.

Helen had indeed gone to town. She had prepared prime rib with all the trimmings, vegetables, perfect Yorkshire puddings, horseradish, gravy et all. The group was a good way into the sumptuous meal before any real discussion took place and it was Caroline who got the ball rolling.

"O.K. so, Jason, did the F.B.I. give you any indication on how long it was going to be before we receive any word about their investigation?" Caroline asked between mouthfuls of food.

"No, in fact, he, more or less, made it clear to me that my participation in the investigation was over and warned me to back off any further involvement," Jason replied as he wiped off a glob of gravy from his lips with a napkin.

"So, you are going to leave it alone?" Caroline asked with some surprise. "Just drop it?"

"Not exactly," Jason replied hesitantly, "first, I was going to try and find Tony's relations and return his artifacts to them."

"Tony?" Caroline asked.

"Sorry, that was the name of my grandfather's shipmate who died on the boat."

Jason replied, "then, I thought I would wait a month or two before contacting Chuck's pal, Jeremiah, to see how the investigation was going."

"Hey, I could help you find Tony's relations." Caroline said with enthusiasm, "I have a clear case file right now, I have loads of time and the resources to help you."

"Whoa, I have a bit of bad news." Chuck interrupted, everyone stopped eating to look at him.

"Got a call from Jeremiah a couple of days ago." Chuck said despondently, "he has decided to retire, with immediate effect. Gone to live down in Mobile. Sorry, I forgot to mention it before, didn't think it was important."

"Do you think his retirement was forced and has something to do with the investigation?" Caroline asked.

"For sure," Chuck replied, "thought the old bugger was never going to retire."

"Wow, this is serious," Caroline said absently. They had all just about cleaned their plates and with that new snippet of information it too was being digested, so a brief silence fell over the table.

"So, when all is said and done, you have nothing to show for all your good detective work Jason!" Archie offered.

"Oh, I don't know," Jason replied. "As I mentioned to you the other day, my quest was to find out what happened to my grandfather. That I have achieved, despite what the authorities may say to the contrary. I have had a great adventure, found new friends." Jason held out his arms indicating all the people around the table. "I now have the confidence to return home with my boat and maybe plan an extended trip down the river to the Gulf, who knows?" He then raised his almost empty glass for a toast and everyone else smiled and responded in kind. Dexter noting that a lot of the glasses were either empty or almost done, rose from the table to replenish the drinks. While Dexter left to get more drinks, a quizzical look appeared on Caroline's face.

"I've never thought about it before, but why do we call the raising of our glasses a toast?" Caroline asked, "it seems a strange expression." The group bandied about a solution until Dexter returned with a tray of beverages and they asked him, he was the bar-owner after all.

“Simple, in days of yore, in merry old England, they use to add pieces of spiced toast to their beer to give it some flavor.” Dexter explained, “then they would raise their glasses to their host. Hence, toast.”

“Not surprising, given the flavor of British beers!” Chuck remarked.

“Well it is surprising actually Chuck,” Dexter said, “what do you think you’ve been drinking ever since I have owned this bar?”

“What Fullers? I have been paying good money all these years for English beer?” Chuck asked in surprise as the others all laughed.

“I think the logo is a bit of a giveaway Chuck,” Bill said stoically, “you know, ‘Fullers London Pride’.” The others were now smiling at Chuck’s bemusement.

“Nothing wrong with that Chuck, the myth about poor beer came back with the G.I.s returning after the war, because they claimed English beer was warm when it was actually room temperature because they didn’t have the refrigeration in those days. They actually make really good beers.” Dexter explained. Then he hesitated for a moment. “But, on the subject of good money, do you still have all that cash from the safe Jason?” Dexter asked.

"Yes, why?" Jason replied quizzically.

"Still think you should get that evaluated, might be worth a bit," Dexter replied.

"Maybe David knows someone!" Caroline offered.

"He's just a jeweler, what you need is a numi, a numas, nusm-" Archie was saying before being interrupted by Dexter.

"A numismatist. I think you're trying to say, someone specializing in coin collections." Dexter said.

"Yes, that's right a numis-, what you said," Archie replied pointing his finger at Dexter in a kind of eureka moment.

"I am sure in his business David would have some connections," Dexter said.

"What do you think Jason?" Caroline added.

"Well, like a lot of things lately, I hadn't given it any thought until now," Jason said as he mused about the possibility. He had come on a quest, not to make a profit on his grandfather's demise and anyway, his father and Tony's family should be entitled to any proceeds. "Not sure the commission on the transaction would be enough to pique David's interest."

"From my experience with jewelers, any profit is worth their interest," Dexter added with a wry smile. There was a brief silence before Carol spoke out.

"Tell you what Jason," Carol leaned forward as she spoke to the group. The others responded in kind as they awaited her comment. "If all you are worried about is that it is a waste of David's time, I will give him the opportunity to sell the jewels if he is also prepared to find a buyer for the money."

"Like a job lot," Bill said.

"Yes Bill," Caroline responded laughing. "Like a job lot."

"Then I can give half of anything we receive to Tony's descendants and the other half to my dad," Jason said, his face beaming.

"Whoa, what about yourself?" Chuck questioned with some belligerence. "You're the one who has done all the work here. Where's your cut?"

"I don't think that will be an issue." Caroline said nonchalantly as she took another sip of her wine, "the finder's fee from the sale of the jewelry will be more than adequate. In fact, I believe you all deserve a cut!"

They all looked at her in complete surprise, the quest had just gained another member.

"Well, I don't know what you are all looking at me like that for!" Caroline said, admonishing the group, "starting Monday, we have lots of work to do. Jason, why don't you come to my house, say 10:00 and we can get started?"

"Well yes, I could," Jason said hesitantly.

"Does that mean you are going to stay a while longer Jason?" Chuck asked.

"Well, I guess so," Jason replied slowly and the two men on either side of him, Chuck and Archie, cheered and slapped him playfully on the back. "But, to do what exactly?"

"Well, today you can contact David and discuss our next step with the sales of our artifacts. Then on Monday, we can begin to find Tony's descendants, I believe I have better resources than you to do that." Caroline responded authoritatively.

"Yes, but do you need me here in person to do that?" Jason asked, remembering he had promised his daughters that he would be returning home this weekend. The others were now watching and listening intently at the backward and forwards banter being delivered, as though they were attending another tense, tennis match.

“Yes, but I am also going to need your invaluable assistance,” Caroline said, “I need to document all your information so that we can go after the bastards who did this.”

“Well, I’m not sure who that would be exactly!” Jason replied, “the army, the F.B.I.?”

“No, not those entities, they were just the players,” Caroline replied.

“Then who?” Jason asked bewildered.

“The U.S. Government,” Caroline said.

Chapter 43 – Post Meeting Activities – Modern Day

There was a strong discussion on who would foot the bill for the meal, but Caroline eventually won the day insisting it was her idea originally and she had, after all, promised to pay. They all left the pub, except for Dexter who felt obliged to help his wife clear away and run the pub. Outside, it was another beautiful day and Bill reminded Caroline that she had promised to go for a ride in his classic car.

"You're right Bill, I would love to," Caroline replied, and Bill's chest puffed out like a frigate-bird. "But can we take a boat ride to the State marina first? I want to see it for myself."

"Well, there's not really much to see there," a deflated Bill replied. "You may as well come and see the local sights with me."

"Bill is right Caroline," Jason added, "there really isn't much to see. The Coastguard is making sure any onlookers move along."

"Regardless. I'd still like to get close to it." Caroline replied.

"Boat trip!" Chuck shouted with some gusto and he waved his arm towards Jason's boat, "let's go."

“Wait a minute, I’ve had too much to drink!” Jason told the group, “I won’t be able to handle the boat, well not legally anyway.”

“I can.” Bill said nonchalantly, “I only had one.” But before Jason could protest, everyone was walking towards his boat with Caroline smiling back at him.

When they reached the boat, Jason went below to retrieve the seat cushions and began passing them to Bill who placed them appropriately on the benches. Once everyone was seated, Bill went through his checks and turned on the engine while Jason found himself in the unfamiliar position of being on the dock ready to cast off. Bill gave him the nod and Jason adroitly boarded and pushed the boat away from the dock, all in one motion. Bill responded with perfect timing and before they knew it they were headed towards the State Marina.

Although it was a warm day it was still, nevertheless, spring and Jason could see that the wind blowing across the boat was making Caroline cold. He went below and found one of his wind-cheaters, he returned with the jacket and Caroline gratefully accepted it. After she had put on the jacket Jason sat down beside her and she snuggled into him for a little-added warmth, without thinking he placed his arm around her shoulders and that's how they remained until the boat arrived at the marina.

Bill had slowed the boat down to just above idling speed and traversed the boat as close as he could to the marina while still remaining within the channel. There was a large Coastguard vessel guarding the entrance which had been widened considerably since their last visit. Furthermore, the marquee that had been erected to hide the authority's excavation was no more and that section of the wall had been demolished together with the sign welcoming boaters to the State Marina of Missouri. Although they couldn't really see what was going on inside the marina they could hear plenty of noise resounding around the walls and they could see the tops of numerous cranes.

"Would they be floating cranes?" Caroline asked.

"The bigger ones that we can see sure are. Judging by the size of those cranes." Chuck said. "No wonder they widened the entrance."

"Would those cranes be for salvaging the Streamer?" Jason asked.

"Ach, they may help out but usually a diving team would fasten lift bags or inner tubes to the sunken vessel then fill them with compressed air. Then the salvage team would make a temporary fix to the hole that caused the sinking, once that is done they can start pumping out the water. The crane may be used to stabilize the boat or add a bit of lift." Chuck explained.

"So why the big crane?" Caroline asked.

"I'm not sure," Chuck replied.

"I wouldn't be surprised if they are removing all the docks and the wall so that there is no trace of a marina ever being here," Jason stated.

"What would be the purpose of that?" Caroline asked.

"So that there would be no trace of anything remaining. That would absolve the government from offering a reason why access has been prohibited for all these years." Bill said. "Then they could deny, deny, deny."

For a couple of moments, the occupants of the boat mulled Bill's profound piece of reasoning over in silence until Jason spoke.

"It would be interesting to see if they have re-opened the road to the marina," Jason said to no one in particular.

"Well, that could be our little road trip when we get back." Bill replied, and he immediately turned the boat around to head back to their marina.

Chapter 44 – State Marina of Missouri – Modern Day

Very little was spoken on the return journey back to Chuck's marina, they were all deep in their own thoughts. As Bill adeptly docked the boat, Jason jumped off to secure lines, leaving Archie to assist Caroline onto the dock. The top was down on Bill's Chevy, so Caroline decided to hang on to the wind-cheater as they all walked from the dock to the car-park and into the car. Caroline elected to sit in the back of the car, ending up between Jason and Archie, much to his delight.

"A rose between two thorns!" Bill said as he looked at the trio in the back from the view in his rear-view mirror.

As they traveled through the back roads to the State marina both Jason and Caroline were treated to further history lessons, although it leaned more to the reminiscences of the men's youth than to local antiquity. It kept the journey entertaining until they turned onto the road leading down to the river and the marina. There were 'No Exit' signs posted but driving down the road did not violate any traffic rules. The road descended slightly until they came to where the old army barracks used to be; where old-man Laarsen had been stationed. The road then dipped as it led to what was once the entrance of the State Marina of Missouri.

Entrance may be too strong a word, the protective wall had been ripped down and where it had once been, was a quagmire. It was obvious some heavy machinery had recently traveled this way and was probably still ensconced within the secrecy of the remaining wall. The state of the road forced Bill to reduce his speed to a crawl, which gave Jason the opportunity to quickly peer into the marina. He could clearly see that the building he had searched through was no longer there and, as suspected, many of the docks had already been removed. The angle they were at did not permit him to see what was happening in the vicinity of the dives he had taken, and he was just about to ask Bill to drive forward when a couple of men in hard-hats came towards them.

"Get this can of crap outta here, you're on private property!" One of the men shouted belligerently and angrily waved his arm at them. Bill took serious umbrage at this slight on his pride and joy and was about to say something until he felt a tap on his shoulder.

“Let me deal with this,” Caroline said softly in Bill’s ear. “Wind your window down Jason,” Caroline ordered she wanted to be more visible to their protagonist, Jason responded without question.

“Who are you? Give me your name, you have no authority here this is a public road, we have every right to be here.” Caroline asked the man authoritatively which blew the wind completely out of his sails and his arrogance immediately dissipated. Meanwhile, the other man had begun talking into a radio and not knowing how to proceed the belligerent one went with his tail between his legs to stand next to the one talking into the radio.

“Well, what is your name?” Caroline doggedly asked, now standing in the rear of the car, but the men had no further interest in talking to her and it became a moot point when an SUV appeared in the entrance of the marina with the familiar F.B.I. logo emblazoned on the side. Without being told, Bill decided it was a good time to take their leave.

Chapter 45 – Research – Modern Day

At just before 10:00 AM on Monday morning Jason was driving up Caroline's driveway in his truck. During the weekend he had explained to his daughters the reason for his extended stay, which hadn't gone down at all well. Jason had also taken the U.S. currency to David for evaluation and sale. David confirmed that Caroline had indeed contacted him with instructions to move on the jewelry and he felt that with the buyers he had amongst his clientele he didn't think it would be long before everything was sold.

As Jason left his truck, Caroline was there to greet him, she was dressed casually in a tight white T-shirt, jeans and not so elegant bunny slippers which were a little the worse for wear, they immediately caught Jason's attention.

"Good morning, nice slippers," Jason said, pointing to her footwear.

"Hey, don't make fun of my bunnies, they're comfy." Caroline playfully berated him. "Come on through." She walked through the hallway, passed the room where they had met last week and headed towards the back of the house. Jason followed her until they came to her office that was adjacent to a spacious kitchen. The office was large with two walls filled with books and a very big oak, writing bureau in the center of the room that was stuffed with stationery and a desktop computer. The bureau faced a patio door that looked out to what appeared to be open countryside and behind him, against the wall with the door he had just entered, was a bank of filing cabinets. Caroline pulled up an office chair and indicated to Jason to sit down.

"The coffee should just about be brewed, make yourself comfortable while I go and pour out a couple of cups," Caroline said.

"How is your family?" Caroline shouted out as she headed to the kitchen.

"None too pleased, but I promised I would go home next weekend, even if it was only for a visit," Jason shouted back. But before anything further was spoken, Caroline had returned with a tray containing two mugs of coffee and a plate of the obligatory English biscuits.

"I'm a bit more prepared for this visit," Caroline commented as she laid down the tray on the edge of the bureau.

"Wow, I'll have to steal a few cookies to take back to the boys," Jason joked, "otherwise they'd never forgive me."

"No need," Caroline replied, "I have a packet for you to take to them. They are a nice group of chaps, aren't they?"

"They sure are. They have not only been a great help, but they've turned out to be great friends too," Jason replied with not a little sincerity, "rare in this day an age."

"Right you are!" Caroline responded. Jason followed Caroline's lead and picked up a mug of coffee in one hand and a biscuit in the other, which she proceeded to dunk. Jason merely followed suit as she started the proceedings.

"So, what do you know of your grandfather's shipmate?" Caroline asked, between munches of her biscuit. Unfortunately, Jason had let his cookie dwell too long in the coffee and as it was extracted, it broke off and fell back into the cup with a plop. Embarrassed, Jason merely mumbled an apology.

"Worry not, it takes practice," Caroline said as she passed Jason a couple of tissues to mop up the splashes of coffee and thought no more about the mishap.

"Name, family, whereabouts?" Caroline continued as she prepared to dunk a second biscuit. Jason watched carefully and actually timed the dunk, not believing what he was doing.

"Tony Lawless, that was his name," Jason said, now thoroughly enjoying the experience of a dunked English biscuit for the first time.

"That's it?" Caroline asked incredulously. She had finished her biscuit and was now all business with a pencil in one hand and a big legal yellow pad in the other. "That's all you have?"

"'Fraid so," was all Jason could reply.

"And you have no idea where he was from?" Caroline asked with some frustration.

"Nope," was all Jason could muster.

"So, Jason, how did you expect to locate this guy's family based on just a name?" Caroline asked as she placed her writing implements on the bureau.

"Hadn't given it a thought." Jason replied, "but now that you mention it, yes, it is a tough ask."

"Tough! That's a bit of an understatement." Caroline replied. "This would have taken you forever!"

"I'm retired, it would give me something to do," Jason replied as though it was no problem at all. Caroline just shook her head.

"Well, we could start with naval records." Caroline suggested, "we can search for Anthony or Tony Lawless and we can assume he would be listed as MIA on the same date as your grandfather. Do you recall what date that was?"

"Don't know for certain," Jason said and thought about it for a few seconds, "but it would have to have been around the 20th May 1944. That was the day they arrived at the St. Louis marina. By the way, what's MIA?"

"Well, that's a start I suppose," Caroline replied as she picked up her pencil and made a note of the date. "Missing in Action, in answer to your question."

"Ah, of course it is, should have known that, seen enough war movies," Jason said. By then, Caroline had turned to her computer and had begun typing in commands.

"Where are you looking first?" Jason asked.

"National Archives," Caroline replied.

"Good luck with that, it took me ages to get the information I needed, and I was a relative," Jason said despondently. But Caroline carried on regardless and was looking down at a list of websites on her desk and after finding what she was looking for, she keyed in a few characters and the next thing they knew she had a list of seamen with the name 'Lawless' being displayed on her screen.

"How did you do that?" Jason asked surprised.

"Told you, I have good resources," Caroline replied. She then filtered the list by adding 'Anthony' to the search criteria which reduced the return count to a mere 24 items. Fortunately, the start and end dates of the seamen's service record were listed on the same screen and they only had to scroll down to the second page to find an Anthony Lawless whose service terminated 1944-05-20. To be certain, they also checked the remaining 'Anthonys' as well as the 'Tonys' but there were no others with a date anywhere close to the one they were interested in.

"So, let's see what they can tell us about Mr. Anthony Lawless." Caroline said out loud, and she pressed the key indicating 'Personal Details'. The only relevant data to them that they could find was the next-of-kin details which displayed:

NAME: Mr. & Mrs. Angelo Lawless RELATION: Parents
ADDRESS: 6137 Wyatt Street
CITY: Chicago STATE: IL

Caroline selected a screen print of the details and a whirring sound caught Jason's attention as a printer in the right-hand-side cabinet of the bureau delivered the printed page.

"So far so good," Caroline said, and she signed out of the naval site and deftly entered another search engine to seek information regarding Tony's parents. Initially, their findings confirmed that Tony's parents had indeed once been at that address, but they must have moved shortly after Tony's death and all trace of them seemed to have disappeared. After a further couple of hours of fruitless searching, Caroline decided they would stop for lunch.

"Hungry?" She asked Jason.

"Sure," Jason replied, and he followed her into the kitchen as she began to prepare lunch.

"There's a bottle of white wine chilling in the fridge why don't you pour us both a glass?" Caroline asked as she scurried around the kitchen. "The glasses are already out." She said, pointing to an area on the spacious island that also served as a breakfast bar. "By the way, I hope you're not allergic to anything," Caroline asked as she continued to scurry around the kitchen preparing the food.

"Nothing I know of," Jason replied as he began to search for a corkscrew.

"Drawer next to the fridge!" Caroline said without turning around. "That's good because the soup I have made contains lots of herbs and spices. Don't know what it's going to turn out like."

"I'm sure it will be fine." Jason replied, now attempting to open the wine, "it has to be pretty bad for me to not like soup."

After a little more chit-chat, lunch was ready, and they sat at the breakfast bar to eat a meal of tomato and pepper soup, Caesar salad together with ham and cheese sandwiches. This was followed by a strawberry sponge cake and a cup of tea.

“Would you like another piece of cake Jason?” Caroline asked, “you seemed to have scoffed that piece down quick enough.”

“No, no, please.” Jason replied holding out his hands as though he was asking for mercy. “I couldn’t eat another thing, that was delicious. Did you make all that yourself?”

“No, I have a team of fairies that prepare everything,” Caroline replied laughing. “Of course I cooked it myself, who do you think did it?”

“Oh, sorry, just wasn’t expecting, you know, someone like yourself to well...” Jason was spluttering his way through his reply.

“I’m of English heritage and I love to cook, simple as that,” Caroline replied then she rose to begin clearing away. Jason gathered some of the dirty plates and utensils while Caroline stored away the condiments.

“You know,” Caroline mused as she closed the pantry door, “if I’m not mistaken, that Chicago address for the next-of-kin is in Little Italy. They were a tight group, especially during the war years. Maybe I should direct my investigation to contacting a couple of the Italian Associations to see if they could help locate the parents.”

“Sure!” Jason replied, not quite knowing how to respond. “But Lawless isn’t a very Italian sounding name is it?”

“No, it’s not, but they lived in the community, so you would think someone would have known them,” Caroline replied slowly, still trying to think the problem through.

“Look, I haven’t been much help to you out there, why don’t I clean up here and let you have at it?” Jason offered.

“Right.” Caroline replied absently and then came back to reality, “oh just put everything in the dishwasher, I can tend to it later.”

By the time Jason joined Caroline back in her office, she had printed numerous sheets containing the addresses and phone numbers of various organizations in Little Italy. Some of the associations had a contact email address so they agreed to share the load with Jason emailing those he could and Caroline phoning the others. But they were not getting much luck there either, most of the emails were bounced back as invalid addresses and of the organizations that were still in existence they did not have full-time staff and they would have to wait until the evening or weekend to speak to somebody. They both agreed that enough research had been carried out for one day and Jason decided to take his leave. He declined another beverage but agreed to return in the morning to continue the research.

"Oh, before you go," Caroline said, and she quickly returned to the kitchen to retrieve a packet of the English biscuits Jason had enjoyed earlier that day. "For the guys."

"They're going to love you." Was all that Jason could muster, then he said his farewell and headed back to his boat.

Chapter 46 – Surprising Developments – Modern Day

That evening, Jason spent the time snacking and talking to his daughters, promising faithfully that he would return home the coming Friday for a long weekend. He retired to bed early and he was up with the larks the next morning, showered, had breakfast and ventured up to the Blue Moon Café where he expected the boys to be. Sure enough, they were holding court at their usual table, each nursing a cup of coffee and discussing the world's problems. They were all eager to hear news of any further progress Caroline and he had made on locating Tony's family's whereabouts. Archie, however, gave him a bit of an elbowing and a wink.

"Yes Jason, you made any progress yet?" Archie said lecherously.

"Yes, we did get some successful hits," Jason replied, ignoring Archie's question, "but it looks as though it is going to take a bit of time to locate any descendants." It was then that he revealed the packet of biscuits Caroline had given him to pass on and placed them on the table. They were pleasantly surprised to see the offering and Archie wasted no time in opening the wrapping and grabbing a couple of the biscuits. As they began to devour the biscuits Lorla, the café's proprietor passed by giving them a contemptuous look, in return, the three men looked away like puppies who had been caught eating something they shouldn't. As Lorla passed, she smiled conspiratively at Jason, she really didn't care, the men brought in too much custom for her to worry about a few cookies.

As the men continued to devour the contents of the packet, Jason gave them a quick update as to where they were in the research and what they hoped to be doing that day. That proved to be an excellent segue for him to take his leave and head out to St. Louis, it had begun to rain, and he would like to arrive before the weather worsened.

Jason said his farewells, bought a coffee and a muffin to go and was on his way. On arrival at Caroline's place, he rushed from his car to the door that Caroline had opened for him.

"It's pouring now," Jason said, stating the obvious.

"Yes, I was getting a little concerned, thought you'd be here sooner," Caroline replied.

"Well, it seems drivers in St. Louis are like everywhere else. Any sort of bad weather and traffic snarls to a halt." Jason stated, although stopping to purchase a bottle of wine hadn't contributed to his promptness.

“Weather forecast is for more of the same,” Caroline said, giving a quick look at the sky before shutting the door, “thunderstorms and possibly a tornado warning could be issued later.”

“Tornados? Really?” Jason asked as he removed his jacket and kicked off his shoes simultaneously.

“That time of year and the right type of conditions,” Caroline replied nonchalantly.

“So, any luck with any of your phone calls?” Jason asked.

“’Fraid not.” Caroline replied, “I’ve left a few more messages but no replies, as yet. I seem to have arrived at a dead-end, but not to worry, we just have to keep plugging away until something comes up. Coffee?”

“Love one,” Jason quickly replied, the one he had purchased at the café was long gone having been consumed while stuck in traffic.

Jason gave the bottle of wine to Caroline, for which she thanked him, and he followed her to the back of the house. As she went to pour the coffees, he fired up his laptop to check on his emails. He scanned down the incoming mail, but he didn’t see any replies from the inquiries he had sent out the previous day. "What do you think should be our next steps?" Jason asked Caroline as she returned with the coffees and biscuits. On seeing the goodies, he added, "oh, by the way, the guys really appreciated your biscuits."

"My pleasure," she replied with a laugh, "but in answer to your question, not too sure with this research. Normally, after I have exhausted all my avenues I would hire some research bureaus and bill the client. Of course, we can still do that, but that can be quite expensive." Caroline said, "what would you do?"

"Pretty basic stuff really, I'd start with 'Lawless Chicago' and see what comes up." Jason replied shrugging his shoulders, not knowing quite how else to approach the problem. In response, Caroline turned on her swivel chair and keyed exactly what Jason had suggested into the search line of her browser. Jason successfully dunked a biscuit, took a bite, then moved his chair closer to read the results of the search with Caroline.

Jason found Caroline's perfume intoxicating and as they were both wearing t-shirts their bare arms brushed constantly as she manipulated the keys of the computer. Either she was oblivious to their closeness or she chose not to make an attempt to move her chair further away. Jason was definitely aware of her close proximity to him, but he too made no attempt to move away. For a few seconds, Jason wallowed in this intimacy until the phone rang.

It materialized that the call had nothing to do with their current research so Caroline extricated herself from her chair and went into the other room to take the call. Meanwhile, Jason moved over to the other chair to continue browsing through the search results. Normally, with any search, only the first few pages of results are relevant, after that, the contents begin to appear less meaningful, but as he was waiting for Caroline's return he continued scrolling down the pages of data. It was then that an entry for 'Lawless & Sons Tugboats of Chicago' caught his attention. He clicked on the entry and discovered that it was a brief reference to a company that had operated in the Chicago area from 1940 until 1944, formerly, it had been named 'Lorento Shipping'.

Given that Jason's grandfather had been chosen for the fateful assignment based on his river experience he wondered if Tony had been selected because of his relationship to this company. He was just about to follow this new lead when Caroline re-appeared in the room. He stopped what he was doing but then her phone rang again, he turned back to the computer as she exchanged initial greetings with the caller. After a slight pause, she tapped Jason on the shoulder and placed the call on speakerphone mid-way through the caller's explanation.

"....personally, I cannot help you in your research Miss Ashdene but there are senior members of our association who may recall knowing something of Tony Lawless's family and possibly their whereabouts now. Our next meeting is at the weekend, so I can ask around then. That's the best I can do I'm afraid." The caller was a man and he spoke perfect English with a gentle voice but a slight Italian accent.

"That would be great Monsignor Costello, thank you." Caroline replied.

"Monsignor Costello, my name is Jason, my grandfather was with Tony when they disappeared," Jason explained.

"Oh, my son, I am so sorry to learn this." The man replied sympathetically.

"Thank you. Look, we've just discovered another piece of information that may or may not be relevant," Jason said with some excitement. "It's possible, but not definite, that Tony's surname was originally Lorento and his parents would have been Angelo and Sophie Lorento." Monsignor Costello repeated the names, sounding as if he was making a note of them.

"I will ask around, but you have to remember, the people who may have any knowledge of these names, well, it was a long time ago and let's just say, they are not quite as young as they used to be. Hey, but you never know." Monsignor Costello told them as diplomatically as he could.

"You never know indeed, thanks again for your help Monsignor," Caroline added, and after polite farewells, she terminated the call.

"Wow, that was an interesting snippet you threw in there!" Caroline said, "good work, I might hire you yet."

"I don't know about that!" Jason replied, "just thought it was a bit of a coincidence, that's all, the tugboats and the name."

"No, good thinking, I agree," Caroline responded as she resumed her position in her chair to look at the item thrown up by the search. Jason returned to his chair, but this time, he gave her a little more space to maneuver. They continued surfing the net for further scraps of information and after, yet another unproductive session, Caroline decided it was time to break for lunch, with no argument from Jason.

They followed much the same routine as the previous day, Jason opened the wine while Caroline prepared lunch, which today consisted of assorted meat subs. and home-made potato chips followed by strawberry cheesecake. Today, however, instead of returning to Caroline's office they retired to the drawing room where Jason and the guys had been seated the first time they came to the house. Caroline and Jason felt that they had put out as many feelers as they could, for now, so if it materialized that their efforts to date didn't pan out then they would resume their research. So, Caroline put on her lawyer hat and they spent a little time discussing the facts they had available to them based on Jason's findings. Caroline made a few notes and said she would work on a suitable legal argument to present to the government once the F.B.I. had completed their research at the marina. For the remainder of the afternoon they exchanged history about themselves as they continued to drink their wine while outside, the storm raged on.

At about the time Jason was scheduled to leave, the rain was so bad, visibility couldn't have been much more than fifty yards.

"I'm not sure driving back, just yet, in this weather is a good idea, Jason." Caroline said, "why don't you stay for dinner and see if the conditions improve."

"No, I don't want to impose," Jason said, although realizing that driving in those conditions was not a good idea.

"Impose, and anyway, we've both enjoyed a few glasses of wine this afternoon, you're probably over the limit," Caroline replied. "You need to wait."

Caroline prepared a beautiful meal of beef bourguignon, more wine, and after coffee Jason once more prepared to leave. As Jason gathered his stuff, Caroline checked the weather channel. The good news was, the storm had passed, and the tornado warnings had been canceled but as Caroline looked out of the window she made a comment that brought a smile to Jason's face.

"It's still raining cats and dogs out there." She said casually. Jason understood the expression, but it wasn't one that you heard every day in the U.S. "Look, let's have another coffee, I think I have some Baileys somewhere, then you will definitely have to stay the night. Jason joined her by the window and saw how bad the weather was. At times, gusts of winds drove the rain almost sideways and the smaller trees were being bent over to their maximum, consequently, Jason reluctantly agreed to stay. Jason also stayed the following night, but he didn't sleep in any of the spare bedrooms.

Chapter 47 – Back at the Bar – Modern Day

On Thursday morning Caroline and Jason arose, they had a leisurely breakfast and talked about their next steps. They agreed to go on a short shopping excursion to St. Louis, have lunch in town then, return to the house before Jason set-off for the marina. Now, Jason was reluctant to leave but he had promised his daughters that he would arrive home on Friday, so he needed to get his things together. It was agreed that he would be back at Caroline's place on Tuesday and hopefully, by then, there would be some news.

On arrival at the marina, he dropped in at the pub to give the boys an update. His arrival in the bar was greeted by a cacophony of oohhs and cheers mainly led by Archie.

"I see you're still wearing the same clothes you left in a couple of days ago," Archie remarked. "Something come up, did it?" Archie said, and once more gave that lecherous grin.

"Don't know if you noticed but the weather has been quite bad, so I was forced to stay overnight," Jason replied nonchalantly.

"Sure, sure," Archie said. "Two nights! Nudge nudge, wink wink!"

"Any updates?" Dexter said pragmatically, as he walked over with a beer for Jason.

"Yes, we have made some progress and we hope to get some feedback next week," Jason replied as he took a gulp of beer.

"Surprising you had any time for research at all." Archie persisted.

"Enough Archie," Bill said gruffly. "What kind of progress exactly?" Bill asked.

"Well, we think we have traced my grandfather's shipmate back to Chicago and we have made contact with some people in the community." Jason explained, "they are going to ask around and hopefully, we will get some more news."

"So, what's next?" Dexter asked, still hanging around the table.

"Well, I'm just going to drink this beer, then I am going to get packing. I promised the girls I would be home for the weekend." Jason explained, "I'll be leaving early in the morning."

"And when will you be back?" Chuck asked, a little disappointed that Jason had to leave.

“Late Monday I expect.” Jason said, “then once we have sorted out finding Tony’s descendants we will be working on a case to go after the government.”

Chapter 48 – Returning Home – Modern Day

Jason arrived home late Friday night and was pleased to see that in preparation for his return, Jeannette had stocked the fridge with a few basics, bread, milk and the such. After a good night's sleep, he was up early the next morning reading through his backlog of mail while luxuriating in the pleasure of a percolated coffee instead of the instant he had been drinking on the boat. He read the last of the backlog of almost a month's worth of mail and decided to get cleaned up before having breakfast, which was just as well as Jeanette came bursting in during his banquet of poached eggs on toast.

Before he could rise from his chair Jeanette was embracing him in an unusual show of love and affection. She was surprised at how good he looked, he had put on a bit of weight, he had color in his cheeks and when he went to clear away his dishes she felt there was a new bounce in his step.

"Dad?" Jeanette said.

"Yes?" Jason replied.

"Are you seeing someone?" She asked him demurely.

“Ha, don’t be ridiculous!” He said.

“You are, aren’t you?” Jeannette said with a smile, wagging a finger at him. “You don’t fool me.”

“If I found somebody, you would be the first to know,” Jason said, turning away as he replied, he knew he couldn’t face his daughter when he said that, it would have been a dead giveaway.

“Fine, but before I forget, we are all having dinner at gran’s tomorrow, so you will be able to give everyone the skinny on what you have been up to and where the investigation stands.” Jeannette said, “so, tell me all about these guys you met at the marina.”

Jeannette stayed for about an hour and for the rest of the day, Jason took the time to catch up on a few things and touch base with a few of the neighbors who were outside doing chores. It felt funny, he had lived in this community all his married life but suddenly he felt he didn’t belong, and he couldn’t wait to return to the idyllic lifestyle he had been enjoying during the last few weeks, of course, a certain Miss Ashdene may have had something to do with that.

The next day he arrived early at his parent's house with a bunch of flowers for his mother and a case of his dad's favorite beer. He wanted to arrive early so that he could have a private chat with them, especially with his father, to explain the details of his father's demise.

"They shouldn't be able to get away with this!" Jason's father retorted in anger after he had been told the details, which brought Jason's mother running into the room where the men were seated, she was brandishing a wooden spoon she had been using to bake a cake.

"Who they? What?" Jason's mother blurted out, quite concerned at her husband's outburst, he was usually such a mild-mannered man. So, Jason explained his findings to her.

"But you have to keep this under your hat for now until the F.B.I. has finished their investigations."

"What?" Jason's father shouted, "they'll cover it all up, as they have done for the last 70 odd years."

"Dad, I know, that's why I'm working with a lawyer to build a case against the government," Jason replied, trying to soothe his father.

"You need a lot of good contacts to go after the government." Jason's father replied, but at least he was calming down, "is he any good?"

"It's a she and yes, she has contacts. Her grandmother was one of the victims on the other boat." Jason replied, "so, she also has a vested interest."

"Hmph," Jason's dad replied in a huff, "well, I hope she knows what she's doing."

After that conversation, they both had a beer and they moved onto more mundane things, each other's health, the current Cleveland Indian's team and the general state of the nation.

Shirley was the first to arrive and she immediately went over to give her Dad a loving hug, then she stepped back and punched him quite hard on the arm.

"What was that for?" Jason asked, rubbing his bicep, thinking her reaction was because he had been away for so long.

"For going diving by yourself, you silly man." Shirley replied, an avid diver herself she knew the dangers involved, "not once but twice, you should know better."

"We would never have known the truth if I hadn't have discovered it when I did," Jason said in protest.

"We might never have seen you again," Shirley replied. At this point in the conversation, Allison stepped forward and tentatively offered Jason a hug, something she had never done before, which he gladly accepted, more to ward off his youngest daughter's playful vitriol. It wouldn't have lasted long anyway because Jeannette and her fiancée had just arrived.

Over dinner they talked about general things, Jason's mother positively beaming at having all the children together for dinner, although she had been terribly disappointed that neither of her granddaughters ever looked liked providing her with great-grandchildren. Inevitably, the conversation returned to the quest and Jason explained what he had uncovered in more detail. Of course, they were all horrified at Jason's theory and insisted that something should be done. Jason reiterated the urgent need for secrecy at this stage and was about to tell them of his legal preparations when his father jumped in.

“Jason’s got some fancy lawyer working on the case, apparently she is in the same boat as him, one of the descendants from the other boat.” Jason’s father said, although Jason thought he could have chosen a better choice of words, but it wasn’t through any maliciousness.

“So that’s who it is, is it?” Jeannette said in a eureka moment looking directly at her father, while everyone else was looking questioningly at her. Jason picked up his glass of wine and took a drink then told everyone that he had a call of nature. By the time Jason had returned to the table Jeanette had shared her thoughts and now everyone was looking to Jason for more details.

“Look, despite what Jeannette has told you, her assumptions are totally unfounded, it is purely a working relationship that I have with Caroline.” Jason explained with his arms outstretched to try and emphasize the point, “so let that be the end of it.”

“For now.” Shirley added, “Caroline eh?” And they all laughed.

Chapter 49 – Back to the Quest – Modern Day

Jason arrived back at his boat late Monday evening and he was surprised to find a Ziploc bag attached to the door containing what appeared to be a hastily written message from Chuck. The note stated that David the jeweler has some news. Hopefully, it was regarding the sale of the jewelry or the currency, he would drive up to see him in the morning, before leaving for St. Louis and after visiting the boys at the café of course.

After exchanging pleasantries with Chuck and Archie, Bill wasn't there today, he called the jewelers to let them know he would be there presently. He took the short drive up to the jewelers and he was welcomed at the door by David himself.

"Good morning Jason," David said, "how are you?"

"Fine thank you," Jason replied, "you wanted to see me?"

"Yes, I'm pleased to inform you that there has been progress on both fronts. There are two potential buyers for the jewelry and they are currently vying for the right to purchase. As for the currency, a local numismatist has come forward to purchase the money and has placed an offer of $23,500 for all the coins and notes. I told him I need to contact you to receive your approval before completing the transaction." Jason just stood there dumbfounded, staring directly at David like a deer caught in headlights. After a few seconds, the pleasant smile disappeared from David's face.

"Sorry Jason, I thought you would be pleased," David said gently, "this is an extremely good offer." Again, Jason merely stared catatonically.

"I will get back to the gentleman and tell him the offer is unacceptable," David said with some resignation.

"No, no, no." Jason finally said, emerging from his silence. "Sorry David, I can't believe the cash was worth that much. My gast is flabbered to say the least. So, Dexter was right about its value!"

"You'd like me to proceed with the purchase then?" David asked, his smile now returned.

"Absolutely, yes," Jason replied without hesitation.

"Well, there is documentation that has to be completed so by maybe, the middle of next week the transaction will be complete and I will have the payment for you. Hopefully, by then we may also know a little more about the sale of the jewelry."

"Great, thanks David," Jason said as he shook his hand and left to make a quick stop at the café to give the boys an update.

Jason fair burst through the door of the café to give the men the news.

"So that's a nice windfall for you," Archie said genuinely pleased for him.

"No, it's not for me," Jason said, "I'm going to give half to my dad, after all, he is the next in line, and the other half to Tony's descendants, if and when we find them."

"That's not right." Chuck said, "you've done all the work you should get something out of it."

"Too right." Archie agreed.

"O.K. Tell you what, I pay Chuck three grand for marina fees, $500.00 goes to Dexter and we have another meal next week, the rest is split as stated," Jason suggested.

"I don't need you to pay marina fees," Chuck said, "this has been fun."

"No, I have used hydro, water and other help. Pay some to young Charlie if you feel bad about it." Jason said.

"That young whippersnapper doesn't deserve it," Chuck replied and they all laughed.

"So why don't you organize another lunch for next Thursday. Let Dexter know and invite David." Jason suggested.

"Why can't you do it?" Archie asked.

"Well, I may not be back for a few days," Jason said looking down at the coffee he had bought earlier, not wanting to look the others in the face.

"I told you, Chuck, I knew it," Archie said, "it's that Caroline Ashdene woman."

"Whatever!" Was all that Jason could reply, wondering how everyone else can pick up on his tryst with Caroline when he hadn't really recognized it himself, until now. The situation was also accentuated during his arrival at Caroline's door that morning, yes, she had the coffee and the cookies prepared for him, but he was greeted first with a hug and a loving kiss.

"I missed you," Caroline said.

Chapter 50 – Connection with the Past – Modern Day

Caroline was thrilled to hear about the sale of the currency, but she was also excited about the news she had received from Chicago.

"Monsignor Costello has come through," Caroline said enthusiastically, "apparently, the parents of one of his parishioners were very good friends with an Angelo and Sophie Lorento who used to live in the neighborhood. In fact, he had known Sophie since he was in kindergarten, Sophie had been born in the U.S. Apparently, Angelo used to work on the rivers, she thinks he used to own a company called Lawless Tugboats & Sons. Too much of a coincidence I think!"

"Sounds promising." Jason agreed, "but I'm a bit confused about the Lorento, Lawless thing."

"Well, apparently after Angelo arrived from Italy he started his tugboat business but felt he could get more trade if he anglicized his name," Caroline added, "but what happened was that both of his sons, Antonio and Mario, were killed during the war. Angelo was devastated, and as he had made enough money to live a comfortable life back in Italy, he persuaded Sophie to go and live in Italy for the rest of their lives. They then reverted back to their Italian name, Lorento."

"That would explain why we had difficulty finding a hit on the Lawless name!" Jason said.

"You got it," Caroline said.

"But where does that leave us, is that the end of the trail?" Jason said

"Not quite," Caroline said mischievously. "It appears that our Mario was a bit of a lad, a woman in every port type of lad. He had gotten a girl pregnant in Joliet and being the honorable grandparents that they were, Angelo and Sophie sent money to her for the child's upbringing, right up until their deaths, which were in the '70s. When they finally passed away, the grandchild, a daughter, by the way, inherited what was left of the estate, apparently a sizeable sum."

"How have you discovered all this since yesterday?" Jason asked, quite amazed.

"Follow the money," Caroline replied, "Uncle Sam likes to monitor financial transactions coming in from abroad. I've been assigned too many lawsuits involving fraud and money laundering not to know the ways and means of investigating money transfers. So, finding a regular payment to a bank in Joliet from Italy wasn't too difficult."

"Do you have a name?" Jason asked.

"Sure do, Esther Grant, she still lives in Joliet, I have an address and a telephone number," Caroline replied, passing Jason a post-it with the details written on it.

"Maybe I should give her a call," Jason said looking at the number.

"Maybe you should, otherwise all the work I've done would be a waste of time, wouldn't it?" Caroline said, joshing him.

"Now that we have found someone, I'm not sure what to say to her," Jason said.

"Just pick up the phone, make the call, it will come, you'll see," Caroline said sympathetically and handed him the phone. "I'll go and prepare lunch." Which was really just an excuse for Caroline to leave him alone in the room.

Jason just stood there, looking at the phone in one hand and the post-it in the other. Eventually, he summoned up the courage and dialed the number, albeit with some trepidation, then waited for someone to reply.

"Hello." A gentle voice answered.

"Hi, Esther, Esther Grant?" Jason asked.

"Yes." Esther replied with that, *'is this yet another scam'* type of reply.

"Hi, my name is Jason Clifford, you don't know me, but your uncle was on the same boat as my grandfather during the war."

"I don't really know anything about that," Esther replied.

"Am I right in saying your paternal father's name was Mario Lawless or Lorento? Jason asked.

"Yes." Esther's tone, even with just a one-word reply, was one of suspicion and Jason could tell he would be losing the call if he was not careful.

"I have been doing some research on the disappearance of my grandfather and your uncle Tony which led me to the discovery of the boat they were on. I have recovered a few artifacts, photos and such that I thought you might like have returned to you as you are the heir as it were." Jason explained.

"I wasn't told much about my father's family and I only met my grandparents once. I suppose it would be nice to have some memento." Esther said as though she was thinking it through. "Maybe you could drop it in the mail?"

"How about I bring it to you a week Monday?" Jason asked, a scheme suddenly developing in his mind.

"Sure," Esther replied.

"I have your address," Jason said, then read it out to her to confirm, "see you about 2:00."

Jason joined Caroline in the kitchen and told her the news.

"So, I said we would be there at 2:00 a week Monday," Jason told her meekly.

"We?" Caroline asked, surprised.

“Ah yes. Well, forgot to mention.” Jason began nervously, “next Thursday, to celebrate, we are all having another lunch at the pub, my treat, we’ve also invited David.”

“And that’s relevant to going to Joillet, how?” Caroline asked, looking a little confused and now standing arms akimbo.

“I’m getting to that,” Jason said as he continued to stutter through his plan, “I thought perhaps, rather than return home after the meal you could spend the night on my luxurious yacht. I mean, you would be able to have a few drinks and not have to worry about the drive home.”

“Again, Joillet?” Caroline asked, beginning to get a little frustrated with Jason’s meanderings.

“Well, what I was thinking is that we could drive up to Cleveland and spend the weekend at my place and then on the Monday we could drive across country to Joliet.” Jason managed to finally blurt out. There was a pause as Caroline stood at the kitchen sink staring out of the window.

“So, we would be meeting your family,” Caroline said softly as she continued to gaze outside.

“Yes, possibly, yes, that might happen.” Jason replied, sounding more like one of the players in a Monty Python sketch than a mature adult, “it would also give me an opportunity to give my father his share of the money.”

“Isn’t this all a little sudden?” Caroline asked, finally turning to face Jason.

“No, we should have the money by then,” Jason replied.

“NO silly, I mean us!” Caroline replied.

“Not if my daughter’s intuition is correct, which it usually is.” Jason countered, beginning to regain his composure. This was followed by another pause as Caroline merely stared at Jason until she finally spoke.

“What the hell will we do in Cleveland for an entire weekend?” Caroline said.

“Are you kidding?” Jason replied, relieved, “the Indians are playing a series at home and there’s always the Rock and Roll Hall of Fame. You know, I’ve lived in Cleveland all my life and I have never visited the hall.” They were both laughing now and decided to abandon lunch at home to spend the rest of the day in St. Louis.

Chapter 51 – Huge Test – Modern Day

Jason didn't return to the marina until the day of the lunch, he had anticipated this eventuality and had brought sufficient clothing for a long stay at Caroline's. He had been in contact with Dexter to ensure all was on schedule and on their arrival, he was pleased to see not only David in attendance for lunch but also Helen, Dexter's wife. Dexter explained that he thought it would be nice to have an additional female at the table to keep Caroline company. Jason never did find out who was cooking the food that day but nevertheless, it was still as good as on the previous occasion.

It appeared that the size of the quest's group had grown, and a good time was had by all. David handed over an envelope to Jason, it contained the money for the currency transaction. David also insisted on paying for a couple of rounds of drinks, claiming that he hadn't had as much fun in a long time. David also took the opportunity to take Caroline to one side to present her with an offer for the jewelry, which she readily accepted. David promised her that a banker's draft would be available for pick-up at his store the following week. Caroline returned to her seat at the table and with a huge smile on her face she whispered to Jason the price she had received. Then she tapped a fork on her wine glass a few times to get everyone's attention.

"Everyone, I have great news," Caroline began, "I have accepted an offer for the jewelry and you, Chuck, Bill, Archie, and Dexter will each be receiving $20,00.00 for helping us with the recovery of these items." There was a large cheer that caught the attention of everyone in the pub but only for a few seconds, then they all turned back to mind their own business.

The only blight on the occasion was Bill. Whatever the poor man was stricken with, he wouldn't tell anyone, was obviously eating away at him. His appetite was gone, he looked deathly pale and had lost an awful lot of weight, even during the couple of weeks since Jason had last seen him. After lunch, which extended to well into the afternoon, Archie helped Bill to his car and was actually allowed to drive Bill home.

Caroline and Jason retired to the boat and after they both checked emails on their corresponding devices they sat top-deck sharing a bottle of wine between them as they watched the boats go by on the river. Jason cracked out some cheese and crackers and they stayed there until the sun finally went down.

Early the next morning, after a quick visit to the Blue Moon, again sans Bill, Caroline and Jason were on the road to Cleveland and arrived there late that evening. Once more, Jeanette had been in to ensure the fridge was well-stocked, only this time, she had gone to town. There were all sorts of extra treats, wine, beer, assorted meats and cheeses. On the kitchen table were two envelopes, one contained a couple of tickets to the Rock and Roll Hall of fame, the other, three tickets to the Saturday afternoon Indians vs Red Sox game. There was also a handwritten note attached:

> Hi dad, you're taking granddad to the game, he's expecting you to pick him up at noon and granny is expecting you over there at 1:00 on Sunday. We'll all be over later for dinner.
>
> See u then
>
> Love you J.

"Well, it seems our weekend is all planned out for us. And you thought it would be boring!" Jason said and then did an exaggerated "hmph".

"Well, at least we get the mornings to relax," Caroline replied with a wink.

"Assuming one of the girls can't wait until Sunday and decide to turn up here to check you out tomorrow," Jason said.

“They won’t,” Caroline replied with some certainty, and she was correct, they didn’t.

Just before lunch the next day, they arrived at Jason’s parent's house to pick his dad up to go to the game. Jason’s mother and father were briefly introduced to Caroline, but the ensuing chit-chat was cut short by Jason’s demand to get moving to proceed to the game. William Clifford was resplendent in his Indians t-shirt and berated Jason for not wearing his. They enjoyed the usual stadium fare for lunch and enjoyed a good game of baseball, albeit a defeat for the good guys. Jason drove his dad back home after the game, then, he drove to a restaurant on the lake where he and Caroline had dinner before visiting the Rock and Roll Hall of Fame.

The next morning, on arrival at Jason’s parents’ house his mother was fussing around, as usual, as though royalty had just walked into her home. Jason’s father merely offered them a beer and continued to lament on the defeat his beloved Indians had suffered at the hands of the hated Red Sox. Jason’s mother was interested to know what Caroline thought of the visit to the Hall and what her favorite exhibit was.

"Well, I'm a huge Beatles fan so I just loved what they had done for them," Caroline responded.

"I suppose Jason had to go and visit the Bob Dylan exhibit?" Jason's mother asked.

"Yes, we did, it was quite good," Caroline said.

"Good? It was fantastic." Jason said.

"Can't see what you see in him, can't sing to save his life and how he got a Nobel prize I'll never know!" Jason's mother ranted.

"It was his writing, his way with words, just listen to the songs." Jason countered while the others laughed.

A few more pleasantries were exchanged with Caroline before Jason took control of the conversation.

"Mum, dad, as you know, Caroline has been helping me find out about granddad. She also lost her grandmother in the accident."

"Oh, I'm so sorry to hear that my dear." Jason's mother said and laid a hand on Caroline's arm to console her.

“Well,” Jason said continuing, “Caroline has located a niece of the man who was on the boat with granddad, she is the same age as you dad, and his only immediate descendant. You see there is some good news coming out of this. I found a safe on the boat granddad was on and I managed to salvage it. With the help of a locksmith, one of the members of the group at the pub, we found money in the safe. The notes and change were in pristine condition and it turns out that they were worth something. So, we found a buyer and, after deducting a small amount for expenses,” Jason smiled and looked at Caroline who reciprocated, “we have split the proceeds in half and your cut is $10,000.00.” At that point, Jason handed an envelope containing the money over to his father. Jason’s mother walked over to her husband and put a hand on his shoulder, the other went to her mouth suppressing a sound of total surprise. Jason’s father looked at it for a moment before responding.

“We can’t accept this,” William said abruptly and held it out to return to Jason.

“Why not dad, it belongs to you!” Jason replied, “if not you then who should get it?”

"I don't like it, it's probably dirty money. If it was all above board why couldn't you just give me a cheque instead of carrying around this much money?" William asked, "why cash?"

"Perhaps I can answer that one, Mr. Clifford," Caroline interceded, "you're absolutely correct, although dirty money may be a bit strong. First of all, apart from us and a small group of people who helped in the salvaging of the safe, no one is aware of the money. There is absolutely no paper trail back to this cash. Secondly, even if there was, the contents of the safe were the belongings of the two men on board, your father and the other seaman, Tony. If the government's case is that they are denying all knowledge of your father's trip and any reason for it, then by default they can make no claim to anything that was on board the vessel at the time of its sinking. Furthermore, the salvager, in this case Jason, is entitled to retain anything he has salvaged. So, yes Mr. Clifford, as the direct descendent of Ray Clifford you are his sole heir. The reason for the cash is simple. Any cheque transactions may draw the attention of some government agency and it may have to go into escrow until it is settled, but that settlement would most certainly be in your favor. This way the government is none the wiser."

William retracted his arm and the envelope rested on his lap for a few seconds while he gave Caroline's eloquent speech some serious thought.

"We could finally go on that cruise we keep talking about, William!" Jason's mother said softly.

"Damn it, the bastards owe me at least that much. Why not?" William said, "who wants another beer, I think we should celebrate!"

By the time the rest of the family arrived, Caroline was in the kitchen assisting in the dinner preparations and Jason was in the den with his father watching the next installment of the Cleveland vs Red Sox series. The two girls and their respective companions arrived together, Jason didn't know if that was planned or pure coincidence but for him, it meant there would only be one moment of truth.

"Hi, I'm Jeannette and this is my fiancée, Allan," Jeanette said enthusiastically and reached out a hand.

"Hi, Caroline Ashdene." Caroline accepted the hand from Jeannette and then did the same with Alan with a quick 'Hi'. Next was Shirley, Jason figured that if there were to be any fireworks, this was the time the touch paper would be lit. But before Shirley had an opportunity to even introduce herself, her partner, Allison, pointed at Caroline with one hand and put her finger to her mouth as though she was considering something.

"Are you the Caroline Ashdene who worked on that LGBT case in New York against that big transport union?" Allison asked.

"Yes, guilty as charged!" Caroline replied.

"And you won, didn't you?" Allison said almost in awe.

"Well, it was a slam dunk really," Caroline replied modestly but it was enough to break the ice and the rest of the afternoon was spent as though Caroline had been a member of the family for years.

Chapter 52 – Meeting the Past – Modern Day

The drive to Joillet was uneventful and at precisely 2 o' clock Jason was knocking on the door of Esther Grant. The young, attractive, lady who answered the door was obviously not Esther.

"Hi, I'm Jason Clifford, this is Caroline, we're here to see Esther Grant?" Jason said in a way as to make it sound like a question. The house was one in a row of town-houses that all looked as though they had seen better days and he wasn't sure if he had chosen the correct door to knock on.

"Yes, she's expecting you, come in." The young lady said. Caroline and Jason walked into a narrow but well-decorated hallway. "My name is Abby, I'm Esther's youngest granddaughter." Abby beckoned them into a room where an elderly lady sat, this thought Jason, would be Esther. She looked a bit haggard, grey wizened hair, crumpled clothes with a blanket wrapped around her. Not the sight Jason was expecting when you compared her to his father who was of the same age.

"Hello, my name is Esther Grant, how are you?" Esther said, "forgive me, I won't stand, had my hip replaced a week before you phoned, my granddaughter has come to live with me for a few weeks until I'm back on my feet." Which, thought Jason, would account for her appearance.

"Can I get you a coffee, tea, anything?" Abby said, as if on cue.

"Oh, I would love a coffee please," Caroline replied, and Jason nodded his head in agreement.

Jason got down to business and displayed the photographs and belongings he had that were once Tony's and explained in a little more detail on how he had come by them. Esther didn't take much notice of the photo of Tony and his brother, they meant nothing to her, but she did look longingly at the picture of her grandparents whom she had met that one occasion when she was quite young. They had paid for a trip for her and her mother to go to Italy to see them, but she only went the once. She explained to Caroline and Jason that her mother's husband didn't like the idea of his wife going to Italy with another man's daughter and pocketed future payments that came from Mario's parents. Of course, the grandparents caught on to this and future payments were restricted to sending money for child maintenance.

"I understand you received an inheritance from Mario's parents?" Caroline asked.

"Yes, but my stupid ex-husband squandered most of it," Esther said bitterly, "but what he didn't know is that there's still a little money over there and a beautiful little house in the mountains to go with it. But I doubt if I'll ever get to go there again, can't afford it. A codicil in the will prevents me from selling it, the house must remain in the family. So, I'm hanging on to it in case one of the children can use it, which is highly unlikely."

"So, what happens to it if your family wants to get rid of it?" Caroline asked, the lawyer in her being inquisitive.

"One of my grandparent's extended family would inherit," Esther explained. At that moment, Abby returned to the room with two mugs of instant coffee and placed them on coasters on small coffee tables next to Caroline and Jason.

"Everything alright gran?" Abby asked.

"Yes dear, fine," Esther replied.

"Look, I hope you don't mind," Abby said, addressing Jason and Caroline, "but if you're going to be here for a half an hour or so, I could go out to get some groceries. I don't like leaving gran on her own. She tends to try and do things herself. Don't you gran?" Abby said.

"No not at all," Caroline said, "we'll stay here until you get back."

As it turned out, Abby's departure was a welcome blessing as they really didn't want to disclose the inheritance money with any other member of the family knowing, that would be Esther's prerogative. So, after they heard the front door close, Jason decided to get down to business.

"Look Esther, we have some good news for you," Jason said as he extracted the now familiar envelope from his inside jacket pocket, "there was money on board the boat that we have divided into equal shares for you and my father, as you two would be the rightful heirs. Your share is $10,000.00." Jason passed the envelope to Esther. Like Jason's father, at first, Esther too was a little dumbfounded but certainly did not have the same qualms about accepting the money as his father had.

"That would be enough to get me to Italy, wouldn't it?" Esther said as though a dream had just come true, "with a little left over!"

“Don’t know how long it would last over there though,” Jason added.

“Wouldn’t have to, I could sell this dump. What with my pension and what I have saved up I could live over there for a good long while. No rent or mortgage, fresh fruit, and vegetables everyday...” Esther’s mind seemed to retract into a longing reverie. “You don’t know how much this means to me, thank you so much.”

“What about your children? Wouldn’t you miss them?” Caroline asked.

“Let me tell you a little about myself,” Esther replied pragmatically. “As I said earlier, my ex-husband took almost everything, even the three kids. They moved out west, only my youngest daughter had children and then it was just one, Abby. She came to Chicago for college and ended up staying with me, she has been great. If she wanted to travel to Italy with me, she would be welcome.”

“Wow, that’s so sad!” Caroline said, looking genuinely hurt.

“It’s life. I have had to accept it, but now, once this hip is sorted out, I’m outta here!” Esther said with some gusto. They all laughed, just as Abby returned, laden with grocery bags and wondering what was so amusing.

"Well, I think it is time we took our leave, but look, here is my telephone number and email address. I'd love to know what you decide and if you need any help with anything please let me know." Jason said, handing Esther one of his old business cards. They all shook hands and Abby was still looking a little bewildered. As Caroline and Jason shut the front door they heard a squeal of delight coming from within. They both smiled, it appeared Esther had told Abby and they assumed she had decided to go to Italy.

Chapter 53 – Events Happen Quickly – Modern Day

Nothing much unfolded during the ensuing couple of weeks. Caroline and Jason worked loosely on building a case against the government, between trips to the pub and the odd boat trip down the river to check on progress at the old marina. It was on one of their regular Thursday trips to the pub that they encountered their first piece of news. They entered to join the boys at their usual spot at the bar only to see a pair of sad-looking faces. As soon as they were in the door, Helen approached them before they could reach the others.

"Hi, look, I have some bad news, I'm afraid Bill passed away last night." Helen said, "we knew you were coming in today, so we didn't want to email you or call, but to tell you personally."

"No!" Caroline whispered as she put a hand to her mouth. Jason slowly walked over to Chuck and Archie and gave each of them a hug. Dexter had already poured the drinks for the new guests.

"On the house," Dexter said solemnly.

"I'm so sorry," Caroline said to Chuck and Archie, like Jason, she gave each of them a hug. Jason took the bar-stool next to Chuck and Caroline sat beside him. As Jason took a sip of his beer he happened to notice Bill's old Chevy parked outside.

"What's Bill's car doing here?" Jason asked.

"It's Archie's car now," Chuck said.

"Yeah, the silly old fart left it to me," Archie explained, "he figured I could pull more ladies in a class car!" That brought a smile to everyone and Chuck asked how the trip went with Jason's dad and the visit to Joliet. Jason brought them all up to date and the rest of the afternoon was occupied by listening to the boys reminiscing about their antics with Bill. Both Caroline and Jason had imbibed a little more than they should, certainly for driving back to St. Louis, so they decided to stay the night on the boat. It was then that Jason received the next piece of news. Just as they climbed aboard the boat, his mobile phone began ringing. This couldn't be good news, very few people knew his number, among those who did, were his daughters and he thought it must be one of them.

"Hello," Jason said as he answered the call.

"Mr. Clifford?" The voice replied.

"That's right," Jason replied succinctly.

"Agent Redmond here. Look, our investigations are complete, and we are heading out tomorrow. I wondered, could you make a trip to the marina first thing in the morning to discuss a few things?" Redmond asked.

"Why, yes, I guess," Jason replied, sounding a bit confused by the surprise call, "what time do you call first thing?"

"If you could be here by 9:00 AM that would be great," Redmond replied, sounding quite friendly, not the terse business-like attitude Jason encountered the last time they spoke.

"See you then," Jason replied, and the call was terminated. Caroline was looking at Jason with some concern and he explained the contents of the call.

"It's all happening," Caroline said.

"We will have to leave here about 8:30 AM, no rest for the wicked," Jason said.

Jason hardly slept that night in anticipation of the meeting with the F.B.I. agent but was grateful Caroline would be by his side. After showering and a quick breakfast they arrived at the marina well before the allotted meeting time. Redmond was outside his command module and walked over to them as Jason parked his truck. Jason was amazed at what had happened to the place since his last visit to the marina. The boats had all been removed from the water, together with the piles and docks they had been moored to. The wall that had surrounded the area had been completely torn down and the land restored to its original state. All evidence of the dockmaster's building and the store had disappeared, there was nothing to suggest there had ever been a marina at the location.

"Like what we've done to the place?" Redmond asked with a smile. Jason just shook his head, astonished at what he was seeing, believing this to be another part of the cover-up. To accentuate his thoughts, Agent Jordan was approaching them with a security wand that Jason recognized as the type of apparatus that was used for searches at airports. It also sparked Redmond to return to his more formal approach.

"Before we start our meeting we need to ensure you are not wired for recording any conversation we will be having, and I am afraid our meeting will be restricted to just the two of us." Redmond said indicating to Caroline that she was not invited.

"This is Caroline Ashdene, not only is she my lawyer but she is also a direct descendant of one of the people lost in this travesty of justice. So yes, she is most certainly part of this meeting." Jason said with a degree of officiousness that startled Redmond and impressed Caroline. Having finished waving the wand all over Jason, Agent Jordan looked at Redmond to await further instructions. He merely nodded his head and pointed at Caroline.

"Follow me," Redmond said once Agent Jordan had finished, and he began walking to the water's edge, while Agent Jordan returned to the command center. Without looking at the couple, Redmond began to talk.

"We've carried out a thorough investigation of what we believe occurred during that night of the storm," Redmond began.

"Don't try to bullshit me, Redmond, I know what happened," Jason said with some venom.

"Mr. Clifford, is this how the conversation is going to go? If it is, we're done here." Redmond replied authoritatively. "What I want to tell you is completely off the record and yes, to the best of our knowledge, there was no paper trail of the incident, our investigations certainly bear out your theory. But if you listen, there may be something that will be mutually acceptable to all of us." Caroline put her hand on Jason's arm in an attempt to subdue him and Redmond began to explain.

Chapter 54 – Start of a Project – September 1942

Lieutenant General Leslie Richard Groves Jr. took charge of the Manhattan Project in September of 1942. The Manhattan Project was the highly classified project created to not only develop the atomic bomb but also to win the race to become the first of the Second World War protagonists to do so. Groves had been selected because he had proven to be a person of iron will with an imposing personality who knew how to get things done. He was a larger-than-life figure, a little overweight, a mustache on his top lip that could probably be best described as a stubble.

The whole Manhattan Project was a massive endeavor, involving as many as 130,000 people at various locations throughout the United States. Groves oversaw all the project's phases, including scientific, technical and process development; construction; security and military intelligence of enemy activities. Groves was involved in most aspects of the project's development and participated in the selection of the sites for research and production. In fact, the day after he took over the project, Groves took a train to Tennessee to inspect a potential site at Oak Ridge, he was impressed, noting especially that the Clinch river ran through the location.

The Oak Ridge site was being earmarked to produce the plutonium which was to be an essential component for the manufacture of the atomic bomb. The bomb itself was to be made and tested in Los Alamos, Nevada.

Naturally, the plutonium would have to be transported from Oak Ridge to Los Alamos. Obviously, rail, air, and road were the preferred modes of transportation but after further research Groves also discovered a potential water route that could be navigated between Oak Ridge and St. Louis which would be ideal if he ever wanted to transport plutonium on a water-going vessel.

The construction of the Oak Ridge factory to produce the plutonium began in February 1943 and the reactor was up and running by November of the same year. By early 1944 the factory had produced its first supply of plutonium and delivery to Los Alamos now had to be arranged. It was decided that small amounts of plutonium were to be shipped via several train trips to Los Alamos. But Groves, being security conscious, was only too aware of the possibility of sabotage. He wanted to build in some redundancy by arranging for a portion of the plutonium to be transported, first by boat to St. Louis, then by car and onwards to Los Alamos. To facilitate this, he needed military personnel with experience on the inland waterways system, especially the Mississippi. Groves ordered some staff members to scour naval records in search of a couple of matelots with any Mississippi tug-boat knowledge to be able to fulfill his plan. Groves' plan was for two individuals to innocently sail a cabin cruiser along the Clinch River to the Tennessee River. Just south of the town of Grand River they would cross over to the Cumberland River that would then join the Ohio and eventually the Mississippi with their final destination being St. Louis. From there they would drive across country to Los Alamos. Naturally, it would have been much quicker to just drive to the Cumberland or the Ohio rivers and pick-up a boat there, but Groves felt that two guys on a cabin-cruiser sailing the long way around would be much more innocuous to any interested spies. After all, two playboy types with a fun boat, sailing part of the Great Loop in springtime would not be an unusual occurrence.

Groves would need a reliable resource to lead this secret project and after personally researching for a potential candidate, Groves settled on a Captain Edward Beardsley. Beardsley was one of the few Americans working for the British in the Special Operations Executive, carrying out covert operations across the English Channel. Beardsley participated in many missions behind enemy lines until he was injured escaping from the clutches of a German patrol that his group had encountered on the coast of France. He had returned to the states to recuperate and it was while he was there that his impeccable record attracted the attention of Lieutenant General Groves. Beardsley was an athletic specimen, just over six feet tall and was not only proficient in martial arts but was also an excellent marksman. Furthermore, his experience in subterfuge gleaned from the SOE missions made him a perfect candidate for Groves' needs.

Groves shared the details of his plan with Beardsley, the only other man to know all the facts. Groves gave Beardsley a list of potential seamen and he was told to whittle the list down to two of them. They would need an appropriate boat, it would need to be racy but not enough to attract too much attention and it would need to be modified to safely accommodate a few grams of plutonium. In addition, the engine should be finely tuned and souped-up, just in case some extra horses should be required during the trip. Beardsley would be responsible for all the logistics of the project but most importantly, the selected seamen should never know what they were transporting.

Beardsley went to work. The chosen boat was a 1940 Chris Craft Double Stateroom cruiser and it would represent pure luxury for the two selected sailors who would be joining the team. But it had to be fitted with a hidden stainless-steel receptacle for carrying the plutonium, Beardsley had to consult with engineers to mitigate this issue. The receptacle, Beardsley had built at the Oak Ridge plant, but the difficulty was hiding it on the boat. One of the engineers solved that problem by suggesting a relatively new innovation, liquid fiberglass. A receptacle containing the plutonium could be fixed to the hull of the boat then a false bottom could be built over the existing hull and by injecting fiberglass into the vacuum, it would protect the receptacle. Unless the boat came out of the water, no one would ever know that it had a false hull. Beardsley also arranged to have a safe fixed into the boat for any personal documents the mariners may have and somewhere to put money for the trip.

With the boat organized, Beardsley's next task was to select two seamen from the list given to him by Groves. It didn't take long to determine that Clifford and Lawless were the appropriate candidates for the mission. Beardsley then set about making the necessary arrangements for their assignment to his project and for their transportation to Knoxville. The hotel rooms were booked and the whole subterfuge of changing them from seamen to civilians was arranged by him. Next was communications and he had just been informed of a brand-new radio system, the Joan-Eleanor system, that had been used successfully during flying missions in the European theatre. The security factor of the system was exactly what was needed for this project, unfortunately, it relied on a line-of-sight to aircraft flying overhead. Beardsley couldn't have planes flying above the boat for 24 hours a day, nor during really bad weather, consequently, he reluctantly came up with two codes to be used on the marine radio. One would be used for an emergency, simply, 'Halifax is in Canada', the other for their arrival in St. Louis, 'Cardinals are in town'. The drill was that the security system should be attempted first and if no acknowledgment was received, to resort to the marine radio.

With everything in place, Beardsley reported to Groves, who insisted on meeting the two men prior to their trip. After Beardsley drove the two men in the taxi to the boathouse and sent them on their way he had been kept abreast of their whereabouts by a succession of planes that had been tracking the boat until the day of the storm. As soon as he had received the emergency call from the seamen he drove down to the State Marina of Missouri to inspect the boat. Once he saw the tell-tale signs of the plutonium emanating from the bottom of the boat into the water, he knew the worst scenario had occurred. Beardsley contacted his superior and he was told to contain the situation.

Chapter 55 – Compensation – Modern Day

At the end of Redmond's account of the events leading up to the deaths of all those people on that fateful night, Caroline and Jason were silent.

"There would be no advantage to running this story through the courts. All the evidence has gone, there is no written account that Major General Groves or any other member of the U.S. government ever authorized any of this, let alone have any knowledge of it. Furthermore, all parties are long deceased, there are no witnesses to bring forward," Redmond explained.

"If there is no evidence, how do you know all this?" Jason countered.

"Look, I'll be honest with you, we found a couple of memos originating from Lieutenant General Groves' office that were written shortly after the first bomb was dropped on Japan. They were inquiring on the whereabouts of your grandfather, Lawless, and Beardsley, he wanted to thank them for their involvement. He had no idea of what went down here or even about this place." Redmond said opening his arms and looking around at what was once a proud marina. "Unfortunately, after years of covert operations, Beardsley's definition of containment and that of Groves were poles apart.

Beardsley went to work and did an effective job of containing the situation, unbeknown to Groves, were the methods that were used. The unscrupulous Beardsley had carried out his task to the letter and the cover-up was complete. We found scraps of evidence that substantiated your findings, but what little, written, documentation that existed appears to have, well, disappeared. So, much like your account, it is all summation, conjecture, and hearsay. It would be difficult to prove." Redmond replied casually.

"I still have the photographs, including the ones of the logbook that proved the boats had docked here that night," Jason said confidently. "And the photographs of where the two boats were submerged."

"The photos are indistinct and could have been taken of anything, anywhere. There is no evidence to support the fact that the boats sank here. The photos of a logbook could be of any documentation, you don't have the original documentation, consequently, it is all circumstantial." Redmond said confidently.

"What about all the skeletons?" Jason asked.

"Again, could be of any skeletons. Our salvage crew, based on a tip, found the two boats at the bottom of the Mississippi with no bodies on board." Redmond explained.

"Isn't that convenient?" Jason said sarcastically.

"The current on this river could disperse bodies anywhere very quickly, never to be seen again," Redmond said.

"What about the bodies encased in the wall over there?" Jason asked, pointing to what was once the entrance to the marina.

"What bodies?" Redmond succinctly replied.

"I have the photographs!" Jason said.

"Of what?" Redmond asked.

"You may seem to believe you have this all covered up Agent Redmond," Caroline interceded, and she continued, quietly and confidently, "but we maintain a piece of evidence that would not only blow your retorts to smithereens but would also provide credibility to the photos that we have in our possession." Redmond looked at Caroline who was standing there with the full arrogance of an experienced libel lawyer. Jason had no idea what the piece of evidence was that Caroline had mentioned but he acted as though he did. At first, Jason thought that Redmond looked unsure how to proceed, he stood with his arms crossed then suddenly burst out laughing.

"You're bluffing of course, you have nada!" Redmond said through his laughter, "but look, let's not get hung up on this. You know, and I know the real truth, I think I have a solution to settle this. Do you want to hear it?" Caroline and Jason looked at each other then they turned back to face Redmond and nodded their heads in assent.

"After the events of that fateful night, the government purchased this land right up to the road which you turned down to get here. The area stretches for half a mile on both sides of what was once the wall. Quite a large swath of land." Redmond paused as his audience looked around, trying to assess the extent of the property and the reason for the explanation. "Here's the deal, you can purchase this property for one cent."

Caroline and Jason looked at him, mouths agape, totally astonished.

"That offer is only good for here and now and right now only." Redmond said ominously, pointing to the ground accentuating the point, "if you want to pursue a legal approach I can assure you it will be dragged through the courts and you will not see a conclusion in your lifetime. Alternatively, take this opportunity to buy a nice piece of lake-front property. We can't give the land to you, that would be an admission of guilt. Take the deal."

"What about the descendants of all the other people who have died," Jason asked, almost pleading.

"Look," Redmond replied, solemnly, almost acting human with emotion, "it was wartime, things happened. Except for yourself and now, of course, Miss Ashdene, nobody else needs to know about this. If word got out that a court case was pending, there would be all sorts of relatives, genuine and fake, climbing out of the woodwork wanting a piece of the compensation. People claiming their parents, grandparents, aunts, uncles were on board the Streamer that night, not to mention the band members and catering staff. Think about it, it would be a dog's breakfast."

"It just doesn't seem fair that we alone should benefit from this when so many people lost their lives," Jason said.

"Life isn't fair, Jason," Redmond replied. "You have been the only person in over 70 years to have questioned the events of that night. You have gone to the trouble of finding out the truth, you have discovered facts that even the government was not aware of. Take the deal, with the proceeds from the jewelry you will be able to build a beautiful house here." Caroline and Jason looked at the agent in total surprise.

"Yeah yeah, we know about the artifacts you salvaged and the money." Redmond admitted, "that definitely would not look good if you wanted to drag this through the courts. As I mentioned to you before, entering a government, restricted property and removing valuable assets, tut, tut, tut. By the way, don't blame the jewelry store owner, he didn't tell us, we have been investigating you since our first meeting. That too will come to an end if you take this deal, I promise you. But if you don't….."

"Do you mind if we have a quick conversation about this Agent Redmond?" Caroline asked as she began to usher Jason out of earshot. Redmond held out his arms and nodded his agreement.

"It's a good deal," Caroline said once they were a few yards away from their protagonist, "I think you should take it and put all this behind you."

"I don't know Caroline, it just doesn't feel right!" Jason replied shaking his head.

"Jason, he's right, they could drag this out for years and you would still end up getting nothing," Caroline replied.

"By the way, what was that piece of evidence you have?" Jason asked.

"He's right, it's a bluff." Caroline said, "if you want to do the right thing, take the deal and we could try and locate some of the descendants of the working people on the boat and maybe do something for them with the proceeds from the necklace. Trust me, none of the passengers' heirs are hurting." Caroline explained, "I think you should take it."

Jason looked at her, letting her rationale sink in, weighing up the alternatives.

"***We*** should take it, Caroline," Jason finally replied. "I could sell my house, we could build a beautiful mansion here and we could live in it for the rest of our lives." Jason stared at the beautiful lady before him wondering what her reaction would be to such a profound, spontaneous statement.

"We take it!" Caroline said, smiled and linked her arm through Jason's to return to Redmond to give him their decision. He had pretty much guessed the outcome, so he was not surprised.

"Good decision, I will get the paperwork rolling," Redmond said and shook both their hands on the successful termination of the deal. "Oh, there's just one more thing."

Jason thought, now what? A caveat in the deal that prevents them from ever visiting the property or something equally as restrictive? Redmond was walking to the other side of the command center where a black tarpaulin was covering something that was on wheels, as that was all that was not hidden. As they came close to whatever it was, Agent Jordan appeared and took hold of one corner of the covering and with Redmond on another they slid the tarpaulin off to reveal the salvaged Chris-Craft Double Stateroom cabin cruiser that Jason's grandfather had sailed into the marina.

"Now, I don't pretend to know anything about boats," Redmond began, "but I am led to believe that, surprisingly, the wood on this vessel is still in excellent condition. This is where the plutonium receptacle was housed," Redmond said, stooping down and pointing to an area on the bottom of the hull. "It was encased in fiberglass, needless to say, we had to remove all evidence of that. But if you're interested, the boat is yours. The engine is diesel, it could probably be started up with a few tweaks, if you knew what you were doing."

“I don’t, but I know someone who does,” Jason replied, now probably more elated with this offering than the promise of the land.

Conclusion

Caroline and Jason took some time surveying their new property before returning to the marina. When they arrived at the pub they explained what had unfolded to the others and asked Chuck to return with them that afternoon to the site of their new home. Their ruse was that they needed his advice on the building of a boat dock, which they did, but it wouldn't be given that day.

They arrived at the marina in Jason's truck, Dexter and Archie accompanied Chuck on the trip, none of them knowing the real purpose of the drive. Chuck walked down to the shore to survey the lie of the land while Jason directed everyone else to the parked boat, concealed once more by the tarpaulin.

"Over here Chuck. I want to show you something." Jason shouted out. Caroline and Jason then imitated the F.B.I.'s earlier positions and as Chuck approached they walked off the tarpaulin.

For a moment, time went backward, and Jason felt as though he was looking through the eyes of his grandfather while he watched the amazement of a seven-year-old boy gaping at the object of his dreams.

Chuck slowly walked up to the boat and in silence lovingly ran his hand along the hull of the boat. The only blight on the boat's appearance was where Redmond's people had removed all evidence of the fiberglass and the plutonium receptacle, a few scrapes and holes had been made, but it didn't seem to phase Chuck.

"It's not in bad shape." Archie remarked. "do you think you could restore it?"

"I can restore it." Chuck replied as though he was in a trance. "I can restore it."

Chuck insisted that they tow the boat back to his workshop right there and then, Jason had expected that, but nevertheless, he teased him, trying to think of objections to delay the delivery. It wasn't until Caroline told Jason to stop that he reversed the truck up to the trailer to hook it up.

A couple of years later, Caroline and Jason had married and moved into their custom-built house overlooking the Mississippi. They did indeed pursue descendants of the occupants of the Streamer. The band members' heirs were easy to locate, and funds were provided where Caroline and

Jason felt they would be of the most benefit. Finding the catering staff turned out to be impossible, there was no record of their names, they were transit workers being paid under the table and subsequently, nothing could be found.

Now, because of their new luxurious setting Caroline and Jason were regularly visited by Jason's daughters and his parents; and of course, the pub crew. Chuck, Archie, Helen and Dexter would arrive either by Archie's Chevy or Chuck's beautifully restored Chris Craft. During one of those visits, Jason's parents were also in residence. Chuck and Jason's dad sat for a quiet moment talking of that encounter a young Chuck had with Jason's grandfather, all those years ago. A degree of separation from the distant past, it was a poignant moment.

There was another reason to celebrate, Caroline gave birth to a boy that they named Reginald, in honor of her father. Caroline had suggested naming the baby, Sebastian but Jason declined saying his son Seb. had taken that name and was now at peace, this was a new life.

One beautiful, peaceful evening, the three of them, Caroline, Jason and Reggie were sitting on their swing at the edge of the water enjoying the serenity until Caroline decided it was Reggie's bedtime. As they rose, Caroline took hold of Reggie's little wrist to wave it at the paddling of ducks that were swimming idly across from where they were sitting.

"Night, night duckies," Caroline whispered, they rose and began to head back to the house. Just at that second there was a splash right above where Jason had first seen the St. Louis Streamer. Jason glanced round and stepped back towards the waterline. Later, Jason said he could have sworn he had seen a ghostly arm, almost transparent, making a throwing motion towards them. Caroline suggested it was just a trick of the light, it was dusk, and daylight was fading. But there at their feet, glinting in the water, like phosphorescence on the sandy shoreline was a pair of ruby earrings. A few yards away, drifting to and fro with the gentle waves was a diamond-encrusted cigarette-holder.

AVAILABLE SOON:

Murder of a Late-Night TV Host

Genesis Déjà vu – The Early Years (third book in the series)

To join the mailing list, email:

DEXTER-JAMES@OUTLOOK.COM

Made in the USA
Middletown, DE
01 May 2020

93161816R00208